STRIPPED
DOWN

STRIPPED DOWN

LESBIAN SEX STORIES

For Michaela —
xxx
Tristan Taormino

Edited by

TRISTAN TAORMINO

Introduction by

EILEEN MYLES

CLEiS
PRESS

Published in the United States by Cleis Press, Inc., 2246 Sixth Street, Berkeley, California 94710.

Printed in the United States.
Cover design: Scott Idleman
Cover photograph: Reza Estakhrian/Getty Images
Text design: Frank Wiedemann
10 9 8 7 6 5 4 3 2 1

Trade paper ISBN: 978-1-57344-794-2
E-book ISBN: 978-1-573444-806-2

This book is dedicated to the memory of Cheryl B., fierce poet, writer, performer, and community organizer. Your spirit continues to move us through your words.

CONTENTS

FOREWORD

Tristan Taormino

What follows a multiorgasmic romp with the
baddest butch in town? What comes before it?

There is no one formula for choosing the
order of the stories in an erotica anthology.
After doing this for seventeen years, I've devel-
oped my own variety of techniques, like pair-
ing stories that focus on a similar theme from
different perspectives. Or arranging them by
tone, from soft to hard, like a carefully orches-
trated spanking, where you start with gentle
strokes and build to stingy slaps. Sometimes I
like to fly from one end of the spectrum to the
other, switching from reality to fantasy, from
girlfriend to one-night stand, from epic to snap-
shot, from flirtatious first time to all-night fisting. It's about seeing the similarities and differences, and deciding how to offset them just so.

What struck me about Eileen's selections is how much territory they covered. They are full of love, loss, innocence, initiation, self-discovery, fear, revenge, enlightenment—and that's just for starters. As I put the stories together, I imagined each one as a step in an erotic journey. The journey begins with a long-term couple and the intense love and passion they share. Along the way, you'll meet characters who feel adored, challenged, schooled, surprised, and satisfied. Some take us to the edge of sanity and the brink of breakup; one goes beyond it to the death of a lover. But with death comes rebirth, and what better way to represent that than a story about a virgin nun and one about a baptismal? Personally, I love when journeys end with new beginnings.

Butches and femmes are featured throughout the book, but several stories focus specifically on how these roles define us, confine us, or sometimes do both. In one, two butch buddies left at home together by their girlfriends explore their desire for each other as they face their own fears and hang-ups about their identities. Assumptions about butch/femme, its rigidity and fluidity also play a crucial part in two surprising, edgy tales of erotic revenge.

Other sexual dynamics are explored as well, all fueled by the roles we play in the world—roles like mother, daughter, teacher, student, employer, employee—and the power dynamics we enact both in and out of the bedroom. A danger of using such familiar, timeless archetypes in sex stories is that they'll dive right into pornoland, where all housewives are desperate and gardeners hot. What's great about these explorations is that rather than being cliché, they are full of quirky characters and clever twists. If you think you know the story of sex with the boss, sex with the truck stop waitress, sex with the delivery girl, or sex with the doctor, think again. Guys also pop up in unexpected places, as watchers and those being watched, as fodder for fantasies, and as objects of affection. And by *guys,* I mean those masculine-identified beings who may or may not have been born male, those who identify as trans, and some whose gender is purposely ambiguous.

Relationships are at the heart of the sex in all these stories. Since my work is known for its hard-core, raunchy fuck tales, I hesitated to even write that sentence because I was afraid it might be misunderstood. I don't mean just love or romantic relationships (although they're in here, too), and I don't want to imply there isn't plenty of panty-soaking material here. There is. The relationships I'm talking about may be established or brand new, committed or temporary, complex and layered or simple and straightforward. They're real and familiar. The writers in this collection explore what connects the people involved, what drives them to collide with one another for a moment of pleasure; they do it with honesty and compassion, sarcasm and wit. It's the relationships, however imagined, ambivalent, or intense, that makes the sex so hot.

Having a good fuck can be breezy and fun. But what makes sex transformative, what makes it possible to explore my outer limits or push my lover's boundaries is my ability to get under the skin. Similarly, what separates strokeable smut from smut that gets me off sexually, intellectually, and emotionally is the bond beyond the damp boxers and shaved pussies. I want to know what's underneath all that sweating and moaning. I want to see how our connections as much as our conflicts (with each other and ourselves) fuel our fucking. These stories do that for me. They strip down way past naked to show us what we can discover about ourselves through our sexual encounters. The folks in these stories fuck, yes, but when they fuck, they find that they are tougher than they thought, gentler than people expected, hungrier, hornier, and more flexible than they've been given credit for. Here is love sex, revenge sex, stranger sex, and fucked-so-good-you-can't-think-straight sex in all its raw, sexy, messy glory.

So, what comes after the final story? Well, hopefully *you*.

Tristan Taormino
New York City

INTRODUCTION: THE REAL THING

Eileen Myles

What a bunch of horny bitches dykes are. What a bunch of dirty little men. Filthy girls. As I read these stories in manuscript I observed a trend in which Massachusetts and New Zealand are both producing lesbian erotic texts on a massive scale. Somebody must've conducted special workshops in both those places 'cause it can't just be that this was a very hot year in Somerville or Auckland, or can it? Are there erotic writing sweatshops there? I once worked for an erotic writing sweatshop. There was an ad in the *Voice* for writers of adult fiction. The sweatshop in fact was a fairly hip loft in the thirties—in Murray Hill to be exact (Hi, Murray!). To even get an interview you had to drop off two thousand words at their office and wait for a call. The call came and next I met with this older woman who was perhaps fifty and was white and her hair was curled and her face in my memory seemed huge in its pleasure at how good and talented I was at *this*. Her enthusiasm made me cringe. All I can remember about my sample (in which I believed I was writing for heterosexuals) was that some cops wound up fucking twin girls in the bushes of Central Park. I remember the girls blowing the cops and the story going into some detail about how the girls milked the cops' dicks. I felt convinced I was insane and now it showed, yet I remember needing to allude to the girls' innocence which was borne out by their mistaking the cops' dicks for tits. The woman smiled and smiled. *You're hired, Eileen.* And then she showed me the big machines. It was like you would be writing into something that made me think of Kafka's "In the Penal Colony," the story that reminds everybody of everything. Because it's a story about a writing machine which everyone feels like already a little bit when they pump out prose. I would go in daily to the loft on Murray Hill and I would have to write about three thousand words a day for three hundred dollars a week. This was 1979 so the money seemed good, but still the work seemed impossible. Word-processors didn't even exist then so I was being hired to pump my dirty thoughts into something I had never seen before. It was like a combination of a teleprompter and a conveyer belt. My words would go away. The woman kept smiling at how good I was at "it." *Writing dirty,* I thought. I felt like she was going to eat me, I meant literally or the machine would eat my mind. Or my brain would get milked. How would I feel after a day of it? An empty window in the combat zone, or a red light district. The curtain shut. No business. The job was going to solve a certain kind of life that wound up getting solved some other way and now it is bringing me here.

Years ago, Patrick Califia (then Pat) led an erotic writing workshop in Boston (!!) at one of the last OutWrite festivals. I think I went with Heather Lewis. I was kind of obsessed with Pat Califia, having accidentally attended a single meeting of the Lesbian Sex Mafia and she wore a yellow sundress and was just unaccountably hot. It was her confidence, her calmness in that insipid dress. In Boston she made me want to do nothing else but write dirty. What else was worth it really?

And still I probably write less about sex than most of the lesbian writers I know. I write about so many parts of my relationships with women that it seems that that one, the most tangible reason I want to be with her or her, should probably remain private. But it never does. It always somehow comes bursting out. 'Cause that's sex.

Tristan sent me first one package, then another, then another. *Groan. I* needed to be writing this summer. When would I read all of this? Then I got sick. Or hurt my back. Something had me in bed for a week, maybe more, and what I had for companions were Peggy Munson's Christian cousins playing with each other's tits in the pool. I think it was the pool and their youth that made it hot. Or how one cousin felt weird about her tits so the other happily groped them. It was like healthy and even sweet, you know. Not in the family album, is all.

But, you know, it would be in ours. If there is an *us.* I feel it. Suddenly someone is fucking herself with a mermaid dildo. Quickly her "cunt balloons," Julian Tirhma writes, but the ballooning almost decorated the sidelines, then flips to the foreground of the story. I liked that. Like doors kept opening

INTRODUCTION: THE REAL THING

and closing. Then, in "After Lunch," a doctor who's in the country to buy a house gets eaten by a waitress who used to be a cop. The doctor hasn't showered but the waitress likes her pussy tangy, she insists. In "Phoebe's Undercover Bon Voyage" a blonde's getting rigged up for a scenario with four enthusiastic cops and Skian McGuire details the differences in each of their uniforms ("a broad navy stripe up the legs of her sky blue trousers") in randy masculine detail. What I loved about all the stories here is that your readerly inattention, or your attention on the peripheral thing, always buoys up the ballooning pussy. Two dykes are fucking at the beach ("A Case of Mistaken Identity") while two guys watching them through binoculars from behind some rocks are thinking the butch is one lucky dude (he is), which clinches the dykes' mundane patter and graphic pumping being well, really hot.

My number one story here is sci-fi, Catherine Lundoff's long and exhibitionistic "Planet 10." Our narrator, a Knossan, is dying to have sex with an Altaran. Has been for years. She winds up one night at an intra-species lesbian bar under the watchful eyes of a number of other horny aliens, and at the whim of the Altaran lizard who has agreed to play with her ("Unfasten that one's upper garment...") she eventually fists herself to orgasm on command. Later, in an alley, she's ripped open and begins her transition. All the while the gold-eyed Altaran's gills are quivering. It's hot. The Knossan has decided to surrender her life to this. To grow a tail herself. To breed with an Altaran is to become one. And *that* is simply profound. I loved the faggot riot grrl getting her ass ridden in the back of the truck by the mean biker daddy in "Puppy Slut." His fuck pad "was soft and smelled like big dogs and sex and woods..." as she climbed in the back. Do you have a medical experiment fantasy? The poor college student of "Clinical Trial" enters a campus facility for testing, and behold, the hot scientist with the clipboard quietly observes her orgasm. Or did she detect an eyebrow flicker? A gill?

Packing in yoga class? Hot! This one's appropriately named "The Plow Pose." How about the pussy packed with organic blueberries by the Miami butch who does home delivery for the produce co-op in "Ripe for the Picking"? Seeing the healthy lesbian aesthetic crashed into a dripping mound of excess was really, really good. And the little nun of "Virgo Intacta." Who could forget the little nun who changed the beds in the Italian B & B for the vacationing professional dykes? "But let's make no mistake, little nun. No one's ever going to touch you again, without you wishing they were me." We wind up sitting with the couple flying home in the plane. They each know what the other's thinking, why the other's smiling, yet no one wants to share.

Then there's the girl headed to Folsom Street Fair in San Francisco with her trans boyfriend. The ex-girlfriends who end up in bed with a riding crop. And the woman in "Gone" who mourns her lost lover who is not just some mean cunt long gone, but dead. Dead! The ultimate fantasy. I wish my ex was dead. I really do! And finally there's the couple encounter in which one lover eats dog food. Because she must. Then they process it a lot. A real lot. The top might. She might do it. But they need to talk more. You know all this stuff is hot because it's not like anyone ever stops talking. It's just that the real conversation is the sex. These are all fiction, but that part is entirely true.

Eileen Myles
San Diego

WHERE THE RUBBER MEETS THE ROAD

Aimee Pearl

We're walking down the street and he's fucking me. Everything's slippery and delicious. This is all true.

We're at the Folsom Street Fair—the annual BDSM outdoor playground event—and it's a hot San Francisco September day. Hot in a way that only San Francisco can be, and only in September. They call it Indian summer. There's a monsoon swelling between my legs. He's going to make me gush.

We're walking in broad daylight. The crowd is thick around us. He rubs a wet thumb against my clit. We move side by side in stride, no pauses. I wonder...

If people looked down toward my crotch, they might see his right hand sneaking around the edge of my bright cherry-red latex micromini. They might realize that he's got a finger sliding between my lower lips. What would they think? What would they say?

My skirt is so short that it doesn't cover the full curve of my ass. You can see my cheeks peeking out from the bottom of the shiny rubber coating. I can't wear panties in this, and I can't sit. Can only stand. Can only keep on walking. While he fucks me.

He's devilishly handsome, this one. His skin is the color of a toasted hazelnut, and twice as tasty. We've fucked many times before, but never like this. Never outdoors, in the middle of the street, digits stretching wet rubber wide...

The red of my skirt is polished to a gleam, and I love the way the color looks metallic against my velvet-soft brown skin. This was the first piece of latex I ever bought, the first one I ever tried on. Its tightness around my narrow waist, rounded hips, and plump ass makes me look and feel space-alien exotic, and draws attention to the fullest part of my body. Yes, my butt has stopped traffic. Who doesn't like to look at a black diva in red rubber?

For now, though, we're blending in, seeping into the throng around us. He's giving me a teasing fuck and my cunt is starting to ache with desire. Pretty soon, I'll want more fingers, I'll want to swallow his fist whole. We've got to find a doorway to lean into. I can't come while walking. I'm perched on spike heels and might fall over.

The orgasms he gives me have been known to cause great commotion.

We find an alley and he pounds me quick and hard, leaves me wet and feeling dirty. This boy has a way with those hands of his. He once made me come while I prepared a cup of tea.

Holding kettle, boiling hot and full, precarious. He came behind me at the stove and rammed four fingers into me. Undid me. Unraveled me. I don't know how I managed to pour steadily after that.

But I did.

We're discovered in our crevice by onlookers, dykes from around town, smiling at the queer couple that is us. I wish he was packing, so that we could give 'em a real show. Unfortunately, he left his dick at home today. Who needs it, I guess, when you've got hands like his?

Still and all, I do crave his cock sometimes. For a moment, as he fucks me roughly one more time for our audience, I imagine him, silicone in hand, rubbing his rubber-covered rubber dick against my rubber-covered rear. Rolling up latex for greater access. Sliding toy into tightness. A fetishistic ass fuck on a city street, sweaty.

I do it again. Come.

Later, we leave our latex-alley love nest and slide back into the crowded thoroughfare. He runs into a friend, a gorgeous high-femme white girl with a buzz cut. Six-two in heels, she works as a pro-domme at a local house. Today is her day off, and she and her girlfriend/submissive are strolling through the fair. She's wearing an ankle-length latex dress, and she's drenched in sweat. She squats down and lifts her skirt to circulate air around her sweet blonde pussy. I want to swoon, but not from the heat. She complains about the weather, and about the clients who keep spotting her in the crowd and begging to be dominated.

Beside me, he chats casually with her and smiles. He knows I'm a sucker for a pissed-off femme domme, not to mention one wearing even more latex than I am. From my angle above her, I can see down into her cleavage and admire the beads of wetness on her full breasts. I'm starting to feel wet again myself. He knows. He knows it's time to fuck me again. He knows it's time to go for a walk...

On our next date, we meet at midnight, this time in another alley, in a different part of town. He's hanging out in a club up the street; I've been instructed to drive into the alley and wait for him in the backseat. I send him a text message to let him know I've arrived, and arrange myself to be ready for him. He leaves the club and approaches my car.

I'm wearing a cream-colored knee-length A-line leather skirt. The material is so soft and buttery that most admirers don't even recognize that it's made out of leather—at first glance anyway. This skirt always gets a second glance. It's not short, it's not tight, and it's not an eye-catching color. But it manages to exude a subtle yet no-nonsense sexiness. It's a great skirt for a dominant woman to wear, because of its strict lines. But I'm a submissive, and I like to wear it to feel encased in it, bound by the leather, however loosely, as it falls around my thighs.

There's a rap at the window, and I reach over to unlock the door and let him in. Let him come in and fuck me.

As requested, I'm not wearing any panties. Although this time it's not because of the length of my skirt, of course, but because of other constraints of the scene. Namely, he wants quick and easy access to my cunt; he wants to fuck me quickly and then leave me to go back to his friends at the club. It's all been prearranged. We move like we're dancing. Only there's no music. Just the sound of leather rubbing against vinyl, and breathing. His breath and mine. Mostly mine as he's fucking me hard and I'm struggling to endure it.

To take it all in. He's packing this time, all right, using one of his biggest cocks.

The day was hot but the night is cold. The windows steam over, and as I'm parked illegally in a one-way, dimly lit alley, I'm beginning to worry if we'll attract any unwanted attention. He doesn't seem to be concerned. He was cavalier from the moment he entered the car. He hasn't said a word to me, in fact. Just leapt in, closed and locked the door behind him, shoved me down onto my stomach, and used one hand to pull his cock out while the other pushed my skirt up.

He's gripping my skirt, the thin leather bunched into his fist. One of my arms is pinned under me, but with the other I start to reach out and run my hand along his pant leg. I discover he's wearing leather chaps over his jeans, and that they fit nice and snug. I try to reach far enough to get to the edge of the leather, so I can stroke his crotch, feel his real cock, the one that's slowly been getting bigger as he's been transitioning and taking testosterone. But he's not having any of this, doesn't want me to move. He rams his cock into me to the hilt and uses both his arms to hold me down, immobilizing me. My face is buried in the vinyl of the seat, my legs spread wide with one on the seat and the other leaning over the side toward the floor, and all else is sound and heat and motion and fullness. His chaps are rubbing the vinyl, my skirt is rubbing the vinyl, and there's no room to breathe. I'm gasping for air, wondering which one of us will come first, when suddenly, without warning, he pulls out.

He pulls out, and pulls back, and I can finally catch my breath. But I'm confused. I shift around to see what's going on, and witness him pulling two things out of his pockets. My eyes go wide as I see that one is a rubber ball gag with leather straps, and the other is a small packet of my favorite anal sex lube. He lays the lube packet on my bare ass and speaks for the first time all night.

"Open up."

I open my mouth to receive the gag, and then he secures the straps in place at the back of my head. Now he twists the tab off the lubricant, and dribbles it onto his dick. His second sentence comes at me:

"Get ready."

The head of his cock is already pressing against my asshole. When we talked about meeting in the alley, he said he wanted things to go quickly. But if he's seriously thinking of fucking my ass with that big toy, this is going to take a while.

Or so I think.

He works it in with surprising speed. Behind the gag, I'm grunting and half-screaming, but he knows I can take it, and I know he's going to make me. The perverse thrill of submitting to this sadistic "forced" ass fuck actually causes me to open a little more, which eases his way inside. He's one step ahead of me, and pushes as I acquiesce.

When his cock is completely in my ass, he pauses for a moment, to give me a chance to feel the extent to which he's stretched me out, to confirm my own surrender. One moment, and then it's over. That's all I get. After that, it's his turn.

He pounds me hard, fucking me for all it's worth. He's determined to come and he knows how to use my ass for his own pleasure. My job is to endure. Gagged, held down, plowed, I am a thing to him. An object. A leather-clad fuck-hole. He slams into my ass, over and over, until he shoots his orgasm into me. It's not liquid, of course; it's an energy, and thus, twice as potent. I take every drop, deep into my ass, for him.

And when he's done, he pulls out gently, undoes my gag gently, slides me over onto my back gently, smoothes down my skirt gently, and gently, very gently, reaches under my skirt and flicks one slick finger against my clit.

I explode.

I come against his hand with a roar, violent waves of pleasure crashing through me. He holds me as I come, body to body, leather to leather, gripping me tightly until my moans subside.

Then, just as quickly as he entered, he puts his silicone dick back in his pants, zips up, and leaves.

Next time we'll play in PVC.

JUBILEE

Quinn Vertiz

"Getcher dicks on, boys, we're goin' in!"
Drake shouted from the front seat as we pulled
up in front of a double-wide with *Momma's*
flashing over the door in red neon. The light
illuminated a few cars parked in front and
smaller trailers strewn around the empty desert like abandoned child's blocks.

The door of the double-wide burst open as
we piled out of the van and a stout woman
with an enormous amount of bleached-blonde
hair stepped out and yelled, "Come on, boys,
I've got some real beauties waiting for you in
here." She struck a bell hanging by the door
with six quick raps. "And that will get up a
few more," she said with a big fleshy smile.
"Do my eyes deceive me or it that Drake?"
She clapped her hands together. "The girls

will really come running for Drake and his boys. Get your cute little butts in here."

I lagged a little behind the other guys, walking funny from the big cock Drake had picked out and strapped onto me. It went down the leg of my jeans and pinched my thigh with each step.

"Hey—Baby Boy, where are you? Don't hang back this time." Drake got me in a headlock and dragged me up the stairs. I could smell his sweat and the musty scent of his leather jacket, and it soothed me. "Momma, look what I got here for one of your special girls." Drake pulled me into the sparsely lit living room, thrusting me in front of Momma so my face was eye level with her cavernous cleavage. "This is my boy and I've brought him to you to find just the right girl to pop his cherry." She grabbed my head, getting a good grip on the tuft of hair on top of my head, and pulled me down into her breasts where it was all softness and perfume. I sighed contentedly in the dark space.

"What a cutie! What a sweet boy. Why, I'd want him for myself, if you weren't here." She winked at Drake and he leered back. "I think I have just the girl, yeah, there's a new girl and she's perfect. Deanna!" she yelled to the skinny girl sitting at the bar by the phone. "Run out and get Jubilee…and tell her I've got a special treat for her—a baby butch cherry to pop."

I felt Deanna's bony hand grab my clammy one. I looked back at Drake sprawled out on the sectional that was crammed into the trailer's crowded front room. Drake jumped up and slapped my ass. "You go on, boy, do your dad proud. Remember what I told you. And you've got your dad's lucky dick, so get out there and fuck her senseless, Baby Boy!" He grabbed the dick where it stretched the material of my jeans over my left thigh, said, "You go get'er," and with that he shoved me out the door so I almost tripped over the skinny Deanna.

"Come on," she whispered. "You'll like Jubilee, don't worry." I suddenly felt panicked and it must've shown on my face. "Oh, you are worried, poor boy, you're white as a sheet." She stopped and took my face between her hands for a minute and kissed my forehead so softly. "I mean it—you don't have a thing to worry about, a sweet handsome baby butch like you, Jubilee's gonna take real good care of you. Is it really your first time?"

I thought of all those times kissing and groping Marie in her bunk back at juvie, and I knew that wasn't what Drake meant by fucking. "Yeah…it's…it's my first time." I couldn't help myself, I blushed. Suddenly I wished Drake were there. I wished he was standing right by me telling me what to do. I almost turned and ran back into the big trailer right then, but Deanna grabbed my hand again, as if she knew what I was thinking, and said, "Let's go—Jubilee's waiting."

We walked through the dark bit of desert, stepping around old tires, empty liquor bottles, and shot-up beer cans, skirting the trailers scattered here and there. They were a motley collection, everything from cool, bulletlike Airstreams to truck-bed campers up on blocks. Some of the trailers were dark and quiet and others blazed with light, music, whoops, and sharp cries. Toward the end of the camp we came to a small green trailer, the single-axle kind, with the rounded edges of the early sixties and blocks under the front and back to make it level and stable. More cinder blocks had been piled to make steps up to the door and beside them was an ancient and wind-battered jade plant.

Deanna knocked on the door. "Jubilee, Momma's got

someone for you." We heard a voice from inside, though I couldn't make out the words. Deanna opened the door and poked her head in. "Momma said to tell you that this one's real special, a sweet baby butch, and you get to have his cherry, all right?"

I heard laughter from inside. "Send him in, sweetie."

Deanna grabbed me by the shoulders as if she knew that I was thinking of bolting again ("Remember what I said, don't you worry now"), and shoved me up the cinder block steps. I came to a stop on the few square feet of linoleum that designated the mini-kitchen, and wiped the ice-cold sweat off my palms onto my T-shirt. Drake's dick felt like a fist pressing into my crotch in the tight harness. I tried to swallow but found that my mouth was so dry I couldn't. I tried to make sense of what I was seeing. The inside of the tiny trailer was strung with pink Christmas lights, and the table and counters of the kitchen/dining area were crammed with thick leafy plants. The other end of the trailer was draped in cloth of every texture and weight, and I didn't know where to look.

"Hey, sweet boy, come here and let me take a look at you."

Her voice was rich and warm, like coffee, and as I turned to look into the red and pink cloth womb of her bed she shone out like a full moon breaking through the clouds, her pale skin dusted white in the dim light and seeming to glow from within. She sat up and swung both legs over to the floor. Her hair fell long and dark behind her. The deep red of her lipstick was the only color in her pale face, and her filmy pink slip showcased her lush creamy cleavage and strong thighs. I stood, stock-still, trying to work up enough spit to swallow.

"Come sit with me," she said as she handed me a glass of water, and clearly not trusting my ability to locomote any more than I did, she took my hand and pulled me across to the bed to sit awkwardly on the edge. She curled up against the cushions half behind me. "What a big handsome boy you are," she said, lightly brushing my arm and thigh with her fingers. "Just relax and take your time and tell me what you want when you're ready."

I could see my boots were resting there on the floor, but I couldn't feel my feet in them. I thought my palms must be making an oily slick of cold sweat on the front of my jeans but I couldn't move them. Shit—I was scared. I wished Drake was there to make things happen. I wished I was Drake and that I knew exactly what to do. It had seemed, when Drake strapped his big dick onto me and then pulled up my shorts and jeans and slapped my butt and said, "Go get 'em tiger!" that the dick would know what to do, but now it just lay there like the most obvious lump in the world, stretching my jeans all out of shape.

"Poor sweet boy—come here," she said, and I felt her soft hand on the back of my neck, petting the clipped hair like I was a cat. "Don't worry, Jubilee will take care of you. Don't be scared, just let me hold you for a while."

I curled myself around and let her fold me into her arms. With her hand still on my neck she pulled my head down to rest on the soft cushion of her breasts. She smelled like mango ice cream and I breathed in the wonderful scent of her and suddenly felt so relaxed that I thought I might just fall asleep right there.

She picked up my hand. "What big strong hands you have," she said, bringing my hand up to her mouth and sliding first one, then two fingers past her lips.

I gasped at the warm silk of her mouth and the surprise of

her throat closing on the very tips of my fingers as she pulled them all the way in. Suddenly the dick that had felt like a hard lump of silicone in my pants turned into an electric extension of my now bulging clit. It was like the monster when Dr. Frankenstein flips the switch and lifeless matter roars to life. She released my hand and it went straight to my crotch to half-cover, half-stroke the newborn monster. She slid away from behind me and my shoulders fell against the side of the trailer. I grabbed her hand and put it on the bulge in my jeans. She bent over and, pressing the cloth down over my cock with her hand, she traced the outline with the point of her tongue, all the while looking up at me sideways to see my reaction. I looked straight at her for the first time and was lost in her huge brown eyes. Oh, she was so beautiful, with her pale perfect skin, broad cheekbones, and lush glossy lips. I couldn't stop looking even as I felt stripped by her gaze, exposed in my helpless need for her to take me in her mouth. I fumbled with my belt and she pushed my hands away, peeling back the belt, opening my jeans and expertly threading my hard cock out of the fly of my boxers. She grabbed a condom from the shelf, tore it open with her teeth, and worked it down over my dick with her mouth. I couldn't take my eyes off her.

I didn't know what to do with my hands, which were flopping around next to me on the bed as my body jumped and pulsed with the sheer force of her mouth on my dick. She worked up and down the shaft, sometimes taking the head of the big dick all the way down her throat with the sweetest muffled grunts, sounds escaping in choked bursts around the thick head. Then she would back off and caress the head with just her lips, letting her excess spit trail off the tip of my cock like it was my own come. My hips bucked with wanting to fill her throat again.

I felt like I would go crazy, or die, or maybe come, if she'd just go on sucking me. Suddenly she grabbed my hands and put them on either side of her head, my fingers tangling in her cool thick hair. She took her mouth off my dick long enough to say, "Go ahead—pull my hair—I want you to. Fuck me as hard as you want, I can take it." That was all I needed to hear and the last of my fear drained in the face of my mounting need. I dug my fingers into her hair, winding the thick heavy strands around my hand and pulling her head down to my crotch. My hips rose to meet her mouth and I bucked like a bronc, feeling the resistance of her tight throat on each thrust against my throbbing, bursting clit. I came in an electric flood, hearing a cry and not knowing if it was my own voice or someone else's.

In the dark silence that followed I felt Jubilee sit up and then curl around me with her head on my chest. I brought my hands up to stroke her face and the gorgeous hair I had just been yanking on. "Your hair smells so good," I said. It was like a summer garden at night, all full of mysterious sweet and pungent smells.

"That's my good boy—you just relax now." Her hands stroked my shoulder and arm. I pushed the spit-slicked dick down between my legs. We were silent and still and our only conversation was the sound of our breaths slowing and calming together.

Suddenly the door burst open and Drake bounded into the tiny trailer. "Hey—Baby Boy—you've done it! I peeked in and saw that you got yourself a real first-class blow job. Yeah, they don't get much better than that, do they, Jezebel—or was it Jasmine? What did you call yourself back in Vegas? Well, it don't matter. What matters, Baby Boy, is that she gives the best head in the state of Nevada and now your dad's got a big hard-on just thinking about it."

"Drake—you shit! I came to Winnemucca so this wouldn't happen anymore. You are the last thing I need right now." Jubilee was up and into her mules in a second so that now she and Drake stood eye to eye in the small space. From my vantage point sprawled on the bed their heads seemed to almost touch the low ceiling and it seemed like the trailer would soon burst like an aerosol can in a bonfire.

"The last thing you need? I bet your panties are telling a different story right about now. I seem to remember exactly how much you did need it. I bet you're dripping just thinking about how I'm going to throw you down on that bed and fuck you. Don't give me that shit. I know you too well."

"Fuck you Drake, and get the hell out of here. Can't you see I've got a client? Just leave us the fuck alone."

"Oh, you mean Baby Boy? Don't worry about him, he's the son I never had and I'm teaching him everything I know. And now I'm gonna teach him exactly how you like to get fucked. So get back on that bed." Drake's hand had come up to cup the side of her face as he spoke and now he pulled back and gave her a sharp slap. "You know I can hit a whole lot harder but I don't want to shock the boy, so get down there," he said, and he pushed her toward me on the bed.

She and I locked eyes for a second. I must've looked scared because she mouthed, "It's okay," and winked at me. She turned and got on her hands and knees with her ass to me.

"Okay boy, let's see just how wet that got her. You check— you can touch her anywhere you want and don't worry about being gentle 'cause believe you me she likes it best rough." I got up on my knees and tentatively reached out to touch her bare ass. Her short slip pulled away from her ass as she bent down and put her head on her hands. I slid my hand down between her thighs along the tight furrow of the lace crotch of her panties bisecting the lips of her pussy. Just like Drake had said, she was dripping; the lace was soaked through and her juice was dripping off her clean-shaven outer lips. My hand came away with a thick layer of it.

"What are you waiting for, sport? Get to work!" Drake reached out and smacked Jubilee on the ass. "Give her ass a slap, boy. You gotta soften her up before you stick that thing in." I looked down at her and didn't know what I should do. She turned her face toward me and gave me a half-smile and nod. "You don't need to wait for permission, boy, just do it." He picked up my hand and let it drop, then I brought it down again with a dull thud on her left buttcheek. "Okay, you can do better than that. Here—spread your fingers a little more and bring your hand down a little cupped, make it meet the curve of her ass...all right—go ahead." I tried a second time and got a nice ringing slap.

"That's better, now you just need to do it harder." Drake laughed and smacked her again just to show me. "Now doesn't that look beautiful? Look how nice and pink her ass gets." I tried a few more times while Drake yelled, "Harder, boy."

Once he pronounced her ass sufficiently red, he fished a glove out of his pocket, snapped it on, and dug down between her legs with his gloved fingers. "Oh—Baby Boy— you've got her so wet you won't need no lube with this one, just go ahead and give her the whole thing." He reached back and grabbed my cock where it had been bumping against her thighs, pushed the head right up against her, and slapped my ass. "Go for it, Baby Boy, that ass is all yours."

My butt flinched away from his hand and before I even thought about it I had buried the big cock in her cunt right up to the base. Now her juices were overflowing onto the front of my shorts. Drake took my hands and put one on each side of her hips, keeping his own hands over them to show me how to hold on.

"All right, boy, you work her over from this end while I get that blow job. Oh man, I am so hard it hurts." Drake threw his leather jacket and flannel shirt to the floor as sprawled on the bed against the opposite wall. He still had on a T-shirt over a long underwear shirt with *Motorhead* splashed across his skinny chest. He splayed his long legs on either side of Jubilee's lowered head, grinning at me as he tore at the bursting crotch of his tight black Levi's. Drawing out a black cock even longer and more wicked looking than the one he had given me, he winked.

With another shrug and twist of his hips to get comfortable, he took a big double-handful of Jubilee's long black hair and yanked her face up to his crotch. "Remember this bad boy?" he growled. "You can't have it till you beg me for it."

The moment Drake raised her head I could hear her steady whispered pleas.

"You're gonna have to beg a little louder then that," Drake said, and swiped the head of his cock across her mouth, letting her dive a few inches for it and then pulling her away with his other hand.

My hips swung harder into her, my crotch and thighs slapping with metronomic regularity into the taut fleshy expanse of her ass. I pounded as if my thrusts could drive her down onto Drake's dick, wanting his cock inside her as bad as I had wanted my own to be buried deep in her.

Her voice rose, torn and gruff: "Please, please let me suck your big cock, Daddy, please give it to me, please, please...." It was like she would never stop saying *please* until Drake's dick stopped her up like a plug.

A smile spread across Drake's face as he looked down at her and with jumping muscles at his shoulders and forearms he reversed his pressure and pulled her head down on his cock. He looked up at me before the eyes rolled back in his head and grinned a shit-eating grin. "Ain't it sweet, boy?"

We were so close we could have easily reached out and shaken hands over Jubilee's writhing back, and I glowed under his approving grin. Drake eased up on Jubilee's head, letting her work him up and down as I had already learned she did so well. I watched my own cock slide in and out of Jubilee's dripping pussy, glistening. I looked at my dark dirty-nailed fingers gripping the smooth swelling flesh at her hips, and loved how they stood out on her paper white skin. I watched her head bobbing over Drake's crotch, saw the bulging veins in his hands as he gripped her hair. She looked so beautiful between us there on the bed in the tiny trailer, her back shining in the dim light and her hair flying every which way, a few dark locks snaking back toward me but most of the dark tangled mass spilling around Drake's lap.

I slowed my thrusts and gave her most of my length on each swing. She groaned deeply as Drake held her all the way down on his dick. His eyes were on mine, but this time the look was something I couldn't read, he was so far gone. I closed my eyes, exploded and fell forward over Jubilee, lapsing again into the silent beyond, the blood in my ears drowning everything out.

For a long moment I was still, but then there was a hand

at my shoulder shaking me. "Boy—Baby Boy, get up!" Drake was looking down at me. "Get your damn dick back in your pants and get out of here! You're dad's got more business with his girl and you're getting in the way. All right, boy? You got what you need—now go sleep in the van. Go on—git!"

He shoved me off the bed, almost sending me into the table at the other end of the trailer as I tripped on the jeans that had settled around my knees. I caught myself on the doorknob and tried to stuff everything back in my jeans, my sticky dick getting all tangled up in my shorts. I looked back at Drake and Jubilee: her hair covered her face and I couldn't catch her eye. I opened the door and stepped out, missing the first cinder-block step and falling out onto the hard rock-strewn sand.

I found my way back to the van and climbed in the back. I unbuckled the harness and pulled it and the dick out of my pants, reaching up front to throw them in the glovebox. Exhausted, I fell into the pile of blankets at the back of the truck. It seemed like I would fall straight into unconsciousness, but instead I thought only of lying back in that trailer with my head on Jubilee's chest.

BUTCHES DON'T

D. Alexandria

*Butches don't do this. Butches DO NOT do
this.* I kept repeating this in my head as my
girl, Sonja, knocked on the door. She flashed
me a wicked grin as she leaned back, pressing
her ass into my crotch.

"You packed," she murmured, grinding
against me.

"Of course," I replied, momentarily allowing myself to enjoy the feel of her.

"It feels different...," she began, but the
door swung open and her friend, Lani, greet-
ed us with her trademark Kool-Aid smile.

"Girl, you look great!" Lani cried as she
and Sonja hugged. Then she turned to me,
gave me the once-over, and smirked. "Sonja,
you're lucky I got a woman of my own, 'cause
you best believe I couldn't let a butch this fine

go past me without trying something."

Sonja rolled her eyes in amusement as Lani showed us into the living room. "Better not let *your* woman hear you. You ready?"

"Almost, have a seat." Lani rushed out of the room as Sonja and I sat on the sofa. I removed my jacket, since I was staying.

"You sure you're okay with this?" she asked me softly.

No. "Yeah, I'll be chill."

She kissed my cheek sweetly. "Thank you for doing this."

You are so not going to be thanking me later. "Of course, baby." I kissed her back.

I was full of shit. I wasn't chill and I certainly wasn't going to be okay. While Sonja and Lani were going to have dinner with some friends of theirs, Sonja thought it would be great for me to hang with Lani's girlfriend, Vicki. Lani, who relocated to California five years ago, had temporarily moved back for a couple of months for a job, and she and Sonja were enjoying getting reacquainted. But of course, as girls do, Sonja felt that since Vicki didn't know anyone, it made sense for the two of us to become friends; she and Lani felt we had a lot in common.

Little did they know.

"I'm ready." Lani finally walked out of her bedroom, sporting a very little black dress. She struck a model pose as she stepped into the center of the room.

"We're going out to dinner, *not* the club," Sonja commented as she got to her feet, but she whistled as she eyed the outfit.

"That's what *I* said."

I turned to see Vicki emerging from the bedroom, her arms crossed in front of her as she gave her girlfriend a half-disapproving look. "There's no reason for that. Look at your girl, *she's* covered." Which was true. Sonja was wearing black slacks and a semisheer blouse that still looked classy. But that was Sonja's style; always a bit conservative.

"Sonja's always been the sugar...," Lani began.

"...and Lani's always been the spice," Sonja finished, before they erupted in a fit of giggles, looking like teenagers again instead of the thirtysomethings they actually were.

"Baby, I told you, no worries." Lani gave Vicki a very deep kiss that forced Sonja and me to look away. "We'll be back around midnight and..." I turned in time to see her whisper the rest of her statement in Vicki's ear, making Vicki blush.

"C'mon, heifer, before we're late." Sonja gave me a gentler kiss, before giving me the "try to have fun" look. After a few more rushed comments and reminders, they were gone.

And then it was just me and Vicki.

She still hadn't moved away from the bedroom doorway and from my position on the sofa, I was giving her an uneasy look. *Why am I here?*

"Did you bring the beer?" she asked.

"Uh, yeah." I had completely forgotten the six-pack at my feet. "You want it in the fridge?"

"I'll do it." She picked up the beer and headed for the kitchen. "Lani made all this snack shit, you hungry?"

"What you got?" I asked, as I tried to calm myself.

"Come look, fool, this ain't no restaurant."

Dammit. Reluctantly, I got to my feet and went into their kitchen. It was entirely too small, barely room enough for the stove, fridge, and sink, let alone the meager cabinet space and their tinyass table. On the table was a spread of rolls, sandwich meats, chips, and potato salad. Vicki was making herself a sandwich, and for a moment I forgot myself and just watched her. Vicki was your stereotypical Californian: body conscious and into just about any kind of physical fitness you could imagine. Dressed in a tank and jeans, you could see how toned she was as she simply fixed herself some food, her muscles moving beneath the skin of her arms in a rhythm that made me bite my lip.

"You gonna just stand there or make something?"

My eyes rose. "Huh? Oh, yeah...sandwich."

She gave me a questioning look before finishing up and squeezed by me on her way out. As soon as I was alone, I started mentally kicking my own ass. Why was I here? Why hadn't I just told Sonja that this wasn't a good idea? Well, because then she'd want to know why. And there was no explanation I could give that she'd be satisfied with, short of my claiming to be sick—which wouldn't fly since Sonja was a nurse. And, of course, telling her the truth would be suicide, so I had no choice but to come.

As I made a couple of sandwiches, I kept telling myself I'd have to be cool. But that was pointless, because deep in my gut I knew what was going to happen...and I still wasn't sure if I wanted it to happen or not. Butches didn't do shit like this. At least not any butch that I knew. But despite feeling like I couldn't do it, I also couldn't ignore what had been happening. The lingering looks, the nervousness in each other's presence, the accidental touches that always ignited sparks...and that fucking kissing episode.

Yes, yes, yes, you heard right. I couldn't replay it exactly; all I remembered was Vicki and I meeting before having to hook up with the girls for a late dinner, sharing some beer and before I knew it we were kissing. Never in my life had I even looked at another butch in a sexual way, but from the first moment I saw Vicki...something was there. Her look, the way she carried herself, damn even the fact that she shaved her head completely bald. And if that alone didn't freak me out, the revelation of her attraction to me sure did. But for the couple months we were around each other, despite the situation, we were able to deal.

"There's no game on, wanna watch a movie?" Vicki called from the other room.

"Depends on the movie," I answered as I finished up. I grabbed a beer from the fridge and walked back into the living room. It was also small, so there was only the sofa to sit on. Vicki was on one end and I took the other, setting my bottle and plate on the coffee table before me. Vicki was flipping through TV channels, and of course there was nothing we found interesting. She started listing all the DVDs they had, but nothing caught my interest.

I occasionally glanced at Vicki, wondering if she was thinking what I was thinking. I knew all the searching for movies and the small talk was just a way to ease the tension. We both knew what could happen tonight. We had never acknowledged the attraction we had for each other, never talked about the kiss, but every time we saw each other, I could see that her eyes mirrored mine. We both wanted to know what could happen, given the chance.

We settled on watching some music videos as we ate, barely talking, only commenting on whatever video was on. But when 50 Cent's *P.I.M.P.* came on, Vicki grinned.

"I love this video," she announced. "That scene with the chick pimp and the two girls on the leash is hot."

"Hell, yeah," I agreed, watching the video with anticipation.

Even though I had seen the video countless times, that one scene was worth seeing any time. And as soon as it came on, we both whistled.

"That shit always turns me on," she said.

"Oh yeah?" I asked.

She nodded. "I got no shame in admitting I get freaky and shit. That's why I dig Lani. She's up for anything."

I turned in my seat to face her. "She be letting you tie her up and shit?"

Vicki grinned. "That and more. Believe me, man, much more."

"What else?" Even though Lani was my girl's friend and all, I couldn't deny the fact that she was hot and her doing the shit Vicki was suggesting was something I definitely wanted to hear more about.

Vicki shrugged. "I've tied her up, blindfolded her, spanked her, flogged her—you know, shit like that."

Unconsciously, I was groping my dick through my jeans, feeling it press against my clit. "Damn. I can't believe Lani's into that shit. Sonja's open and all, but I don't think she's *that* open. Although it would be cool to find out."

Vicki was staring at me intensely, as if she was measuring me. "There's something I got you may want to see."

"What?"

"Hold up." She got up and disappeared into the bedroom. A few moments later, she was back with a DVD in hand, walking over to the entertainment system. I watched her load the movie and sit back on the sofa, remote ready.

I was finished with my food, and now held a second beer in my hand as I watched the screen. It was black and then the title, *The Black & the Bound,* appeared. My eyebrow rose as the title faded and the screen was lit up with a dark-skinned sista on a table. She was on her stomach, naked and spread-eagle, her ankles and wrists tied with rope. As soon as I took that shit in, my nipples tightened and I let out a measured breath.

Vicki had just played her hand.

At first, the girl on the screen was still, just lying on the table—and no lie, that alone was arousing to see. But then we could hear loud footsteps offscreen, causing the girl to writhe against her restraints. After a few seconds, we saw another sista approach the table. Sporting a PVC catsuit and extreme killer heels, she was holding a wooden paddle in one hand, while her other began caressing the naked girl's body.

"I'm not really into dominatrixes all dressed up like this," Vicki said suddenly. "But it's all good."

Apparently it was. Out the corner of my eye I could see her groping herself like I had been doing myself earlier. My eyes went back to the screen just in time to see the dominatrix swing the paddle and it landed a blow on the girl's ass with such a loud smack, the sound echoed throughout the room. The girl on the table cried out, but got no time to relax as the paddle quickly came down on her ass again. The dominatrix was pretty relentless, wielding the paddle with finesse as she decorated the girl's ass with hit after hit, and even through the dark skin, we could see the discoloration beginning to appear.

As much as I had some interest in that S&M shit, I had never seen an actual video, so I was watching in semishock. But that was nothing to the shock I felt when I turned to say something to Vicki and found her slumped beside me, her hand shoved down her unzipped jeans. Damn, I'd been so into the porn, I hadn't even heard her unzip.

She looked over at me and just smirked before turning back to the TV. My eyes went back to the screen, but I was thinking that not even two feet away, Vicki was getting herself off. I couldn't believe she was doing it with me in the room. I had never seen another butch get herself off. It was one of those things you just did on your own. But as I sat there, feeling the sofa jiggle with Vicki's movements, and now watching the dominatrix switch to a flogger, it was as if my dick was screaming at me to touch it. All I had to do was unzip and slide my hand inside. All I had to do was grab my shit and just stroke it, feeling the base of the dick press into my clit. I've mastered jacking off that way and could reach a climax within five minutes if necessary, and not touching myself was too much to bear with all the sexual energy in the room. But I was feeling rather embarrassed about it. I didn't know any other butch who masturbated using her dick that way. And I wasn't sure if I was strong enough to handle the possible ridicule.

"You gonna just sit there?"

My head turned. Vicki's hand was still shoved down her jeans, but she was looking dead into my eyes.

I just shrugged, the embarrassment spreading. Usually I was not the type to be shy about sex, but in this situation, I felt out of my element and couldn't find my footing.

"You can't fool me. I know you wanna do it."

I didn't say anything, but I could tell from her eyes that she understood how I was feeling.

"If you show me yours, I'll show you mine."

My eyes widened. "You're strapped?"

"Hell, yeah," she said. That's when I realized the exact movements her hand had been making within her jeans. She was stroking her dick.

I relaxed for a moment, enjoying the newfound knowledge. I took a deep breath and closed my eyes as my hands moved to my waist. I quickly unbuckled my belt, unbuttoned my pants, unzipped, and slipped my hand inside—but then I stopped.

"I'll go first," she said suddenly. My eyes opened and I watched as she lifted her hips and tugged her jeans down to midthigh. She reached inside the opening of her boxers and pulled out one of the most perfect dicks I've ever laid eyes on. It matched the color of her skin almost exactly. It looked to be about six inches, average width, not too veiny, and her hand fit around it as if it belonged there. She resumed stroking it and I sat there in amazement, watching someone else do what I thought I alone had done.

"Your turn." Her voice had grown softer with arousal.

I tugged my pants down like she had, revealing my own boxers. And just as she had done, I pulled my dick out through the flap. My own was jet black, completely smooth and seven inches—bigger than the one I usually packed. But, for some reason, deep down I had wanted to impress Vicki tonight.

And she indeed looked impressed. She winked at me as she reached behind a cushion, retrieving a bottle of lube. I watched her apply some to her hand and dick before tossing the bottle to me. I couldn't help but smile as I did the same, and then we just sat there together, watching each other as we jacked off, the porn completely forgotten. To say that it was arousing is a gross understatement. Just watching her slick hand move up and down the shaft, the way she would occasionally play with the head or slow her movements teasingly, was a sight that had me about ready to cum. My own stroking was more leisurely; I was just enjoying the moment I was in, wanting this to last for as long as it could despite every down-stroke threatening to push me over the edge.

"Damn, look at that," Vicki said suddenly.

I looked back to the television and watched the dominatrix press a large dildo into the girl's ass. At some point, the dominatrix had placed a ball gag in the girl's mouth, so as the dick was sinking into her, her cries were muffled. Her limbs were taut, hands balled into fists, as the dominatrix kept telling her to be a good slut and take it. You could see the pain on the girl's face, but she was pressing her ass back, trying to take as much as the dominatrix was willing to give.

"You like anal?" I asked.

Vicki's eyes met mine again. "Yeah, I'm into that. Lani loves taking my dick in her ass. You?"

I nodded, but looked away. Only Sonja knew that I enjoyed getting fucked in the ass, and, surprisingly, she had obliged me a few times. It wasn't something I was entirely proud of, since just about all my butch friends refused to bottom for their girls. So, the fact that I not only enjoyed bottoming, but also enjoyed receiving anal was something I kept on the down-low.

I heard a sudden movement beside me and before I knew it, Vicki had gotten to the floor and was kneeling before me. Our eyes met briefly before she moved my hand away and wrapped her strong hand around my dick. I let out a soft groan as I watched her stroke me. She pumped me for a few moments before lowering her head to take me in her mouth.

"Yo, that got lube on it," I protested, half wanting to shove her head down on my dick, half wondering if I could let her.

"It's flavored, don't worry." And with that, I watched her swallow my entire dick with skill. I watched in awe, not able to believe this was actually happening. Never in my life would I ever have thought that I'd see another butch suck my dick, let alone do it with such hunger. She bobbed her head with ferociousness, her sucking beyond audible, the sounds bouncing off the walls, and she stroked the remaining inches in perfect timing. My clit was rock hard, screaming from the pleasurable pressure, and I was afraid that I was going to cum too soon. I raised my hands to try to get her to back off, but I ended up grabbing her head, feeling the slickness of her scalp in my hands as I pressed down instead. She gagged for a slight moment, but didn't back away; then she gave a loud, muffled moan that I swear I felt through my clit and down to my very toes.

I held her head tightly and started fucking her mouth. Vicki's hands gripped my hips for balance as I just lunged at her, moving with an aggression I'd never felt before. I was intensely watching her lips stretched around my dick, the way her cheeks hollowed as she sucked me with urgency, how her saliva was coating my dick so perfectly that entry between her swollen lips was effortless.

My head fell back as I lost myself in the sensation, trying to ignore the words screaming in my mind that this was beyond gay. Hell, I've heard people say that butch-on-butch sex was Super Gay. Butches didn't do this. But feeling the strength in Vicki as she sucked my dick, I didn't care. This shit right here was purely animalistic, hedonism at its best—raw heat and desire, just the need to get off. I understood all this as I felt myself start to cum. I held her head firmly as I shoved my dick down her throat, feeling my thighs twitch and my clit swell. I came, holding Vicki's head to my crotch, feeling the heat of her on my pussy through the boxers, knowing that she probably couldn't breathe but not caring. I was loud and unashamed as I gave my cum to her, feeling my entire body just cave in on itself.

After a few moments I slumped back against the sofa, letting Vicki's head go. I was expecting her to give me an angry look for the roughness, but her eyes were filled with pure lust and delight. She sat back on her heels just smiling at me smugly, her lips puffy and red. Her dick was in her hand and she was stroking it slowly as she looked me over hungrily.

She was ready to get hers.

I forced my weary body to sit up. "Sit down."

Vicki shook her head, that wicked smile still on her face. "Naw, baby boy, I don't want it like that."

My eyebrow rose in confusion. "What do you mean?"

She reached in her pocket and pulled out a condom. "I want that ass."

"Hells, no."

"You can't say you don't want it," she said. "I saw that look in your eyes. Now get on your knees."

"I ain't going down like that with you. I'll suck you off, but that's it."

"Tell me you don't want to feel my dick in your ass." She held my gaze challengingly. "Tell me you don't want to bend over right now and feel me slide in that tight hole."

"I don't care, yo. That shit's too far."

"It's just me and you, son. No one else gotta know that you did it. I know you want it, you know you want it. So stop worrying about your fucking pride and get what you want."

My jaw was tense as I returned her gaze, but I couldn't deny her words. God I wanted it. I wanted to feel what it would be like to get fucked the way I fuck. Sonja was great, but it wasn't the same. And I knew, at this moment, I was being handed the chance.

My pride wouldn't let me answer her. So I just stood, slowly turned my back, and lay on the sofa, my ass facing her. I felt Vicki's hands on my boxers and as she pulled them down to my knees, my eyes closed in shame. I tried to pretend it was Sonja kneeling between my awkwardly spread legs, that her hands were caressing my ass, gently pinching and swatting each cheek. But as soon as I heard the snap of the condom, I couldn't pretend anymore. And the way my pussy was swelling again from that very sound, I knew I didn't want to. I felt Vicki reach for more lube, heard her apply some to her dick, and the cold shock of her applying some to my asshole, making me tense up.

I felt her body over mine, her voice in my ear. "You're gonna want to relax that ass, baby boy, or it's gonna hurt."

I took a deep breath, trying to relax my entire body, telling myself it was just going to be like it was with Sonja: slow, measured, and as soon as I was ready, I'd be able to take it all. But I should have known better. I should have expected the same thing I'd have done if I'd been in Vicki's position at that moment. As soon as I felt her dick at my hole, she pushed in quickly, and I growled from the pain, pressing my face into the cushion. Vicki pressed all the way in, till I felt her boxers against my bare ass and she held herself still for a moment. Then I heard her groan as her hands found my waist, holding me to her, literally grinding her completely embedded dick into me. I was gasping at how full I felt; the dildos I had used before had never felt this big, despite my always secretly craving more. Well, I was getting more now, and on the other end of that dick was a butch who knew what she was doing.

Vicki pulled out halfway, then pushed in just as quickly, and as before, she held herself against me tightly, forcing me to feel all of her. The pain had already subsided and all I felt was pleasurably full, my body starting to relax in the blissful feeling. But as soon as I did, Vicki started up again. She pulled out, this time letting only the head of her dick remain, before she snapped her hips forward, driving it back into me. I gritted my teeth, my hands balling up in fists from the forcefulness. She pulled back again and repeated the quick thrusting, this time so hard that my head hit the back of the sofa. My hands reached out to brace myself as Vicki fucked me, each thrust powerful and unyielding. I knew that this was not the way she fucked Lani. This was the way you fucked someone who was as tough as you were. Someone who could handle it as rough, aggressive, and uncaring as you wanted to give it. Someone who understood that you just wanted to fuck.

She was methodical in her fucking, each stroke as measured as the one before, slamming into me so hard she might as well have been swinging a hammer. But hell, I was enjoying it. I loved being opened this way, impaled. Her grip on my waist was tight, and she began pulling me back to meet her thrusts. Instinctively I moved with her and in no time, she didn't have to guide me, because I was throwing my ass back, trying to get as much as I could. Our grunts and groans echoed through the apartment, and maybe even through the building. It felt beyond incredible. She was giving it to me just the way I've always wanted it done. And when I felt her lie on top of me, her dick in deep again, and hold herself still, I was gasping. She rotated her hips and it felt as if she was stirring my insides; my body flinching from the sensations.

One of Vicki's arms moved up to encircle my shoulders,

and when she started fucking me again, she kept her dick in deep, only withdrawing a couple of inches for her thrusts. Her body molded to mine as she fucked me slowly, and I let my head fall forward, unsure of what to do with all that I was feeling. I felt her other hand reach round my body and grab my dick, making me moan. She was stroking me as she fucked me; every time she pushed in, I'd feel the base of my dick hit my clit and my eyes rolled in my head. She pumped me deeply, her teeth nipping the back of my neck, her growls signaling that she was about to cum. In response, I pressed my ass back to meet her thrusts, in turn helping her jack me off. Her arm around my body was tightening, and I reached back and grabbed her thigh, pulling her closer as I worked my ass on her dick.

"Oh shit…," she whispered in my ear.

She was riding my ass faster, groaning louder and louder, yanking hard on my dick now, while I bucked even faster. Vicki suddenly grabbed both my wrists and pulled them behind me. With one hand, she pinned my wrists to my back then started to ram me. If I hadn't turned my face in time, I wouldn't have been able to breathe, because now she was completely gone. She stroked me harder and harder, and before I knew it, my second orgasm of the night peaked and I yelled from the pleasure, clenching my thighs and asscheeks together, which triggered Vicki. She pressed me down into the sofa, pounding me harder and harder as she came, calling me every nasty name in the book, her voice laced with unbridled lust, and I just took it…gladly. She kept humping me until her body finally gave up, and then she slowly pulled out of me.

We didn't speak for a few moments, then she playfully swatted my ass and said, "You a'ight?"

"Yeah," I answered, glancing at the clock on the wall. We still had a couple of hours before the girls were supposed to come back. I felt Vicki move, and I gingerly got to my feet, pulling my boxers and pants up. "I'll be right back," I said, heading to the bathroom to clean up.

When I finally came back to the living room, Vicki was on the sofa, eating a sandwich and watching the news. My stomach growled. I attempted to walk as steadily as I could but sensed her smirking as I passed her on my way to the kitchen. I fixed myself something to eat and grabbed another beer before joining her.

We didn't talk about it. We just ate, watched television and talked shit about everything else under the sun until Lani and Sonja came back a little after midnight. The girls were all teary as they said their good-byes; Lani and Vicki would be leaving in a couple of days. Vicki and I gave each other daps and the mandatory butch nod before Sonja and I left.

"Did you have a good time?" Sonja asked, as she laced her arm through mine.

"It was a'ight," I replied.

"It better have been more than *a'ight* since you're walking all funny," she said, winking at me.

TORI'S SECRET

Andrea Miller

As I was bending down to get the tray out of
the cupboard, my dress rode even further up
my ass and my toes squeezed yet more painfully into my pointy shoes. Standing up and
opening the fridge, I noticed different discom-
forts. In fact, no matter which way I moved
the French maid costume was unbearable.
Tori'd given it to me for my birthday the week
before and when I'd unwrapped it, I balked. I
mean, I was femme but this costume crossed a
line—and besides, I was tired of getting pres-
ents from Tori that were really for her. Somehow, though, here I was in the dinky hat and
frilly apron anyway.

Tori was having friends over to watch the
hockey game and I could hear them cheering
and stomping even with the long hall separating

us. I wished they'd be quieter; it was my name on the lease, after all. Tori had moved in with me a year before, but so far she had weaseled out of making it official.

I cracked open four beers and placed them on the tray. Then I reached up and got Tori's favorite glass out of the top cupboard. She wanted a rum and Coke—a nice tough butch drink to complement the way she could swig it back, the way she could swagger, the way she could pinch my little maid's ass. Boy, did Tori think she was made of metal.

I opened the freezer and grabbed the tray of ice cubes, popped four out and let them clink to the bottom of the glass. Ice: now that was something that could actually spark a good thought about Tori, a memory from the beginning of our relationship. It had been a hot, sticky day and we'd just gotten back from the beach. "Come here, Kelly," I heard Tori call, but I was in the living room and couldn't tell where her voice was coming from. I walked down the hall and poked my head in the bedroom—no, not there. Then I stepped into the kitchen and suddenly she was behind me with her arm around my waist and her mouth on my neck. Her teeth grazing my skin.

"I'm gonna fuck you so hard and good," she crooned. "That for the rest of your life, when someone rams their fingers into your cunt, you're gonna think of me; you're gonna wish they were my magic fingers inside you." Then in one swift motion she yanked my bikini bottoms down and bent me over the table.

I shut my eyes as Tori wedged her thigh between mine, parting my legs. "Look at that little pucker," she said. "So pink and exposed. Just waiting for some attention. Baby, is this what it needs?"

My asshole felt suddenly like it was on fire and I tried to wriggle free. Tori had a hand on my back, however, and she was pinning me down. "Relax," she murmured and as my struggling settled into a slight squirm, I realized that what she was rubbing me with was actually not hot, but rather very cold. Ice cold. And as the ice made contact with my skin, it slowly melted, trickling to my pussy and down my thighs. Christ, it felt good. So good—so slick against the gritty grains of sand left over from the beach—that another kind of wetness formed between my legs.

Tori relaxed her hold on my back and bent down, kissed the undersides of my thighs and the globes of each of my buttcheeks. Then, snaking her warm tongue between my crack, she found my asshole and licked me there until I begged her to make me come.

On a certain level I wish that what followed then had been nothing special, that when push came to shove Tori couldn't follow through on her cocksure promise to be better with her hands than anyone else. But the truth is, she *was* that good and I guess that was the reason I couldn't break it off with her even though everything about her pissed me off. And I guess, too, that was why she was always so popular with the ladies— even those she hadn't (or rather hadn't yet) fucked. One look at Tori's trimmed nails and strong hands and women instinctively knew she was going to be good.

I topped off the cup with rum, then headed down the hall— my heels falling silently on the carpet all the way to the living room where Tori and her friends were talking.

"There are different kinds of trust," Tori said, looking her friend Katie in the eye. And I thought, *Fuck, she's getting deeper with Katie than she ever does with me; maybe she occasionally says something real when I'm not around.* Tori, after all, hadn't seemed to notice that I'd gotten back from the kitchen.

"It's like this," Tori continued. "You can trust me with your wallet, but not with your girlfriend."

Katie visibly bristled and Tori laughed, punching her arm. "Jesus, man, just kidding." But Katie didn't look comforted and I definitely wasn't. The thing is, I know about jokes. I know that what makes them funny is that on some level at least, there's truth in them.

Tori's laughter slowly faded to a giggle—a little butch giggle she probably would've called a cackle—and everyone else just sat there, looking at the TV or Tori's boots or some other random point. But I don't think any of us really saw anything except a picture of Jacqueline in our minds' eyes. Jacqueline, Katie's girlfriend, with her perfect curves and long dark hair. Jacqueline with her easy smile.

Jacqueline wasn't like the others; Tori didn't just fuck her behind my back. Instead, two months after the hockey game, she left me for her. I knew things hadn't been working out, but finding Tori's note on the coffee table just about killed me. There was my pride thinking, *Damn why didn't I leave her first?* There was the eternal pisser that everything always worked out for her, and then there was the fact that made me really raw—that she'd never again bury her fingers in me and then let me suck them off. The force of my reaction, however, went beyond the pain of those three points and crossed into out of control. Sobbing and slamming my fists into the walls, I hurtled back to being four years old—to when my father left. I remembered my mother and me coming home to find both his note and the plate he'd used for lunch on the kitchen table. And now, twenty-four years later, that plate seemed a terrible kick in the teeth. After years of marriage, my father couldn't even throw away the crust from his own sandwich.

In a similar way, Tori (in her PS) left me with shit to clean up, too. "I'll be by soon to get my stuff," she wrote. "Maybe you can pack it for me." And sure enough almost everything Tori owned was still strewn about the apartment. On the closet floor I found one of her T-shirts that still smelled like her—like men's deodorant and cigarette smoke. I put it on and crawled into bed, looking for comfort in the cotton. But the clock ticked on without comfort or sleep. Forgetting I hated Tori, I'd lodge a pillow next to my belly and remember her sexy crooked smile and the deep indent her calve muscles created in her shins. Then I'd kick off the blankets and plot fantastical schemes for revenge.

Three days later I called my friend Tracy. "Tori still hasn't come to get her stuff and I doubt she ever will," I said, the telephone cord drooping.

"I could see her doing that," Tracy answered. "She'd think that by not coming, she could avoid conflict."

"But I need her to come, Tracy. I need resolution. I keep thinking I see Tori and Jacqueline everywhere—on the bus or at the grocery store. I'll never be able to go to Sister's again; that is actually somewhere they might be."

"You know what?" Tracy said and it sounded like she was tapping her nails on a table. "We need to go to Sister's right now because you need to face this. I'll be by your place in an hour."

Later, I wondered what had possessed me to phone Tracy looking for a shoulder to cry on. She was my best friend but she didn't know how to be a shoulder. Tracy wanted to fix problems—to take action—and once she had a plan, she was an unstoppable force. "It's Tuesday," she'd assured me, "they won't be there." But Tracy hadn't remembered there was a drag king show on and that ninety percent of the city's lesbians had bought tickets in advance. So Tori and Jacqueline *were* there—Jacqueline with her hand in Tori's back pocket, her head on Tori's shoulder. Humiliated, I went home before they saw me.

After Tracy left I wriggled out of my dress and unhooked my bra. Then, lifting up my pillow, I found Tori's T-shirt where I'd left it that morning, folded into a neat rectangle. I pulled it over my head as I had every night since finding the note but this time I couldn't catch her scent—just a whiff of my own perfume, which struck me suddenly as smelling sickly sweet. I decided that in order to sleep I'd need something more of Tori, so I opened the closet. My half was lined with dresses on hangers trimmed with lace, while in Tori's half, the few hangers she had were mostly dangling empty and the bulk of her wardrobe was on the floor with the shoes. I rummaged in her heap until I found her khaki cargo pants. Then, putting them on, I checked myself out in the mirror.

At first I looked out of the corner of my eye, imagining it was Tori I was seeing. But finally I looked head-on and what I saw took me by surprise; I actually didn't look bad out of a dress. As my build was smaller than Tori's, her clothes hung differently on me, giving me a wiry look that was wolfishly sexy and compelled me to complete the outfit.

I found one of Tori's ball caps—a black one—and tucked

my blond hair underneath it. I fished her thumb ring out of a bowl of pennies and slipped it on. Then I opened up the bottom drawer where she kept her sex toys and dug through the harnesses and dildos. She'd taken the best of them with her, yet I managed to find a nice thick black cock and a passable harness. I took off the cargo pants and got the goodies strapped on.

Tori and most of the other women I'd ever dated were stone proud, so it had been a while since I'd worn a cock. But I'd always liked the feel of it and even now, when I had no one to thrust it in, I was getting juicy. I pulled the pants over the silicone and admired the bulge between my legs. Then I lightly ran my fingers over that bulge—my gaze fixed on my reflection in the mirror.

Grinding into my hand, I imagined that the cup of my fingers was Tori's cunt, that I was fucking her and that she was loving it—moaning and squirming like a silly bitch. I undid the zipper, let the dick spring free, and then dipped a finger into my pussy to slick the head with my own wetness. Choking the rod, as if doing it hard enough would really make it shoot a load, I felt the rub of the harness working my clit and I cocked my legs wide open. In the mirror I watched my nipples poke hard against Tori's T-shirt and my hips thrust up and up. I let out one deep moan and came simultaneously with my reflection.

Two nights later I was decked out in more of Tori's clothes when the doorbell rang. *Shit,* I thought, *I can't answer like this.* How could I explain my queer cross-dressing to any of my friends, to my mother, or—on the off chance that it was her—to Tori? I stumbled out of the jeans, wallet chain clinking to the ground, and threw on a floral bathrobe. "Hello," I said, opening the door, a little breathless.

Outside was Katie, running her fingers through her short, sandy hair. "I've been wanting to talk to you," she said. "But I wasn't sure you'd want to...."

I was surprised Katie'd come because she'd always been more Tori's friend than mine—she and Jacqueline had just been people I'd see at parties or events. But Katie had nothing to worry about. I was very glad to see her; finally I'd have someone to talk to about the breakup, someone who wouldn't get sick of hearing about it. I invited her in and we settled into the living room, her on the sofa and me in the armchair. "I don't get it," she began. "Things were fine between Jacqueline and me, but it's like women can't resist Tori."

"Tell me about it," I said. "It doesn't matter what a woman thinks her type is; she'll fall for Tori anyway."

"Yeah, Jacqueline likes butch blonds like her, but she usually goes for someone not built quite so much like a brick shit house. You know, someone kind of wiry like me."

The two of us went quiet for a minute—a real "tear in the beer" bout of silence. "Katie," I finally said, "I'm being a crap hostess. Do you want a drink?"

"What've you got?" she answered, following me to the kitchen.

I looked in the fridge. Tori's pop had all gone flat, but two of her beers were left. Cracking them both open, I handed one to Katie and noticed she was looking down. Following her gaze, I realized my robe was sliding open, revealing the curve of my breast. I quickly adjusted it and Katie laughed. Then still smiling she pulled me to her, kissing me. Her lips and tongue were hesitant but precise, and I had felt so lonely with Tori gone that now for a moment I melted into Katie. It didn't feel right, though. I knew I was being pathetic—making out with Tori's leftovers.

"I can't do this," I said, crying. "I'm not ready."

Breakups spur change. You know, people do stuff like cut their hair or move across the country. Me? I wanted to change jobs. After three years at university, I'd dropped out and gotten work at an art gallery. Still there seven years later, it was wearing thin for me, dealing with the same shit daily. Yuppies buying Inuit art. Yuppies buying abstract art. Yuppies buying something a little daring.

About a week after Katie's visit, I was once again scanning the classifieds for a new position. As usual there wasn't much unless you aspired to be a babysitter, but finally in the right-hand corner I spotted it—a want ad for an assistant manager at Between the Lines bookstore. The very same shop where Jacqueline worked.

For a moment I just sat there grinning with my coffee growing cold. Then I jumped up to find Katie's number. I had a lot of things to do. I had the perfect revenge to execute.

The following evening I showed my hairdresser a picture of a seventeen-year-old skater boy and said I wanted his hair. My hairdresser, who had known me and my femme ways for years, clutched at my long locks—drama queen shock written on his face. "I'm serious," I said, and I was. I'd spent hours milking Katie for information on Jacqueline's turn-ons, and now I intended to live up to all of them—including the short hair.

Since I hadn't wanted Katie to know what I was up to, it

had been complicated getting information out of her. I'd had to pretend I wanted to know intimate details because I was nursing an obsessive jealousy for Jacqueline and, as a kind of give and take, I'd had to dole out similar information about Tori. Ultimately, the trouble I'd taken had been worth it. I now knew, for example, that Tori was not the ideal lover for Jacqueline, as Jacqueline liked both getting fucked and fucking. I knew there was no way Tori let Jacqueline strap it on or slip a finger in, but *I* was more than ready to play those games. To do anything, really.

Just about finished, the hairdresser's razor hummed against my neck and his scissors snipped at a few rogue strands. I looked at my hair lying in clumps on the tiled floor. Then I looked in the mirror and sucked my teeth. Fuck, I wanted to blow a kiss to that sexy butch looking back at me. This was going to work. All I had to do was get the job and buy the cologne Jacqueline loved—the one Katie couldn't stand and had always refused to wear.

Two weeks later it was my first day at Between the Lines and the manager was showing me the ropes—giving me the grand tour, introducing me to the staff. Everything was going well, but I was nervous knowing Jacqueline could be anywhere and that at any moment she could spring out like a pop-up monster in a children's book. As chance would have it, however, I had nothing to worry about—I was the one who popped out at her. The manager and I rounded the magazine rack and there she was, kneeling in front of the philosophy section with her back to us. "Jacqueline," the manager said, clearing his throat. "I'd like to introduce you to Kelly."

From her place on the floor, Jacqueline slowly looked up at

me—her easy smile first playing over my boots and then up
and up until she met my eyes and the happy curve of her lips
was lopped off, sliced up by three huge shocks. One, we were
face to face for the first time since she'd stolen my girlfriend.
Two, henceforth she'd have to deal with me daily. And three,
I didn't look the way she remembered.

Fortunately, by this point so many people had expressed
shock over my new look that I'd learned to shrug that off.
Tracy, for instance, had told me such quick comfort in a 180-
degree turn meant I didn't know my own true identity—a
bullshit line, I concluded, meant to conceal her own fear. The
very human fear of gray. Of worlds colliding. Of categories
blurring. Yes, people want tidy distinctions. Butch or femme.
Hot or cold. Love or hate. Villain or victim. And so it was
making people very nervous to see me with short hair. To
hear me say I'd always had butch and femme sides and that
the butch had just been waiting to learn how to swagger.

But Jacqueline's look of bewilderment had various sources,
not just the butch thing—and so it was a zillion times harder
for her than for others. That's what I was thinking, anyway,
when the book she'd been trying to shelve slipped from her
fingers and fell to the floor with a thud.

The manager's gaze flicked in a triangle from me to Jacqueline to the book, which lay pages spread. Spine arched. "Have
you two met before?" he asked.

Jacqueline avoided me for weeks, but it wasn't wasted time. I
was studying her and our game by spending a few minutes of
every shift in the hunting and fishing section. I'd open a random book to a random page and I'd read until I found some
nugget of advice I needed, and in that way I learned how to

circle in slowly, how to interpret every gesture—the tilt of her head, the flick of her hair. And I learned when to start reeling in.

"Jacqueline," I said one afternoon when all the signs were right and we were alone in the staff room. "We should talk." She had a peach in one hand and a book in the other and instead of putting them down she gripped them tighter, apparently not noticing the trail of peach juice that dripped down her fingers and all the way to her wrist. I licked my lips and sat down across from her.

"You obviously aren't comfortable around me," I began. "But I'm not at all mad at you."

"No?" she said, her voice lifted in hope.

"No—you did me a favor. Things weren't working between Tori and me. I couldn't be myself with her.... The two of you, on the other hand—you make sense together."

Afraid of sounding smarmy, I paused then and looked at Jacqueline, trying to read her. The corners of her lips were beginning to curl up into their natural position and her blue eyes were so wide open the fringes of her lashes were forced vertical. She'd put down her book and fruit and she now seemed on the verge of clasping her hands together. Yes, she was buying it. And of course she was, I thought, gaining confidence. She wanted nothing more than to have her guilty conscience soothed.

We talked until the microwave clock said 1:28 and I reminded her that we had better get back to work. "But let's have a hug first," I said when we were both standing.

Without hesitation Jacqueline threw her arms around my neck, showing me how everything about her was deliciously soft—the crush of her breasts against mine, the tickle of her angora sweater, even the fuzzy smell of peach on her fingers. I realized I was going to enjoy fucking her for more than just the ironic revenge of it and in the same instant she realized she was attracted to me. I could tell by of the way she instinctively touched the back of my neck, then quickly stiffened.

I don't know what it was Jacqueline liked about me—the hair, the cologne, the lean press of my bones, or something else altogether. Maybe something perverse like curiosity about where her lover had been. All I know is that hug marked the beginning of months of seduction. Months of standing too close, of double entendre, of private jokes. I remember once being inches away from her in the storeroom. Hemmed in by books, yes, but mostly that close just because we wanted to be. Jacqueline had her face turned up to me and her lips parted, ready to be kissed. I leaned in like I was going to oblige her and then I quickly turned away. My mouth was watering for her, too, but I knew it was better this way, better to make her wait until wanting crushed her guilt, made her reckless. And it was another month before she was that hopelessly ensnared and an opportunity arose—dished up in fact by Tori, who forgot to pick her up one night.

"Jacqueline, it's dark and wet out there," I said. "Let me drive you home."

The streetlight in front of their apartment cast a weird orange glow over everything in the car, while their living room window was a perfect black rectangle with no one home. I locked all the doors with the press of a button, turned off the ignition, and let my thigh brush hers. "You aren't going anywhere," I said, jingling the keys, flashing my best demonic smile.

She playfully grabbed for the keys but I whisked them

behind my back. Then she flung her arms around my waist, pressing into me, and continued trying to snatch them. Now her face was inches from mine and I couldn't resist. Loving the risk of it, the possibility of Tori showing up at any minute, I leaned in and kissed her—a sweet, soft kiss that left me wanting more bite. I pulled away and handed her the cold metal teeth. "I can't believe you fell for that," I sneered. "It's the oldest trick in the school yard."

Jacqueline's face fogged into bewilderment, then darkened into pissed off—just what we needed for something more savage. We kissed again and this time began humping with the urgency of dogs, so hard I thought her slit would strip me of my skin, grind down my bones. I wanted to hurt her, I wanted to make her come and I no longer knew the line between those extremes. I jacked up her skirt and drove my fingers in.

Her cunt was slick, yet it clamped on to my knuckles with the strength of a snake crushing a mouse in its guts. I rammed harder, slithering to my knees between the dashboard and the passenger seat. I flicked my tongue on her clit—once, twice, three times, felt her shudder and pound her fist into my back. Then I pulled away. Looked down at her shaved pussy—a cleft moon in the night.

"Let's go to your place," she said, her voice throaty like I'd never heard it before.

After that Jacqueline and I fucked everywhere. In my car like the hard line of the seats didn't exist, like we couldn't ride too fast. In my bed with all the nasty irony of using Tori's cocks. And even in the store—in the staff bathroom during breaks and between the shelves after hours.

Jacqueline talked about leaving Tori for me, but wanting more, I put her off. I wanted Tori to catch us, wanted to see for myself the smugness wiped from her face. So I left hints—the whisper of teeth marks on Jacqueline's skin, for example—hoping something would raise her suspicions and make her spy on Jacqueline. Months passed and the lies became more complicated.

"Tori went to her mum's," Jacqueline said one Friday night in the car. "She asked me to go but I said I couldn't. I said I should visit my folks, too."

"Are you going to?"

"Of course not. I wouldn't miss the chance to be with you all weekend."

Excellent, I thought, taking a sudden turn that veered us away from my apartment, our original destination. At the very least this would be an opportunity to leave more clues—my hair in their bed, my scent on their towels. And at best this would be the climax of it all and we would finally get caught.

"Where are you going?" Jacqueline asked, looking nervous but not saying no.

Their apartment was new—the walls brilliantly white, the carpet pink like the inside of a shell. Floral sofa, books lining shelves, soft light. Those were Jacqueline's touches. For signs of Tori I could see gum wrappers on the table, clothes slumped on the floor, dirty dishes in the sink. No, I decided, I didn't miss Tori.

Jacqueline leaned down to undo her sandals and I admired her ass—two firm fine grapefruits I couldn't help but touch. Still bending over, Jacqueline wriggled against my hand, giving me access to everything. She was wearing red Capri's and through the cloth her pussy felt like a squishy bun fresh from the oven. I undid the button, then the zipper, then pulled the pants down to her ankles. Pulled down her white panties sprinkled with hearts. And all the while I thought about how Jacqueline and Tori surely must have fucked in this same spot.

Jacqueline stood up and pulled off her shirt. "Now you," she said, undoing all my buttons one by one. Then when we were both naked, her fingers trickled over my skin. My nipples turned into hard pebbles, my cunt into a river. We tumbled to the floor.

Jacqueline swept her hands over my thighs, belly, breasts. Broad strokes that finally condensed into tiny wet circles playing my clit. She slipped a finger inside and, just as Tori had once predicted, I thought of her. But not like she had said I would. No, I was imagining her walking in, watching. Maybe looking crushed or maybe jacking off to the rhythm of Jacqueline sliding in and out—two different, yet delicious images that made my hips rock faster. Yes, my fantasies were so real I could hear Tori's footsteps, the key in the lock, the door swinging open.

Then Jacqueline froze suddenly and I realized fantasy and reality had finally merged. Tori, her hand still on the doorknob, was standing above us with her mouth gaping open. I tried not to grin, yet for those first few seconds victory felt sexier than the orgasm I'd missed out on. Then I noticed something was off—not like I'd imagined it. Tori looked neither turned on nor crushed, rather a mixture of the two and then some. Her face containing traces of things that seemed to have no origin—guilt and amusement even. But of course there was an origin and she soon bounded in on Tori's heels, not noticing until it was too late that Jacqueline and I were on the floor.

"I love it when you fuck me up the ass," Katie declared to Tori.

THE BREAK

Cheryl B.

My ex-girlfriend Kate invited me over for dinner. The minute she opened the door I was immediately reminded of what attracted me to her from the beginning: the blue eyes, dark spiky hair, small sturdy body, and the perfectly round bottom covered in baggy jeans. I wanted to turn her around and smack her ass, but we hadn't seen each other in over two months and had more pressing things to get over first.

After the awkward "Hello" hug, we sat down at her kitchen table for the lasagna, which she had baked to perfection and served with a crisp salad and warm bread. I'd almost forgotten what a good cook she was. Almost forgotten that on our first date, Kate had described herself as a domestic butch.

"I like to cook," she had said.

"And I like to eat," I answered before pushing her down on the bed.

When we were finished with the lasagna, we moved into the living room where we sat on separate parts of her sectional couch to watch the DVD. It doesn't matter what the movie was, and I can't remember it one bit. But I found myself trying to figure out a way to smoothly move myself onto her section of the couch. Maybe if I stretched out far enough, I would touch her leg. I tried this several times but couldn't completely work it. The last time I sat on this couch with her, she lay across my knee as I smacked her fleshy cheeks with a paddle. I'd worked it into a good rhythm, moving from one red-welted cheek to another with an intensity that almost scared me.

"Baby, I don't think I can take anymore," Kate cried.

"Oh, you're going to take it." I picked up the rhythm.

"It feels so good," she acquiesced.

"I bet it does." I continued smacking.

But that night I kept my distance as she didn't seem too interested in crossing over onto my area of the couch.

Following the movie, we stood in her doorway for the good-bye.

"It's late," I said, looking at the clock on the wall.

"What do you mean by that?" she asked cautiously.

I reached out and touched her hand—I couldn't help myself. When she touched me back, it was obvious we were both under the spell of the familiar.

"I mean it's past midnight," I offered.

"Does that mean you want to stay over?" Kate asked.

"Do you want me to?"

"If you want to."

"Are you sure?"

"Yeah, it's too late. The bus is weird now."

"I can sleep on the couch."

"You don't have to do that."

"Are you sure?"

"Yes."

Kate handed me my favorite red flannel pajamas. The ones I'd always worn when I stayed over during our two year relationship. They were soft and warm and as soon as they were in my hands, I realized how much I'd missed them. Or perhaps I'd just missed her. I went into the bathroom to change. Just a few months prior, I would have disrobed right in the middle of the living room, but since we were broken up I felt self-conscious. I was surprised that she had even kept the pajamas; I was even more surprised to find my pink toothbrush waiting for me in her medicine cabinet in the same spot I had always kept it. But then her toothbrush was still in my cabinet, too. I didn't want to throw it out. "Lesbian couples never really break up," someone said to me years ago, "they just find new ways to be co-dependent." I never thought that was true. I'm not one of those people who could be friends with my exes, so this was new territory for me.

Kate's new girl made her presence known in the bathroom as well. There was an unfamiliar hair product sitting out on the sink next to expensive loose powder. On the shelf above were two tacky hair accessories with long strands of blonde hair still attached. I picked up one of the barrettes and studied the specimen. I could tell by the way the hair caught the light that the other girl was a natural blonde. Kate always told me she didn't like blondes, she only liked brunettes, like me. My ex-boyfriend told me he didn't like women with large breasts, he only liked women with smaller chests, like me. You can imagine where that went when we broke up.

By the time I got ready, Kate was already in bed, tucked up to her chin, journal in hand. I didn't know what to expect. Was this really just a friendly sleepover? Were we going to get it on? Even worse, I didn't know what I wanted to have happen. I got into the bed and she stopped writing, ending the entry with an exaggerated flourish of her pen. She put the journal on her nightstand, and I realized that I'd never seen her write in a journal before. Was this a new thing? So much can happen in two months, I thought as I ducked down under the covers.

She shut off the light and moved closer to me, placing her arm around my waist. I didn't know whether to burst out crying or kiss her desperately. Either way, the weight of our separation was apparent, and we melted into each other as if nothing had happened, as if we'd never broken up.

I rolled on top of her and held down her arms. She was my prisoner.

"I'm your prisoner," Kate said playfully.

"Oh, yes you are." I reached over the side of her bed and felt around for her wrist restraints. They were still attached to the bed frame, one on each side. It was nice to see my girl hadn't lost her lust for pervery. I turned her around, belly down, bottom up and tightly fastened each wrist.

"Stick your pretty ass in the air," I whispered in her ear.

She did as I told her, pushing her ass out in exaggeration. I pulled her satin blindfold off the bedpost, fastened it around her head.

"Oh no!" she cried.

I opened the bottom drawer of her night stand, where she kept the supplies and felt around for her riding crop. It was at the bottom. Did this mean she hadn't used it in a while? Was blondie not into spanking?

I spread her knees farther apart and fastened each ankle in its restraint.

"Don't move," I told her and smacked her ass hard with my hand just to emphasize the seriousness of the situation.

"Yes," she answered.

"Yes, what?"

"Yes, Ma'am," she answered. This was all part of our game, and I was ecstatic to hear that she hadn't forgotten the dialogue. Then I picked up the riding crop, got off the bed, and walked a few feet back to regard the situation; my little domestic butch prisoner was waving her ample ass in the air just waiting for it. No one else had ever done this to me—turned me into such a dirty foul-mouthed bitch with a bad attitude and a steady, sadistic hand. Before Kate I was not particularly interested in much outside the typical fucking and sucking that had been part of my existence as a bisexual woman. But something about her just brought out my femme top.

She was really begging for it now, waving her bottom in the air.

"You better smack my ass soon, or else," she implored, barely able to move any part of her body except her ass which was thrusting wildly. I could see her pussy slick and glistening from behind.

"Or else what?" I laughed, my own juices bubbling over inside my panties. "What are you going to do to me? You're all tied up."

"I'll smack your ass," she said defiantly. She knew that was never going to happen.

"You're going to smack my ass?"

"Yes, I'm going to smack your ass if you don't start smacking mine. Please, please don't make me wait any longer."

I stepped closer to the bed. She whimpered in anticipation. I ran my implement across her cheeks, down her crack, and separated her soaking wet lips with the tip of the riding crop. She began to tremble all over, practically falling over on one side, her ass falling toward the bed.

"Get up. Put your ass back in the air," I said, lightly smacking her bottom with the palm of my hand.

"Yes, Ma'am!" she said. She was shaking but she got back up and once again assumed the position.

I continued to play with her pussy lips and rub her clit with the riding crop. The black leather skated easily over the deep red folds of wet flesh. I wanted to reach down and taste her but managed to focus on the task at hand. I backed away, raised my arm over my head, and brought the riding crop down on the fleshy bosom of her left butt cheek. She gasped, then moaned.

I watched as the skin rose, forming a perfect red welt. I raised my arm even farther above and came down on the right side. I thought about the blonde, leaving her hair all over the place and staking her claim in the bathroom. I imagined her paws all over Kate; the bitch had probably even worn my pajamas! My favorite pajamas! I bore down on Kate's ass with a fierce velocity.

With each break on her ass, I thought about "The Break" we had taken in our relationship. What a brilliant idea that was! I thought. "Breaks" never work out; they're just ways to belabor the "Breaking Up" process, throw another wrench into the already gut-wrenching mix, which then just spins around and hits you in the head. I noticed a long blond hair on the sheet by Kate's knee. I thought about the guy I'd been with since "The Break"—as bland as a bowl of vanilla ice cream and even less satisfying—no one will ever bring out his inner pervert.

He has no inner pervert; some people are just like that and you have to accept it. But I keep going back because I don't know what else to do. It's hard to meet people in this city, and I've never been one to be alone.

I'd heard from a good friend that Kate was crazy about the blonde and as I stood there, lovingly beating her ass to a fuschia-tinted pulp, I was filled with an incredible sadness. And I somehow knew, that no matter how much we wanted each other that night, we would never be together again. When Kate yelled for me to stop, I collapsed on top of her, both of us crying like we did when we first fell in love. Her ass was warm against the front of my flannel pajamas, and we both fell face down on a bed that could no longer contain us.

THE PLOW POSE

Sinclair Sexsmith

The room was hot. And I mean sticky, sweat pouring, tongue swelling, palms slipping, steam rising, tropical jungle hot. Robin insisted this would better open up our muscles and let us sink deeper into the poses. There was certainly something I wanted to sink deeper into, but I can tell you right now: it wasn't my hip joints.

I can't really say what started me on the habit of packing to go to my yoga class. It could have been a dare. It could have been that I had somewhere else I was going right after class, so I was just saving time. It could have been my own idea, late one night when my only comfort was my own hand and memories of the perfect curl of her lower back when she moved from cat pose, on all fours, back arched, head down, to cow, bending her neck back and aiming her eyes toward the ceiling. I hadn't expected it to be all that comfortable, packing and doing yoga at the same time. But after the first time, I was hooked. I stretched my hips differently in order to compensate and use the weight between my legs. Straining against my clit, the cock felt different, like it was no longer separate from me. Maybe it was because yoga pushed me all the way to the edges of my body.

I started out with some little softpack, but as soon as I felt confident that my breathable yoga pants wouldn't give away the swelling at the V of my legs, I pulled out the big guns. It isn't as though I pack all the time outside of class. Sometimes, sure—like when I'm going out and trying to impress, or if I expect to request a blow job in the bathroom at a club—but no matter how broken in my leather harness gets, it never quite feels like skin, and there's always some discomfort after a few hours. I don't really recall how exactly I came to packing at yoga class, but it was such a high, such a sensual body experience, I couldn't stop.

Certainly it didn't hurt that I had the hottest yoga teacher in Seattle. Robin had all the things the typical yoga teachers did—a lifetime of dancing, college degrees in kinesthiology, certification in yoga and Pilates instruction—but she had more: she was smokily beautiful, for one. Her hair was dark, nearly black, and streaked with gray. It curled around her jaw and ears softly, often fell into her face when she demonstrated triangle or crane or any forward bends. I doubted she could be more than thirty-five, but then again yoga bodies are deceptive in their aging. Maybe she was as much as forty-three. Her eyes were icy blue, shining bare with scintillant light, always so clear I feared she could see right to the pores of my skin.

And she had the most delicate crow's-feet around her eyes, and just hints of lines at the corners of her mouth. Her mouth, god, I had never seen a mouth like hers: the perfect pink of organs, tender and supple like the fingertip of a child.

I couldn't watch her lips move without having to fight the urge to bring something to her lips—fingers, cock, teeth, anything. Something about the way she was so soft and solid, so pulled together and spiritually in touch with all the Buddhist yoga stuff, made me want to ravage her. What is it about such simple, pure beauty that makes us want to conquer, to take and take, until perhaps we have earned some semblance of the beauty for ourselves?

Today, Robin was deliberately torturing us, twisting the thermostat until I thought the dial would crack and we'd leave here with our skin burned. Her Tuesday evening Yoga II class, filled with twenty-three of Robin's devoted addicts, myself included, would weekly attempt to take whatever she challenged us with, and like the good little fans we were, we always tried our best to impress her. Most of the people in my class were here for Robin rather than the yoga, though we would all admit the yoga was a perk we rather enjoyed. Walking out of here with muscles pushed to the limit, breath pulsing, body opened and expanded, I always felt as though she personally had something to do with the afterglow I would feel for days. It didn't hurt that Robin always took a hands-on approach to her teaching, circling the room and never hesitating to glide her hand along our aching muscles to encourage us to bring the elbow just a little straighter, to strengthen the thigh muscle just a little more, to stretch the groin just a little farther.

The class flowed through sun salutations, and as Robin

took us deeper into the *Virabhadrasana* warrior poses, I could feel her watching me.

"*Trikonasana*," she said, startling me with her closeness, "triangle pose." I straightened my legs from the lunge of warrior and brought my left hand straight up. "In this pose, you want to have a strong line from your ankle all the way up to your shoulder," Robin stated, still behind me, bending down to slide her fingers from my ankle up to my hip, where she took hold of my waist and aligned me to her liking. She left one hand at my hip, resting, though with a heavier weight than usual. She encircled my arm with her thumb and forefinger and dragged her hand up my arm to my wrist, pulling it straight up. She paused long enough for me to get a clear picture of her beautiful body above mine, hair falling into my face, restraining my wrists as she rode me.

"Turn your hips open. Make sure they are stacked, one on top of the other," she said, her hand on my waist moving to twist my hips. Her two fingers casually lingered on the exact ridge of the shaft of my cock, tracing the outline as she pressed my hip open.

Oh god. That had to be on purpose. If it wasn't on purpose, certainly she now knows.

"Good," Robin said softly, to me. "Very nice."

I closed my eyes. This is not happening. She meant the pose, she meant my body, not the strap-on I had diligently concealed in the crook of my hip, bent precisely so I could feel it but it wouldn't look huge if by chance it was noticed.

"Bring your arms back up, stretch then overhead...breathe in...and breathe out, bend from the waist, clasp your big toes with two fingers...and breathe." Robin continued to weave through the room, though I noticed she wasn't taking the same interest in everyone as she had in me. This comforted me. She knew, she didn't mind—in fact, maybe she liked it. I felt exposed in my forward bend, legs spread, ass up, but I tried to breathe, concentrate, and get back into the sweet spot of the poses.

I had never been so glad my cock was made of silicone; otherwise, I was certain a wet stain would have given me away.

Robin took us through a vigorous flow session during which she focused on the hips, the groin, the gluteus muscles, the root chakra. Every time she let us rest, every time my hard-on began to feel tolerable and under control, she took us deep into another root pose that filled me swollen yet again. I swear, once, in the half-bridge pose, on my back, feet on the floor and knees bent, hips pressing to the ceiling then back rolling down to the floor, I caught her staring, serene, sitting on her heels while she watched my face as I nearly cried out with the pressure, and she smirked. I swear she actually smirked. The woman was actually toying with me. While I could already tell I wouldn't be able to walk for days, I had to admit I admired her for it.

I wanted her to open me.

Tears really did well up with the final release of *Savasana*, corpse pose. I was spent, every muscle straining to relax, while she let us acclimate to our emptied, bare bodies. She had peeled me back and spread out everything I had in front of her, and I felt vulnerable and small. Robin delicately chimed her prayer bells and even chanted a little before gently bringing me back to my body and thanking the class.

Back in the heat of the yoga studio, dazed, my fellow worshippers and I wiped the sweat from our faces, tightly rolled our yoga mats, brought the straps to the shelves in the back of the room, and piled the blankets we used to support us. Robin put away her chimes and her discreet timekeeping piece, and chitchatted politely with some of us enthusiasts. I took my time, deliberately sliding my socks over my feet, cautiously lacing up my black shoes. I slipped my rolled green mat under my arm and caught her eye as my hand grasped the door handle, trying to smile my *goodbye, see you next week.*

"Zed, do you have a minute?" Robin broke away from the conversation she was having with the other remaining student, an awkward, starry-eyed boy who had only been coming to class for a few weeks. He twisted his head with a bite of jealousy in his eyes, and swung out the door.

Aside from being surprised that she'd taken the time to notice my name, I was startled, certain Robin wanted to discuss, somehow, my inappropriateness.

She shut the door and leaned against it. The murmur of the students in the hallway faded, and the hardwood yoga room echoed and loomed large with air now that everyone had gone. I could hear her breathing. I could hear my breathing. I was certain she could hear the blood brimming in my veins, fluid and full.

I tried to look confident. Squared my shoulders. Tilted my chin. Cocked my hip. "Course, I have a minute. Great class." Stupid, stupid thing to say.

Robin looked amused, hips tilted coquettishly, hands behind her back. "I have some poses I'd like to show you. Ever done partner yoga?"

"...No."

She smiled, but I wasn't sure if she was pleased or poised

to pounce on prey. "Lay down your mat...no, not there, right in the middle of the room." I took a few steps. "Yes, right there. Take your shoes off. Take your socks off. Take your jacket off."

One more order and I swear I'll retaliate.

As I unlaced my shoes and set them aside, she settled on the mat in a loose butterfly pose, the soles of her feet touching like an open book, and stretched her neck, hands poised on her knees, first finger touching thumb. She sighed, apparently collected, and gazed over at me, twisting her hair behind her ears. I summoned every bit of butch courage that I could and walked onto the mat; stood in front of her, cock at eye level. She looked up at me, neck barely moving but eyes rolling and lips parting just enough for me to know her tongue was swelling. I restrained the impulse to take fistfuls of her hair in my hand.

"On your knees," Robin said, as she gracefully drew herself to her feet. I gave her my best I-know-this-game kind of look, and obliged. "No, keep yourself upright," she said when I lowered myself to sit on my heels. "Breathe, open your chest high. Bring your hands to your waist, behind you, start leaning back. Yes, like that. Push your hips forward. Push. Just press. Harder. Yes." Robin brought her hands to my thighs and encouraged me forward. She touched the crease in my hip and I could tell from the way her hand wandered that she wanted to touch my cock again, but held herself back. "Now, slowly, bring your hands down to your heels. Yes, perfect. And press forward."

I pressed. I bent myself far back, while pushing forward with enough strength to reach the opposite wall in the hope it might mean touching my cock to her fingers. Or her mouth.

Or...I imagined her in front of me and strained against the fabric of my limber cotton yoga pants.

"*Ustrasana*," she said. "Camel pose." My eyes were on the wall behind me, now upside down; I couldn't see what Robin was doing, but I could hear her moving.

"Stay there," she said, softer now, not in her commanding yoga tone but with a trickle of desire. "I'm going to push against you a little, just to launch myself. Are you feeling strong?"

I managed to breathe "Yes." I could fuck through steel. Her weight suddenly, gently pressed against my hips, right into my cock pressing on my cunt and I nearly liquefied, but she stopped me.

"Just hold it there, Zed, lean into me for balance...yes, that's it. That's it." Robin was still moving against me, but I couldn't tell quite what pose she had taken. Possibly her shoulders were leaning, with quite a bit of weight, right into my hips. Or was it her chest? She was pressed against me hard, balanced somehow.

I felt her breathing. "How are your arms?" she asked, finally settled into however her body was arched.

My shoulders were pierced with heat. "A little tired."

"Okay, gently then, gently, release your heels, press into me, use your stomach, push yourself up to standing."

I did, slowly.

She had slipped out of her clothes. Robin, my god, Robin was nude under me, the Robin all my friends had crushes on, the famous urban legend yoga teacher, that Robin was lying back on her shoulders, feet lifted overhead and toes touching the floor in the plow pose. *Halasana*. Feeling me upright, she shifted her legs into a V, pushing them wide enough apart for me to see her hair falling around her head, eyes looking up into my lustered face. She rolled her hips against me and took her toes off the floor, one at a time, bending at the knee. I leaned forward into the weight of her and brought my hands to her hips.

"Don't make me ask," she whispered. She brought her arms out like wings, flat on the floor, and wrapped her legs around my waist. Her unclothed chest was glossy with sweat, the buds of her nipples blushing coral-colored and rigid. Lips trembling. Cunt saturated. "Do it."

I tore at my yoga pants, pulling my dark purple cock free, and swiftly slid inside. All the way. No one had been so open under me before. My clit swelled to fill my cock and she drew me inside, even farther, with muscles I didn't know existed. I shuddered against her, softening; I felt anything hard draining out of me and into her, and she tightened around me. Fuck if I didn't feel her every ripple. She brought one hand to her clit and let her fingertips rest, softly, as my body bucked against hers, and let that be movement enough.

Eyes closed, mouth open, Robin finally let out a moan. A cross between an *ooohmm* and a whimper, rising from the spot against which I was gently pressing to escape her lips. I could hear the connection up through her throat when I subtly changed the angle, moving inside her. Her fingers quickened. She pressed her face into the bend in her elbow and braced herself taut against me.

Robin came like a glacier, flowing liquid ice from her forehead, her chest, over her delicate belly, and down to her pelvis and the thin dark patch of hair between her legs, then finally caving, pieces of her breaking loose and crashing down into the pool of me as I caught her. Icebergs of her softly sailing as

I slowed and stabled. She poured alongside me as I lowered myself onto her and kissed her.

She tasted like rain.

I broke away from her lips. Had I gone too far? Sometimes kissing is so much more intimate than sex. She closed something under me, but instead of pulling away, Robin circled my cock with her fingers and managed to twist around me, laying me on my back, languidly stroking to press against my clit. Robin knew what she was doing. I pressed my thighs together hard and came easily in her hand, uncurling, spilling open.

"Zed," she said, wiping her mouth, "next week, please try to make it less obvious. I can't keep taking the distraction."

Oh, but she could. Could she ever.

RIPE FOR THE PICKING

Kristina Wright

I have the hots for the produce manager at my
local market. She's a young chick, at least ten
years younger than my thirty-seven, but who
cares? I want to fuck her, not marry her.

I've never been much of a vegetable person.
I'm a protein gal from way back. Give me a
thick, rare steak and I'm happy. A potato on
the side is just garnish as far as I'm concerned.
She changed all that. Now I'm as likely to
have a salad for dinner as a steak, and every
bite reminds me of her.

It took me three months to find out her
name: Marissa. What a cute name for a cute
dyke. Her family is from Cuba, but Marissa
was born here in Miami. I know this from a
conversation I overheard one day when she
was talking to one of the little old Cuban wo-

men who shop in the market.

I would have been content to see Marissa a couple times a week for my produce needs, but one day she noticed me. Hell, the entire store noticed me. I somehow managed to run my cart into a cardboard stand of mangos. The entire display came tumbling down, mangos rolling this way and that. I stood there, hands still on the wayward cart, staring at the mess I'd made.

Then sweet, sweet Marissa came through the swinging doors that lead to the dark recesses of the grocery store. She always smiles, my Marissa. Even then, with a hundred runaway mangos threatening to trip little old Cuban women, Marissa was smiling.

"I am *so* sorry," I said.

"No problem," she said, with just a hint of a Cuban accent. "It happens."

When Marissa flashed her dimples at me, I forgot about the mangos. She'd already picked up half a dozen pieces of fruit before I realized I should probably give her a hand.

I retrieved two mangos, the most I could hold at once, and dumped them in the bin. Marissa brushed against me as she deposited a few more mangos. The girl had a hard little body. If it was the result of lifting boxes of produce, the whole world could benefit from the Vegetarian Workout, I decided.

"It's all right, I can get the rest," she said. Her eyes were coffee brown. They were pretty eyes, with long, dark lashes. "Thank you."

A four-alarm fire could not have gotten me out of that building. "Hey, no problem. I need the exercise."

I've had women undress me with their eyes, but never quite like that. Marissa gave me the sweetest, slowest look and another toothy grin. "No you don't."

I scooted out of there with a throbbing in my cunt and a basket full of fresh fruits and veggies. Some found their way into my salad. The cucumber, on the other hand, served a greater purpose. If I couldn't fuck Marissa, I could fuck her produce.

Three or four visits later, I decided it was ridiculous to act like an adolescent girl with a crush. I wanted Marissa and there seemed no reason not to approach her and ask her out. Easier said than done. I tried, but I couldn't quite coax myself into asking. So, I went on making my twice or thrice weekly trips to the market and carrying home more produce than any one person could eat in a year.

Then the day came when my local market went high tech. I could order my groceries online and have them delivered the next day. Quite a convenience, sure, but I didn't go to the market to shop—I went to ogle Marissa. I tossed aside the flyer announcing the new service and forgot about it until one day a month or so later when I got sick.

I'm not pretty when I'm sick. My nose runs and turns red from being wiped so often, my skin gets blotchy and dry, my eyes have bags under them from not sleeping well. It was on the third night of the cold from hell that I broke down and used the market's service. I couldn't possibly face Marissa looking like one of the living dead, so I keyed in a few necessary items on my computer—tissues with lotion, orange juice, chicken soup. I scrolled through the produce list, longing for Marissa, and picked a variety of fresh fruit, hoping a megadose of vitamin C would do the trick. I got a confirmation number for my order, turned off my computer and crawled into bed.

I didn't get out of bed the next day until the doorbell rang.

I grabbed my robe, threw it on over my Melissa Etheridge T-shirt, and shuffled to the door. I was actually feeling better than I had in three days, but post-illness exhaustion had settled into my bones and showed no signs of leaving.

I opened the door and blinked, convinced the high alcohol content of my cold medicine was causing hallucinations, because it couldn't be Marissa the hot produce dyke standing in my doorway with two sacks of groceries in her buff little arms.

"Hi," she said, and that's when I knew she was real.

I also realized I was real—red nose, blotchy skin, ratty bathrobe and all. Oh, and jaw dragging on the floor. I did the only thing I could do, I closed my mouth and ushered her in.

"Where do you want them?" she asked, looking over her shoulder at me.

"Kitchen table," I muttered, trying to hide behind the curtain of my unwashed hair.

She deposited the groceries on my small kitchen table and grinned at me. "You don't look so good."

I made a face. This wasn't exactly the conversation I'd fantasized about our having. "I'm getting better."

Marissa nodded. "You got some good stuff. You'll feel better tomorrow."

I fumbled with my purse hanging over the back of the door, looking for a tip. Part of me wanted to stall her, since I finally had her to myself. Another part of me, the rational, coherent part, wanted her gone so she wouldn't have too clear a memory of me looking like shit.

"You know what you need?"

I noticed the way her jeans hugged her muscular thighs and how her bicep flexed when she ran her hand through her short, dark hair. Marissa had what I needed, only she didn't know it because I was too chicken to tell her. "No, what?"

"A good steam. It will clear you up."

I was hallucinating. I refused to believe I was standing there listening to the sexiest dyke on earth tell me how to clear my stuffy nose. "Thanks. I'll try that."

Marissa studied me for a long moment. "No you won't. You'll go back to bed and then you'll never get well."

Hard to argue with that. "Okay. I'll do it as soon as you leave."

"How about you do it now?" Before I could say anything, she headed down the hall toward my bedroom.

Marissa was going into my bedroom.

The babe I'd been lusting over for six months was going into my bedroom. My bedroom, with the unmade bed, the snotty tissues tumbling off the table onto the floor, the underwear kicked in a corner because I was too sick to do laundry.

"Wait! No! Stop!" I said, getting more nasally with each panicked breath.

Too late. Marissa was in my bedroom.

"C'mon," she called. The echo told me she was in the bathroom. I frantically searched my brain, trying to remember the last time I'd scrubbed the shower. "You're not going to get better standing there."

Even while I was trying to figure out how this had happened—how the produce girl from the market was standing in my bathroom—my body was moving of its own accord. I found Marissa with her head in the shower, turning the water on full blast.

"Okay. Sit down," she said, when the water was adjusted to her satisfaction.

There really wasn't anywhere to sit except on the toilet. I sat down, miserable and humiliated. This was not the fantasy I'd envisioned about when and if I ever got Marissa into my apartment. I felt like her invalid mother.

Marissa, on the other hand, seemed to be enjoying herself. "Cheer up. This will make you feel a lot better."

The bathroom began to fill with steam. Marissa pushed my hair dryer and a bottle of cough syrup out of the way and leaned against the counter. The steam at least provided some atmosphere. It made Marissa look fuzzy, so it could only be helping my sad appearance. Of course, she'd already seen me in all my glory.

"Now, take a deep breath."

I breathed. Or, I tried to. It's hard to breathe through a clogged-up nose.

Marissa shook her head. "Blow your nose."

Now I felt like a sick kid she was babysitting. I obeyed her though, using the last of the tissues in the box on the back of the toilet. "Okay. I'm as clear as I'm going to get."

"Good. Now, a slow, deep breath."

I did as she said. It was really getting hot in there.

"Exhale. And do it again."

This was the most bizarre situation I'd ever found myself in, but I was too exhausted to complain. I breathed, Marissa smiled. I'd do anything for that smile, even take a steam bath in my less than pristine bathroom.

"Good. Keep breathing, I'll be back in a minute."

She didn't give me a chance to ask her where she was going. I figured she was escaping the germ fest while she could. I was in no condition to wrestle her to the floor and have my way with her, not that the thought hadn't crossed my mind.

She returned a few minutes later with what looked like half the contents of my spice rack in her hands. She deposited the glass bottles on the counter and began to line them up.

"What are you doing?"

She had her back to me and I found myself staring at her well-muscled, denim-covered ass. I was starting to feel better already.

"Just some herbs to add to the water." She reached into the shower once more and put the stopper in the tub drain. Then she started picking up bottles one at a time and shaking the contents into the tub.

As the steam began to do its job, I recognized a few scents. Rosemary, at first. Then mint. Something that smelled spicy, but I couldn't quite place it. Soon, the scents were blending together so that I couldn't distinguish between them, but the mere fact that I could smell them at all was amazing.

"See, I told you," Marissa said.

"Thanks."

We stared at each other as the steam thickened and the scent of herbs filled the air. The whole thing was too surreal for words.

"Why are you delivering groceries?" I finally asked.

"I saw your name pop up on the list and I wanted to see you."

Whatever I'd been expecting, it wasn't that. I suddenly forgot about being sick and her seeing me in my ratty bathrobe. "You did?"

She nodded. "I did."

"Wow."

She smiled. I was starting to get used to that smile. "You're welcome."

Now, if this had been my fantasy, she would have led me to bed and done wicked things to my body, but I guess the runny nose, grungy bathrobe and unwashed hair just wasn't a very sexy combination. Half an hour after she had gotten to my house, Marissa kissed the top of my head and left me sitting in the bathroom. I could breathe again, but I was also horny—the real sign that I was feeling better. I was now a true believer in holistic dyke medicine.

By the time I returned to the market the following week, I was humming with sexual tension. I needed to get laid. More importantly, I needed Marissa to do the job. Instead of throwing me against the papaya display and fucking me senseless, she only smiled at me and kept stacking bags of carrots.

"Good afternoon," she said.

"Hi." I stood there, wondering if I should ask her out. Wondering why she didn't ask me out. "Thanks for your, um, advice last week. You were right, I felt much better."

She nodded and turned back to her carrots. "I'm glad. Told you it would help."

"Right." I wandered away, wondering if maybe I had imagined the entire thing after all.

Two more weeks went by and the same thing happened. Marissa was nice, polite, friendly. Problem was, I wanted the sexy dyke who had come to my apartment and I wanted to be healthy and full of energy the next time she got there.

I concocted a plan. It was childish and pathetic, but a girl has to do what a girl has to do.

On the day before my usual Saturday trip to the market, I signed online and placed another grocery order. My entire list consisted of items from the produce department. If Marissa was working, she'd see my name. And maybe, if I was lucky, my greengrocer would be back to give me a different kind of steam.

At 4:45 on Saturday afternoon, there was a knock at the door. My heart hammered in my chest even while I was trying to convince myself not to get too worked up because it might not be Marissa. But when I opened the door, there was Marissa smiling at me.

"Not feeling well?"

"No, I feel fine—" I stumbled over my excuse. "I've just been busy."

She just grinned.

I moved out of the doorway and gestured back toward the kitchen, as if she'd never been in my apartment before. "You can put them on the table."

I followed her, my entire body throbbing. "Um, I really didn't—uh—I was hoping to see you again," I said, rushing through the words so that they barely made sense to my own ears. "I mean, it's nice to see you again."

Marissa set the groceries on the table and looked at me. Her eyes were so dark they seemed bottomless, yet they sparkled with humor. "It's nice to see you again, too."

Clearly, she had no intention of making this easy for me. "About the last time you were here…"

"Yes?"

"Was there something between us, or was that just the cold medicine?"

Her smile faded and she got an intense expression: pure sensuality, exuding lust and sex and confidence. It was a heady combination and I gripped the edge of the table for dear life.

She took a step closer to me and leaned forward just a bit.

"What do you think?" she whispered.

"I think if you don't kiss me soon, I might just have a relapse." I was tired of playing games. I wasn't getting any younger.

She put her hands on my shoulders, drawing me closer until our bodies were touching, chest to chest, hip to hip. Then she was kissing me.

It wasn't a first kiss. Hell, it wasn't a second, third, or fourth kiss, either. It was the kind of kiss you give someone you've been fucking for a while, but not so long you're used to each other. When the heat and throb are still insistent and you're both always needy. That kind of kiss.

She was groping my ass before the first kiss even ended. In my premeditation, I had made sure to wear a skirt. I was also wearing panties, but I didn't really think about that fact until they were somewhere down around my knees. I wasn't quite sure how she'd made that move, but I didn't complain because she was stroking my cunt and nibbling my bottom lip as if someone had given her a road map of my body with the erogenous zones marked as points of interest.

When I was thoroughly kissed and dripping wet from her fingers working between my thighs, she pulled away. "Is that what you had in mind?"

I blinked at her, waiting until I regained some feeling in my lips to speak. "Something like that, yeah."

"Why didn't you say so?"

I ran my tongue over my lips. "I'm kind of old-fashioned."

She looked skeptical. "Does that mean I have to take you out to dinner before I can fuck you?"

I grabbed a fistful of her T-shirt and dragged her closer.

"You've already brought me dinner. We can move on."

"Good."

She wrapped her hands around my waist and backed me up against the kitchen table. Thankfully it's one of those heavy, butcher-block style tables that can withstand a hell of a lot of weight and motion, which was what I hoped she had in mind.

With one hand on my hip, she gently pushed me back on the table until I was lying flat with my legs hanging off. I could feel my panties sliding the rest of the way down to my ankles and I kicked them off. I lay there waiting for her to slide her fingers into me, but it didn't happen.

I propped myself up on my elbows and looked at her. She was going through the grocery bag on the table.

"Um, hello?" I wiggled my fingers at her. "Remember me?"

"I haven't forgotten. Hold on." She pulled out a pint of raspberries and a pint of blackberries.

"Hungry?" I snapped.

Her grin was feral. "Oh, yes."

That was enough to make me lie back down. Whatever she was up to, I was pretty sure I was going to enjoy it.

Marissa walked over and stood between my spread legs. She looked into my eyes, rather than between my legs, which automatically earned her a couple bonus points and made me whimper with impatience.

"I love blackberries," she said, softly. It was the single most erotic thing I've ever heard a woman say.

"Me too."

I closed my eyes as I felt her kneel between my legs. I waited for the feel of her tongue, but it never came. Instead, I felt something cool against my cunt. It took a moment for it to register in my lust-filled brain that she was pushing the black-berries into me.

"Hey, wait," I said, struggling to prop myself up on my elbows. "I don't think that's a—"

"Sshh," she murmured, sliding the berries in deeper. "Don't think, just relax."

It seemed silly to argue while her fingers were in my cunt, so I lay back and tried to relax. The berries tickled. Or maybe it was the juice that tickled. Or was that my juice? I couldn't really tell anymore.

Marissa braced her hands on my thighs and breathed against my cunt. "Mmm, you smell like a briar patch."

It sounded like a compliment. I was from Miami, home of strip malls, highways, and parking garages, so I wasn't sure.

She stood and the bag rustled again. I tried to remember what I'd ordered. Raspberries, blackberries, strawberries. Blueberries? I couldn't remember. I kept my eyes closed and felt Marissa between my legs again.

"You like berries."

"They're good for you," I muttered, flinging my arm over my eyes to avoid the embarrassment. I could feel my cheeks flush hotly as she began sliding more fruit into my already juicy cunt.

It didn't take long before I was filled. I felt like a Christmas goose, stuffed and spread out on the table, a banquet. It should have been embarrassing, but funny things were happening down below. My cunt tingled. It felt full and bloated, but it also felt hot and aroused.

Marissa knelt again between my legs. This time I felt the hot, slick wetness of her tongue slide across my cunt. I could hear her slurping the juice, berry juice, cunt juice. I shivered and grabbed the edge of the table. Another lick and I was arching my back and pushing my cunt into her mouth.

She pushed two fingers into me, berries and juice squeezing out of my cunt around her twisting fingers. I was a human juicer. I giggled as wet, squishy noises filled the air. She kept fucking me until my giggles turned to moans, her hand anchoring my thigh to keep me from bouncing off the table. I was a bountiful harvest of berries, being fucked on my kitchen table by the queen of produce. Who knew healthy living could be so much fun?

I whimpered and moaned and thrashed as Marissa fucked me, fucked the fruit right out of me, as I rocked the wooden legs of the table until I was sure it would collapse beneath my weight. Marissa sucked my clit between her lips as she finger-fucked me and the combination of sensations drove me over the edge. I gripped her head between my thighs and screamed.

In a rush of juice, I came. *Hard.* My cunt contracted around Marissa's fingers and I gasped as the odor of fresh, sweet berries filled my senses. She sighed and lapped gently at my cunt as berries dribbled out of me and the ripples of my orgasm faded.

Marissa pulled me off the table and we fell in a heap on the floor, the table creaking with relief. I laughed, then she laughed, stroking any part of my body she could reach. I could still feel the berries and juice trickling out of me and I couldn't stop giggling. Thank god for tile flooring.

I pulled her berry-stained mouth down to mine for a kiss as I worked my hand down the front of her jeans. "That was pretty fucking intense," I murmured against her lips.

She sucked my bottom lip into her mouth and I could taste the juices of the fruit and my own cunt. "Wait until you see what I bring you tomorrow."

AFTER LUNCH

Kathleen Warnock

The small town of Danbury really couldn't be considered a bedroom community for Chicago, Rebecca thought. It had taken her two hours to get there by train, and if she were going to consider a move to the suburbs, it would have to be much closer.

She would tell the realtor that, if the woman ever showed up. In the meantime, she waited at the Danbury Café, a small but clean-looking place that served greasy sandwiches. She didn't eat much red meat, but she hadn't eaten breakfast that morning and the smell of fried onions and the heaping plates around her tipped the scale in favor of a shot of fat and cholesterol. She signaled the waitress, who was chatting with the cook, a heavyset woman with dark hair.

"Get off your ass and see what she wants, Babe," the cook ordered.

"What can I do ya for, hon?" the waitress asked with a grin, flipping open her pad. She wore an apron over jeans and a flannel shirt, her dark hair pulled back in a loose ponytail. She had a big grin, and her dark eyes smiled as well.

"What's the special?" Rebecca asked.

"Well, there's the burger," Babe said. "Then there's the burger deluxe. And, for you, we have the burger deluxe with a side of Tums."

"I think I'll have the burger," Rebecca said.

"Hey Sissy," Babe called back to the kitchen. "Catch something that's running around back there, smack it on the head, and put it on a roll!"

"I don't suppose you have whole wheat?" Rebecca asked. She was enjoying this. She didn't joke easily, and wished she knew how to banter. She thought, given the chance, she could be funny.

"What do you think this is, San Francisco?" Babe sassed back. "Out here in the heartland, there's only one kind of bread: white!"

Rebecca's phone went off, and she answered it to hear a breathless explanation from the realtor: flat tire…miles from a garage…tow truck on the way…. Rebecca told her not to bother. She looked around at the luncheonette, wishing it were a bit closer to home. Babe was joking with another customer; the cook shouted to them over her grill. The customers were a mix of men who looked like truckers and mechanics, and…a lot of women. There was at least one couple holding hands and sharing their French fries.

"Is this a lesbian restaurant?" Rebecca asked.

"It's a restaurant for anyone who wants a sandwich," Babe clarified. "The only rule is, you don't bother the other customers. Some folks, you know, if they tried to hold hands, say, at any other restaurant in town, they might get hassled...but no one tries any of that here. My sister back there...," she indicated the kitchen, "is pretty good with the bat we keep behind the counter. And I used to be a cop. I can still take a man down if I have to. Or a woman," she said in a totally different tone.

"It sounds like my kind of restaurant," Rebecca said. She eyed Babe's tan arm, the muscles sliding smoothly under her rolled-up sleeves.

"I ain't gonna walk it out to her, Babe!" Sissy called from the kitchen. Unsure of the etiquette, Rebecca sprang from her stool to go and get her own food just as Babe wheeled around to return to the counter. The two women collided awkwardly, and Babe caught at her to keep her from falling.

"Sorry, hon!" the waitress said. "You sit down, I'll bring your burger."

"You're strong," Rebecca breathed. Babe's grip had been sure but not painful. Pleasant and hard across Rebecca's breasts.

"Here...your food," Babe replied, blushing deeply before stepping away for the order and hurrying back. "I didn't meant to, uh...I mean, no personal contact intended...uh...I was just trying to keep you from..."

"Falling," Rebecca said. "Thank you, and no, I won't sue you." Babe looked relieved. "Unless I get food poisoning. I'm Rebecca." Babe let out a loud guffaw, and a smaller giggle, and reached to shake her hand.

"So you used to be a police officer?" Rebecca asked. Babe semiperched on the stool next to her.

"Yeah, I really liked it," she said. "But I got hurt. With my bad back, I couldn't pass the physical anymore." Babe looked quite fit to Rebecca.

"This is very good," she told Babe. "May I have a napkin?" Babe silently handed her one, and Rebecca wiped her lips. "What did you do after you left the force?"

"I drove a long-haul truck, and I liked that, too." Butcher and butcher, Rebecca thought. She liked that in a woman.

"Then I got pregnant, and married, you know, had to stay home with my kid...," Babe went on. Rebecca glanced quickly at her hand. No wedding ring.

"Then I got divorced. My sister and me opened this little dump and it can be fun. We almost make a living."

Sissy came out of the kitchen wiping her hands on her apron.

"So in case you're, like, wondering how to tell us apart, I'm the straight one, and Babe's the one who likes you, but is a little bit of a chicken." Babe turned red, and slugged her sister in the shoulder—hard enough for it to hurt, Rebecca thought.

She couldn't think of anything else to say, then came up with: "What's your coffee like?"

"It ain't Starbucks," Sissy declared. "You still want a cup?"

Rebecca nodded.

After the lunch rush, Babe offered to show Rebecca around town in her pickup. In the bits of conversation they'd been able to grab, she'd been trying to convince Rebecca that the commute to the city wasn't that long. Rebecca didn't believe her, but she liked that the other woman wanted her near.

Rebecca had some trouble climbing into the pickup, so Babe

reached over and pulled her in, and Rebecca was embarrassed at her own awkwardness. Babe steadied her and patted her knee lightly. Sissy, who'd whispered something to Babe just before they got in the truck, waved gaily after them. Rebecca asked what she'd said.

"Sissy said she didn't know if you were just slumming or I was overreaching but she hoped we'd have fun," Babe told her, busily adjusting the rearview mirror.

"Do you think I'm slumming?" Rebecca asked.

"Well, I like to think I have something to offer," Babe said, with the nervous smile she'd flashed a few times already. "I own a business and a home, I'm a responsible parent. I don't know if I have anything in common with you but…"

"But?" Rebecca asked.

"But there's a little heat happening between you and me, isn't there? I mean I'm not wrong about that, am I?" Rebecca smiled back at her in agreement.

"What *do* you do?" Babe asked, eyes on the road.

"What do you think I do?" Rebecca asked. She was so rarely out of her own milieu and away from her comfort zone, she was genuinely curious about how she appeared to others.

"Well," said Babe, pulling into a small, secluded park and shutting off the motor, "let me have a look at you." She took Rebecca's hand and turned it over, stroking the palm.

"You have some calluses, but not like you're a carpenter or something. Or a musician. But you use your hands." She looked more closely at Rebecca's hand, turning it over. "You also have short nails, and they aren't polished. So for some reason, you don't want tips or a fancy manicure." She moved her lips closer to Rebecca's fingers, until they almost tickled. Rebecca rather liked the feeling. "And you smell like hand soap. Like you wash your hands a lot. And you make enough money to buy a house in Danbury, which isn't real posh, but we're getting some yuppies. Maybe you work in a lab; maybe you're a nurse, or some kind of medical technician. They can pull down a pretty good hourly wage."

"You would have been a good detective," Rebecca told her, with a quick intake of breath as Babe brushed her lips over the tips of her fingers. "I'm a doctor." Babe leaned back a little. Rebecca put her hand on Babe's leg, feeling the muscles under the faded denim. She wondered why Babe had pulled back. She ran her hand up the other woman's thigh to her crotch.

"What would your doctor friends say if they saw you with me?" Babe asked.

"What would your truck driver friends say if they saw me with you?" Rebecca responded. She fiddled with the buttons on Babe's shirt and Babe let out a long sigh. Rebecca slid her hand inside the shirt, and pushed Babe's sports bra up over one of her firm breasts. Her nipple was large and standing at attention. Rebecca looked around the small lot they were parked in and realized they might be seen from the road. The idea of people driving by catching a glimpse of them doing...what? made her suddenly more excited. No one knew her here.

"This is very high school," Babe said, blushing but not resisting as Rebecca circled her nipple.

"I didn't date much in high school," Rebecca told her.

"You've never experienced the torture of trying to do it in a car?" Babe asked. "That's why I have a truck." She pulled a blanket from behind the seat. She was around the truck in seconds, holding the door for Rebecca, lifting her lightly to the ground. "Come on, get in the back!" she urged. "There's no one around, and it's a beautiful day. I bet you've never done it outside."

"No, I haven't," Rebecca realized. Beds and showers and living rooms and kitchen tables, yes, but never the great outdoors. Babe lowered the rear gate and Rebecca climbed in, noticing the truck bed was carpeted. Babe seemed well-prepared. She threw the blanket over the both of them, and pulled Rebecca close.

"You mean to tell me you never got to have some sweaty jock pawing at you and prying your legs apart and humping on you like a dog?" Babe asked. "You don't know what you were missing," she said with a low laugh.

"You make it sound so appetizing," Rebecca murmured as Babe nuzzled her neck, then moved up to plant a firm kiss on her slightly parted lips. Soon Babe's tongue was in Rebecca's mouth, and her hands were urgently reaching under her blouse. Rebecca kissed back just as hard, and let her tongue travel up Babe's jaw, then began to nibble on her earlobe. She could tell she'd found a good place, as Babe began to croon with excitement, her eyes shut, her breath coming in short gasps. Rebecca played with the hair on the back of her neck, running both hands up into Babe's hair and pressing her close for a deeper kiss.

Babe's hand was in Rebecca's panties, feeling for the dampening curly thatch.

"Mmm...you don't shave...I like that," she whispered. She worked her own jeans down her legs, and then her boxers. She pressed her thigh between Rebecca's legs. Rebecca's panties were already halfway down, and Babe lay herself on top of her, running her thigh over Rebecca's bush, first lightly, then harder and faster, as Rebecca's clit swelled.

"Rebecca, I want to taste you.... Can I?"

"I've been walking around all day...I don't feel...," Rebecca began.

"I like a woman with some taste to her," Babe told her. "After a shower, all you taste is the water and soap. I like it...tangy." And with that she went down on Rebecca, deftly working her tongue around Rebecca's clit, pushing it in, then stroking it back up, pulling it with her teeth. Rebecca was feeling far too much pleasure to be embarrassed, and she pulled Babe in even closer. Babe took her further and further; she'd never felt such powerful sensations from a tongue, and had never felt such a long, powerful build to climax.

"I'm going to come...," she gasped, as Babe kept up the delicious rhythm. Rebecca tried to hold herself back, but Babe wouldn't let her. She knew she came very wet, and didn't want to drown Babe. But in a moment, it was beyond her control, and she felt herself gushing. Babe's busy tongue lapped it up, and thrust deep inside her vagina, licking and probing the walls in a pleasurable examination. When she lifted her face to Rebecca it was glistening, and her broad grin shone wetly. She crawled up to cuddle with Rebecca, who was still pretty much incapable of speech, kissing her cheeks and eyes and lips.

"You know," she told Rebecca, "when I was with men, I always had a hard time coming, and one of the only ways I could was when the guy went down on me. And they never wanted to do it, or do it long enough. When I finally came out, I determined to be the best pussy-eater in Danbury, then work my way up to Chicago...maybe the whole Midwest."

"You're definitely on your way," Rebecca sighed.

"I know you're not going to move out here," Babe said.

"But I didn't want to let you get away without at least trying to get to know you a little...."

"I'm glad you did," Rebecca told her. "Sometimes I regret not following through on my own impulses. I liked you, too, but I was too shy to do anything about it." Babe seemed to be waiting for her to say something else. "I could come here again. It's not *that* far away."

"Or I could ride you back to Chicago," Babe offered. "You know, I still do some runs in the truck on the weekends," Babe told her. "I like someone to ride along. If you feel like riding shotgun, I could show you around..."

"The interstate?" Rebecca teased.

"The part of a rig where the trucker sleeps...or whatever," Babe told her.

"I've never done anything like that," Rebecca said wonderingly. Babe watched her carefully, looking, Rebecca was sure, for some sign of rejection or disdain. "I think...doing things I've never done before has made me a happier person. At least some of the time."

"Then you should definitely pick up a load of onions in Vidalia, Georgia, with me next month," Babe told her. "They're the sweet kind."

"Like you," Rebecca said, and Babe blushed once more.

TOUCHÉE

Jean Roberta

"Sheila." The large, friendly manager seemed
to be smiling all over. Her short, wheat-blonde
hair and pink face gave a perverse impression
of wholesome sleaze. "You know what this
job involves, don't you?"

Sheila McLean shifted in her chair, hoping that her outfit was the best choice for
this interview. She was a small, shapely brunette with a shrewd face dominated by dark-
chocolate eyes. In her short black leather skirt
and turquoise knit top, she managed to look
tough and vulnerable, young but worldly-
wise. She was quick, naturally graceful, and
wary. She was sexier than she knew. "Yes,"
she answered.

Frances Veronica, the manager known as
Vern, studied her. Vern had grown up in a

series of unsuccessful cafés, coffee shops, and nightclubs run by her parents, and she liked to think there was nothing she didn't know about the service industry. She also liked to think she was a sensible dyke and a good judge of character. She wouldn't admit that falling in love could make her forget her own name.

"I see you have serving experience," Vern remarked, skimming over the resume in her hand. The paper was clean, the laser-print type sharp and impersonal, but a faint perfume rose from the sheet. Vern felt as though she were already touching the new job applicant, but first she wanted to satisfy her intellectual curiosity.

"Have you ever worked in the sex business?" Vern softened the question with an inviting grin.

"No." Sheila licked her lips. "But I...no."

Vern was intrigued. "But what?"

Sheila dropped her eyes. "I lived with an alcoholic for a while. I used to give, um, her whatever she wanted to keep her calmed down. She had a temper." Vern waited for a punch line that never came. "So I'm used to being available for sex," concluded Sheila. "Anytime."

Vern was moved in spite of herself. So this wounded little cat was into women, and at least one had used her badly. "Honey," she sighed. "You probably need some time to get your life together. This probably isn't the job for you."

Sheila's eyes flashed fire. "You don't have to protect me," she returned in a voice of dull steel. "I worked in a restaurant where the cook and the owner were always making stupid remarks about my ass, and another place where the customers couldn't keep their hands off me and all the manager cared about was how fast I could get their orders out to them. Here

I'd know what to expect, and I'd be ready, and I'd get paid fairly. That means a lot to me."

Vern shook her head. "Sheila, we get adults of all kinds in the Petting Zoo. Men, women, and everything in between. They all have the right to touch the servers within limits. Some will want to finger-fuck you, and some will want to go further. Against the wall or bent over a table. You can say no, but if you do, you won't get a tip and they might not come back. Some will bring in nipple clips for you to wear while you serve them. Some will want to spank you if they're not satisfied with your service. If I agree with them, I do it myself."

Vern paused for breath. "You don't have to let customers hit you, or use anything but their hands, but they will try. Especially when you're new. Customers come here for the servers. We serve good food too, but they could get that in other places. We'll protect you from real violence, and we won't hesitate to kick out crazies and drunks. But you'll be touched all the time. Whenever you're on the job."

Vern warmed to her topic as she looked Sheila in the eyes. "Do you know the term *bottom space?*" she demanded.

"Yes," smiled Sheila. She hadn't been dismissed, and this was a good sign.

"That's the only acceptable attitude for this job," Vern warned her. "You can't be a martyr and put up with getting pawed just because you need the money. You have to offer yourself and show how much you want to please every single customer. You have to need this. You'll be the special on the menu every day. It's not a job for everyone."

Sheila stood up, trembling only slightly. "Try me." Vern let her gaze rise slowly to Sheila's breasts, where her hard nipples were clearly visible. "I'll show you. You could try me out."

Vern looked at the girl just long enough to let her reach the edge of panic. "Come here," Vern ordered. She pulled her chair out from behind the desk and sat with her thighs spread and her hands firmly planted on them. She wasn't smiling.

Sheila walked up to her expectantly. "Take your clothes off," the manager told her calmly. "Slowly. Don't show off, but give me a show."

Sheila shrugged out of her top, clearly fighting the impulse to hurry up and get it over with. Her small breasts pointed at Vern with brave impudence, and her nipples were redder than Vern expected. Looking down to pull off her skirt and panties, Sheila wiggled to ease fabric and leather over her hips. Vern felt stirred. The girl's movements weren't smooth yet, but her desire to please burned in every gesture.

Sheila stood naked for Vern's inspection. A silver ring with a ruby-colored bead winked in the girl's small, shallow navel. The shockingly dark triangle of her chestnut bush made her surrounding thighs and belly look pearly white and vulnerable.

"Not bad," chuckled Vern. "Turn around." Sheila pivoted to drumbeats in her mind, showing a butterfly tattoo on the back of one shoulder and a rose-and-briar design below the small of her back, just where her flesh curved into buttocks that certainly deserved to be noticed. The black lines of the rose were smudged, and the image looked like high school artwork, but the butterfly was an exquisitely detailed monarch in clear tones of orange, yellow, white, and black. It looked as though it could fly away. Vern decided to ask about the tattoos later.

"Close your eyes," Vern instructed. Sheila's smoky eyelids dropped apprehensively. She wanted to pass the manager's test, and she didn't realize that Vern was trying to make it easier for her by taking away the distraction of sight. Vern cupped one of Sheila's little breasts in a warm hand, bouncing it gently before advancing on the uppity nipple with grasping fingers. "Are you my slave girl for the evening?" she prompted.

"Whatever you want me to be," agreed the girl. "I'm here to serve."

Vern pulled one nipple, stretching it, while squeezing the other. "I'll have a dark rum and coke, honey," she ordered, "and maybe I'll drink some off your cute titties." She pitched her voice to sound masculine, and slurred her words. "I'll have the stuffed mushrooms to start. And the sixteen-ounce sirloin for the main course. I'll have brandied pears and Colombian coffee for dessert. You got that?"

Sheila repeated the order. She had studied the menu.

"Any questions?" prompted Vern.

"How do you want your steak done?"

"Rare, baby," answered Vern in the guise of a smug male patron. "I like my meat almost raw." One of her hands slid down Sheila's rib cage to tug at her navel ring. Two fingers went south to stroke dark hair. "You wet for me yet, cunt?" she sneered, trying to catch the girl off guard.

"Oh yes," sighed Sheila, shifting her weight to give the manager easy access. "Sir," she added. Vern plunged two fingers into her, skimming over her clit and aiming for a sensitive, spongy area in her depths. Vern deliberately moved her fingers in wetness until the swishing sound was louder than Sheila's breathing.

"What else do you need to ask me?" demanded Vern. "I shouldn't have to remind you." Vern's experienced fucking finger massaged Sheila's G-spot until the girl could feel deep tremors moving toward a crisis point. "You better not come," warned Vern. "What do you need to know, bitch?"

Sheila was having trouble staying upright, and she didn't dare clutch the manager's shoulders for support. She racked her brain. "Do—you—want—soup or salad—" she gasped, "with—your steak?"

Vern withdrew from her victim, stroking her clit on the way out. Sheila guessed that she was wearing a latex glove. "What's the soup du jour?" teased Vern. "I don't want your clam juice."

Sheila was desperate, but she knew better than to hesitate too long. "Tomato rice or country chicken," she blurted, hoping these answers were in the realm of possibility.

"I'll have the tomato rice," ordered Vern. "Good girl," she added. "What else?"

Sheila took a deep breath. "Baked, mashed, or French-fried potatoes or rice?" she asked.

Vern ran a moist hand lovingly over Sheila's hip, and the smell of the girl's lust rose to her own nose. "Mmm," mused the manager. "Crispy, golden French fries," she suggested, making them sound obscenely tempting. "Sit here," she invited, pulling the girl toward her with two kneading hands on her asscheeks. Without opening her eyes, Sheila found her way onto Vern's lap while holding her arms for support. "You still cooking?" snickered the manager.

"Oh yes," sighed Sheila. Her need had become a persistent, throbbing ache that showed no sign of going away.

"Good," Vern approved. "Let it motivate you, Sheila. But remember that your customer's needs come first."

A deep, half-muffled groan emerged into the air like the last sound from a captive who no longer expects to be rescued.

"Should I call you Sir?" begged Sheila. "What would you like me to do? I want to know what you want."

"Easy, honey," soothed Vern, rubbing Sheila's back as though she were a young child. "When I want something, I'll ask you. Meanwhile, just respond. Trust your instincts. And call me Sir until I tell you to call me something else."

Vern tucked Sheila's head beneath her own and idly played with her glossy chin-length hair. It was gelled into long spikes in a haystack style that looked wild in such an artful way that Vern thought it might as well have been pinned and sprayed into a 1960s French twist. Vern ran her fingers through it, wanting to peel off the gel and touch dark feminine softness.

She inhaled the scent of Sheila's scalp. "You smell good," Vern told her, "but you put too much gunk in your hair. I'd like it clean and natural."

"I'm sorry, sir," mewed the girl. Vern ignored the apology.

She wrapped her arms around the lightweight girl on her lap and played with her breasts. "You ever have milk in here, honey?"

"No," laughed Sheila. She was tickled by the unexpected question.

"You like this?" persisted the manager, giving one breast a hard squeeze.

The realization that Vern wanted to give her pleasure seemed to ripple through Sheila's flesh from her still-tingling scalp to the soles of her feet. "Yes, Sir," she gushed, blushing prettily. "I love it."

"Open your eyes," Vern told her. Sheila looked up at her, and Vern bent her head to give the girl a long, slow, juicy kiss.

Then she let the girl go, gently but firmly. "Where'd you get your tattoos?" She rested one hand on Sheila's bottom, below the ragged rose.

"Oh." Sheila seemed distracted. "The rose one was done by a guy I knew who wanted to practice. He was learning to be a tattoo artist." Vern sensed that both the needlework and the relationship had hurt the girl more than she expected. Vern ran a finger over the stylized vine. "I got the butterfly when I was in art school and I met Mike Flash. Do you know who he is?"

"A famous tattoo guy?" joked Vern.

Sheila quickly suppressed her annoyance. "He's known," she pointed out. "My girlfriend was learning to tattoo from him. I wanted a butterfly, so she asked him. They both worked on me."

So Sheila had gone to art school. Vern guessed that in her life of broken dreams, the winged creature engraved on her skin had turned out to be a rare and perfect gift. "Was your girlfriend the drunk?" Vern asked with interest, stroking the butterfly.

"Yes," muttered Sheila. "She worked in various media. She had a lot of talent. Has."

"And you wanted to be her inspiration," Vern filled in. "But you couldn't tame her demons, and you felt like a failure." Vern lifted Sheila off her lap and stood up. "I want your tongue, baby," she said, grinning as though she hadn't changed the subject. Her eyes held a challenge.

Sheila looked confused, so Vern helped clarify her position by pushing her shoulders until she knelt on the floor. Vern unbuckled her belt in a way that made Sheila wonder what the punishment for poor service might be. But the manager casually dropped her belt, pants, and underwear to her ankles. "I'm a customer, Sheila," she explained.

The girl caught her drift. "Uh, S-sir," she stammered, inhaling Vern's female aroma. "I think I need to use a dental dam. To keep us both safe."

"Smart girl," said Vern approvingly. "That's our policy." She stood on one foot to pull her pants completely off, then walked to her desk, rummaged in a drawer, and handed a packet to Sheila.

The girl used her slim fingers to good effect, touching Vern's wet folds as much as possible while holding the dam over a swollen clit and licking it with enthusiasm. "That's it, honey," Vern encouraged her, moaning. Her orgasm was like an underground explosion, intense but contained. She bowed deeply to the kneeling girl in acknowledgement.

Vern offered her a hand up, and pulled her close. This time, Sheila responded to Vern's nudging by wrapping her arms tightly around the manager's back. For a moment they stood still, listening to each other's heartbeats and breathing each other's breath.

"I bet she couldn't forgive you," suggested Vern, picking up the conversation where she had left off, "for the way you paid for your beautiful tattoo. She called you a whore, didn't she?"

Sheila nodded. She couldn't trust her voice.

"I bet she said you had no brains, no self-respect, no loyalty. To him, you were nothing special, but to her, you were a cheatin' phony. I bet she said you didn't belong with a real dyke, and she could never trust you again. As a punch line, she said you might as well be working here."

Sheila sniffed. Her eyes were wet.

"Am I right?" demanded Vern.

"Yes," answered Sheila. "Sir."

"Call me Vern," the manager told her softly. "It's okay," she crooned, rocking her. "You have a lot of talent too, girl, and you can learn what you don't already know." Vern carefully brushed the tears from Sheila's eyes.

"You've got the job, honey," Vern told the girl, watching her face. Sheila rewarded her with a stunned smile. "I think you'll be one of our best servers. And I want to talk to you later about painting a mural on the back wall." Vern gave Sheila a kiss to seal the deal. When Vern's tongue slipped between the girl's teeth, she pressed herself against the manager as though she wanted to melt into her.

Vern had more to say. "I want you to start on Monday. You could put your clothes on and leave now, if you'd like, and I won't blame you at all. But I'd like you to stay for something else, Sheila. Do you trust me?"

"I might as well," she said carelessly, then, seeing the other woman's suddenly grim face, Sheila realized that she had better learn Vern's expressions and respond to them. "Yes, Vern," she answered. "I do."

"Then clear a space on the desk and bend forward over it. Hold onto the sides of the desk." Sheila did as she was told, giving Vern a good view of her delectable, faintly glowing bottom and a little pink opening framed in dark, curly hair.

Vern removed a key from a desk drawer and used it to unlock an unobtrusive cupboard behind the desk. From there she removed one of her favorite things, a clear glass dildo that she fitted into a leather harness. Girding her loins with this device, she felt like a mythical creature, an androgynous wizard.

Sheila stayed trustingly still, aware of her own breathing, her heartbeat, and the prickle of suspense in her lower parts. She was touched by something cool and hard as Vern asked, "Do you like this, honey?"

Knowing that she could let go, that the hungry bitch in her was finally being fed as the glass warmed up in response to her heat, Sheila yelled, "Yes!" She pushed backward as far as possible to meet the inhuman cock that was filling her. She wanted to scream like a hawk or howl like a wolf, but she was afraid of being heard beyond the thin walls of the manager's office.

"Good," laughed Vern, working up a steady rhythm. "I like it when you make noise."

At an opportune moment, Vern reached for the girl's swollen clit and tormented it with cruel squeezes. Sheila responded with near shrieks, feeling out of control and yet safe.

"Good girl," Vern told her as though it were a mantra. "Good girl." She gently removed her instrument. On impulse, she covered Sheila's back with kisses, tasting her salt.

"Get up," ordered the manager, glowing with pleasure. She pried Sheila's hands off the desk and pulled her by the waist. Still flushed, the girl turned to smile shyly into Vern's eyes.

"That's what I like to see," Vern assured her. "That's a performance worthy of an Employee of the Month." Vern gave her a long, leisurely kiss. "This job won't be easy, honey, even for you. Just remember to trust. Trust me, trust yourself, trust that for every Neanderthal man you have to serve, you'll get a reward. Sometimes when you least expect it."

Sheila took a deep breath. "I just hope I won't disappoint you, Vern," she sighed.

"You won't," promised the manager. "Not really. When

you make mistakes, which you will, you'll get more training, or some incentive to do better." She grinned and gave Sheila a quick slap on the behind. The girl felt as if she could come again, but decided to let her lingering excitement motivate her until her job really began.

After a mandatory shower alone in the servers' washroom, Sheila dressed, reapplied her makeup and fixed her hair so that she would look decent enough on her way home to her small apartment in a rundown neighborhood. With a jolt of pride, she realized that after a few months of earning a Petting Zoo salary, she would be able to find more comfortable digs, even if no one else invited her to move in with her/him. The girl hardly dared to imagine this possibility.

Vern looked deceptively calm and managerial when she offered to drive Sheila home to ensure her safety. Sheila had no way of knowing that this wasn't Vern's usual way with new servers. As the two women rolled through the streets in the protection of Vern's Lexus, they sensed another presence in the car: a feeling that was stronger than both of them.

NO MORE SECRETS

Chuck Fellows

I

My late dinner was peanut butter on white
bread again, and coffee of course. I was sitting
on a bale, leaning back on another and trying to ignore the prickly roughness of the hay
pressing through my thin T-shirt. I hadn't felt
the need to eat properly ever since Cassie had
left six months ago. I just didn't want to waste
the time. She had always come down to the
stable with a proper meal, come lunchtime.
Soups, salads, fancy recipes she wanted to try
out. Cassie had been bored here, never really wanting to live this far from the city. She
wanted dancing and parties. She wanted to
play at dressing up and going out but I had to
be here, didn't I? I had a lot of money invested
in this place, and at that time I was boarding

thirty-two horses. Sure, less than half of them were mine, but I was still responsible for all of them. Thirty-two horses isn't really too many with six hands working for me, but for some reason, around the first of the year, all but one of my workers moved on. And Cassie started to feel like I wanted to keep the stable running more than I wanted to keep our relationship moving along. She had already been gone longer than she had shared my bed, but I still missed having a woman to share my life with.

I don't know, maybe it wasn't Cassie I was missing. Maybe it was just the sex I wanted back. When I first met her she said she loved the smell of leather. Back then I misunderstood, thinking she was talking about my line of work. I work with leather every day: bridles, reins, and the like. Something always needs to be cleaned with saddle soap or repaired around here. And now every day when I work the leather, I think of Cassie. Well, maybe not specifically her—but I keep seeing a slender back flowing down to round womanly hips, straining against the ropes as I lovingly stripe pale skin with buttery soft reins.

As I sat working the peanut butter from the roof of my mouth, I thought about the first time Cassie had shown me a little something about kinky sex. I had been working late in the tack room on a Saturday night, cleaning up the mess left by young boarders in a hurry to go out and party. I thought I heard a noise in the barn and when I looked up there was Cassie, walking toward me, naked as the day she was born. She was carrying a coil of my best rope.

"What are you doing, Cassie?" My heart stuck in my throat as I contemplated whether anyone else might drop by the stable at 9:30 on a Saturday night. She ignored me completely and started threading the rope through eyebolts in the wall near the bridles. *How the heck did those bolts get there?* I wondered, briefly. I had never noticed them before. I didn't think about them for long, since Cassie's ass was my more immediate concern. Each time she lifted her arms to thread a bolt her ass moved just a little from side to side. Watching her move, catching just an occasional glimpse of breast, I realized my breathing had changed. I didn't know what she was doing, but I was already enjoying the show.

The coil of rope was stretched evenly between two eyebolts, knotted at each, with a couple of feet hanging on either side. Cassie turned and smiled at me. "I want you to tie me up," she said as she handed me one of the ends.

"Whaaat?" This was so unexpected, all I could do was look at her nakedness and wonder at the flush on her face and chest.

"Circle my wrists a couple of times and tie it off with a slip knot. I promise I won't pull it out. Come on, it'll be fun, you'll see."

It was hard to believe, but Cassie wanted me to tie her up and, and, do...something to her. I knew about such things, but in all of my forty years I had never actually thought about doing them. Now here she was, naked, with a length of rope, and I could feel my clit getting harder by the moment. She turned and faced the wall again, stretching her arms up and out to grasp the hanging rope. Hesitantly, I bound her wrists as tightly as I dared, half hoping she would change her mind and pull her hands loose. But she didn't, and when I was done and she was secured to the wall, I tried to imagine what I could do to her now. We had never talked about this stuff before and I wasn't even sure if I could ask her what came next. But

Cassie was always a pro at whatever she did, and now she told me that I should start by running my hands all over her body. When she told me to pick up the reins I had been cleaning and slap her backside with them, I felt myself getting warm and even more excited. I gently tapped her ass with the last six inches or so of the inch-thick leather straps and she laughed at me. I swung harder, solidly connecting with her skin, and watched in fascination and horror as two red welts appeared.

"More," she gasped. "Do it harder. And don't stop." More redness and more welts came up on her ass, and when I started worrying about ripping her soft, beautiful skin I moved up to her shoulders.

Cassie was panting and moaning now, dancing about in an attempt to move out of my range. But she had told me to keep going, and I could not stop until she had all she wanted. I suddenly felt like I just had to touch that reddened skin. Dropping the reins to the floor, I put my hands on her back, marveling at how hot her skin was. I suspected the coolness of my hands was something of a comfort to her. But with each caress, her moans grew louder, and with them, so did my excitement. There was nothing I wanted more at that moment than to fuck her, then and there. Reaching between her thighs I found her lips swollen, her sex wet and wide open. There was no thought on my part, only reaction. I plunged two fingers deep into her cunt and she staggered, struggling to remain upright. Regaining her footing, she arched her back, giving me better access. Half standing, half squatting, I pumped into her with my hand. She was so wet, each time I pushed in or pulled out there was this glorious slurping sound. The slapping noise my knuckles made against the wetness dripping from her fueled my own desire. I fucked her pussy as hard as I could, almost lifting her off the ground with each thrust. Her fingers scrabbled against the solid wall, desperately seeking purchase and not finding any. And then, suddenly, she was coming, loud and hard and strong, her cunt pulsating, sending wave after wave of silky wetness over my hand, until finally she slumped, still partly suspended by the loosened rope.

II

"Hey, come back." A sweet voice startled me out of even sweeter memories. Jo was looking down at me with concern etched on her face. I realized I was breathing heavier than I should have been and turned beet red with embarrassment. Jo didn't seem to notice, or maybe she was just being polite because I was her boss.

I never should have hired Jo. The job was physically challenging, and Jo was definitely not in any shape to do it. She was on the short side, with little spindly legs and all barrel up above. Her arms were flabby and there was no way she would ever be able to keep up with the rest of us, hauling bales of hay and buckets of water for the horses. But Jo had a nice smile and dark eyes that reminded me of a mare I once loved. That part is true, but let me be honest: she got to me because she looked enough like Cassie to be her sister. And Cassie had walked right out of my life less than a month before. God, did I miss her.

It had been painful to watch Jo struggle for her first few weeks on the job. Occasionally someone else would step in to help her, but she refused all offers. She volunteered to come in early and always managed to hang around late, and we all stopped offering to help her. By late spring the whole stable got busy, with new people always dropping by, new horses to be boarded, new kids wanting to learn to ride, and I stopped looking out for Jo. She was handling the job. She was getting stronger and I didn't need to worry about her anymore. Then one day about five months after she first started working for me, Jo showed up in a tank top and shorts, and suddenly she caught my eye. The round belly was gone. Her arms were tanned. And good lord, the girl had calf muscles! Jo was working much harder and much faster than any of the other stable hands now, and she'd grown tan and fit.

Now she was standing in front of me holding a brown paper bag.

"I brought you some dinner," she grinned, pulling out and handing me a container of potato salad and some cheese.

"Thanks, but you didn't have to do that. How come you're still hanging around, anyway?' I asked, popping open a lid and reaching in the bag for a plastic fork.

She looked at the floor. "I wanted to talk to you alone about a couple of things."

"Oh?" I raised my eyebrows.

"Yeah, that Zangri kid. She's gonna ruin Blaze's mouth the way she jerks that bit around. Somebody has to talk to her. She won't listen to me."

The Zangri kid was really no kid. Katie must have been in her late twenties, not much younger than Jo, but she did have a heavy hand with Blaze and this was not the first time someone had noticed it. "I'll catch her the next time she comes in and have a word with her. She knows better."

"Thanks," Jo murmured, kicking a bit of hay around with her toe.

"Something else?" I asked around a mouthful of potato salad. The silence stretched out.

"No, not really. Well. Maybe." Jo looked away again.

I swallowed, my fork hanging in midair, thinking this must be serious for Jo to hold back.

"Um. Well. Yeah, right."

"What is it, Jo?" The last bite of the salad disappeared.

"I've also noticed you watching me." She still wouldn't look in my direction and so I never saw it coming.

"Yes, I have, and you are doing a great job. I've gotten no complaints about your work."

Jo turned, her dark eyes staring down directly into my own. "No. That's not what I meant. You've been *watching* me."

I blushed because I couldn't deny it, and she knew that. I swallowed hard, not sure of what to do or say next. Should I apologize? Or what?

Jo leaned down and kissed me full on the lips. What could I do? I kissed her back. I had been wanting to do that for weeks now, anyway. Her tongue pushed between my teeth and from somewhere deep inside of me came a moan, full of want and need. I tried to set the empty container down on the edge of the bale and missed, knocking my coffee over in the process. Her fingers, strong and rough, caressed my cheek and slid down to the back of my neck to hold me close against her. Her lips were cool and insistent as she kissed her way down my neck, leaving a trail of moist places along my skin—and producing an even wetter place between my legs.

I gently pushed her away from me so I could stand up. Jo took a step back and looked away again. "Sorry," she said, seeming suddenly embarrassed.

"Don't be." I picked up her hand and, after kissing her palm, walked toward the tack room pulling her along. Once inside, I locked the door behind us. I turned and faced her, feeling brave and wanting her terribly. Turning her around to face the door, I pushed her up against it, holding her there while my tongue followed the line of her jaw and then continued down her neck. My teeth pressed into that tanned shoulder, biting hard until she let out a cry of pain and surprise. I stopped only long enough to lift her tank top over her head and use the material to loosely bind her arms behind her. My breath coming faster now, I leaned in and asked, "Is this okay?"

"Yes," Jo panted. "I want it hard."

My thumbs pressed roughly into the flesh on her back, squeezing and pinching, and then sliding around to pull on her nipples through her silky bra. "I want this off," I said, unclasping the hook in front, pulling the pink lacy thing down to further bind her arms. My hands slid over her smooth sides, moved around to her belly and cupped her breasts, then held her nipples tightly between my forefingers and thumbs. Rolling my fingers together to pinch and twist Jo's large hard nipples made her squirm quietly. I pinched harder and she cried out. "What shall I do with you?" I murmured in her ear just before my teeth clamped down on her earlobe.

"Anything, please, something. Whatever you want. Please!"

I stepped back, taking hold of the waistband of her shorts, and pulled them down, panties and all. She stepped out of them. Her asscheeks, high and round, were white compared to her tanned legs. Using my fingers to follow the crack of her ass, I slipped my hand between her legs and found Jo to be wanting this as much as I did. Her lips were wet and swollen and her clit was a hard pebble under my finger.

"Yes," she whispered, as I used my boot to slide her legs apart. Jo leaned her cheek on the door and pushed her ass out toward me. I squatted on my haunches, running my hands down one leg to the top of her heavy boot and back up the other side. Her ass stuck out in my face, and I breathed deep the scent of her excitement. With one hand on her thigh and the other holding on to her hip, I took a mouthful of cheek and bit down gently. Jo pulled her ass back in far enough to press her stomach to the door.

"Now Jo," I said sternly as I stood up again, "are you going to pull away every time it hurts a little?" Her ass moved backward again and I smiled. My hands, rough with a lifetime of calluses, traced her arms up to her shoulders. I turned her to face me, and her hard nipples puckered when I took each in my mouth, my tongue flicking over and over. Jo's eyes closed as she leaned awkwardly on the door, her arms still bound behind her. She whispered something too quietly for me to hear. I stopped my gentle sucking and stood to look in her eyes, now open and pleading.

"What did you say?"

Jo's eyes closed again, and in a tiny voice she said, "I want you to hurt me. I know you know how."

I wondered how she could possibly know, but that didn't stop me from walking her to a clear space on my workbench and bending her over it. I removed the tank and bra and she moved her arms, muscles rippling, to rest on the bench over her head. Gathering up the bridle laying there, I draped the strips of leather over her lower back, holding the bit in my hand. My other hand rested on her shoulder. "Are you ready for me?"

Jo laughed, "I've been ready and waiting for weeks."

I set the bit down on the small of her back, the reins hanging to one side and puddling on the floor at her feet.

"Don't let that fall off," I whispered. Scanning the bench,

my eyes rested on nothing but possibilities. Bits of leather, pliers, a hoof pick left here for no apparent reason, a rubber curry comb with the handle missing, and yes, there was exactly what I needed. An old cotton cinch, starting to fray, colored by years of horse sweat and rain and who knows what else, gave my own pussy a jolt. The whole piece was maybe thirty-six inches long, with a round metal ring on either end. I doubled the cinch up, threading my fingers through both rings, feeling the heft of it. Not heavy at all, but certainly capable of providing a little stinging sensation when slapped against the tender, exposed, white ass before me.

Jo stood very still, her ass waiting for whatever I wanted. I gently tapped the folded cinch on her cheeks, moving from side to side, gradually striking a little harder, ending with a solid *whack!* She jumped and cried out, almost losing the bit balanced on her back. Changing my angle, I swung back and forth, hitting close to but not directly on her pussy, not wanting to mingle her juices with those of a multitude of horses. Stopping long enough to slip my fingers between her thighs, I pushed my knuckles up into her, feeling the heat and wet of her desire. My only goal was to tease her, I wasn't ready for this to end quite yet. Pulling my hand back out, I laid the cinch across her back. With my dry hand I squeezed her right cheek, pressing my fingernails deep and creating half-moons, while the hand moist with her juices slapped down hard on her left.

"More!" Jo gasped.

I left the cinch where it was and started spanking her in earnest, blow after blow, her ass getting hotter and redder with each slap. The bit was dangerously close to falling off, the reins slithering across her back as she shifted her weight from foot to foot. The air was filled with the scent of her excitement, and my own cunt had soaked the crotch of my dusty jeans. I didn't want to wait any longer, I wanted to hear her come and scream for me.

I pushed a finger deep inside her cunt, feeling the heat and wet. Pulling it out, I plunged it deep in her ass. She moaned loudly, and pushed hard against my hand as the halter slid the rest of the way to the floor. My other hand found her unfilled hole, opened wide, hot, wet, and ready for me. Jo's cunt absorbed two of my fingers without even trying, and I quickly added a third. Pumping hard into her, I alternated hands, almost coming out of her ass, while pushing hard in her other hole. In and out. Slurp and smack. Slurp and smack. Slurp and smack. Moving faster, harder, pressing in, pulling out, the knuckle of my little finger hitting her clit with each thrust.

"Come on, Jo, come for me. I want to hear it," I panted as I pounded both her ass and her cunt.

"Oh, yes, yes, yes," she chanted breathlessly, matching her rhythm to my own.

My hands moved faster, pressing in, sliding out, and shoving her body hard up against the workbench with each thrust. Jo's cries got louder and more insistent with each pounding against her sex and her beautiful ass. The feel of her clit growing larger and harder against my hand flamed my own excitement. I wanted to hear her now. Pulling my finger out of her ass, I slapped my hand down hard on her cheeks, moving from one to the other, while still pumping in her cunt with the other, when suddenly her pussy clenched down hard, trapping my fingers inside her. Jo let out a loud scream, and hot, wet juices flowed over my hand as she came. Wave after wave of tightness ground my fingers together until I was sure they would break in two. And suddenly, Jo was sinking down, her knees finally giving out, unable to hold her up because they trembled so. I caught her as she went, and lowered her to a pile of big clean saddle blankets. Settling in next to her, I wrapped my arms around her, holding her safe while she rested and tried to regain her composure.

"Don't you want to know how I knew you could do that?" Jo asked, looking up at me from the crook of my arm.

I looked down at her, a little confused at first, not understanding what she meant. Jo looked away, unsure how I would take this news. "I needed a job, and one night when I was driving by here late, I saw a light on. I figured no one but the boss would be working so late, so I pulled in and walked through the barn toward the back where the light was on. I figured if the boss was working that late, he must need help; then I heard two women's voices. I quickly realized what I was hearing was not really conversation, but something hotter. I couldn't help myself; I sat down and listened until I thought you were almost through. And then I left, not wanting to get caught. Later, when I came back during daylight hours to ask about work, I had trouble not blurting out anything about what I had heard. I recognized your voice right away, and I was so afraid you would know something was up, but I needed to hear that voice every day. And now here I am."

I smiled at her, not believing my luck. "And here I am, too. Do you have other secrets I should know about?" I didn't wait for her answer. I kissed her, my tongue slipping into her mouth, my fingers sliding down her body, reaching for more. Reaching for her.

THE WOMAN UPSTAIRS

Tara Alton

My grandfather had always taught me not to dwell on things that I couldn't change but I was having a truly hard time following his advice after Marissa left me. Six months ago, she had returned to France to be with her ex-lover, with whom she had opened a cheese shop in a suburb of Paris. I had thought our love of cheese was something shared only between the two of us, but apparently not. Our favorite Sunday ritual had been to sleep in, then venture out to Zingerman's deli around noon and find a new cheese to take home and nibble in bed while reading the Sunday paper. Now Marissa was sharing cheese and living life to the fullest with someone else in France.

As for me, I was hardly living my life at all, choosing sofa diving on the weekends instead of going to my yoga lessons or pottery classes. I barely had the energy to get myself together to come to my grandmother's annual spring house party.

As I sat in my car in the driveway, I pondered over her beautiful two-story house with its sloping roof and massive back porch. How much had changed since my grandfather's funeral two years before? That was the last time I had come here. Knowing my grandmother, it probably hadn't changed much at all. She already had it decorated into country house heaven, making it look more like the photo spread in a magazine than a home.

Glancing at my watch, I realized I couldn't stall any longer. I was already late. The moment my shoe touched the porch, my grandmother appeared at the front door and came outside to greet me. With her matronly figure, she was one of those women you could call handsome. Of course, she was wearing her fake company smile.

"Iris, it's so good of you to come," she said.

"Hello, Grandmother," I said.

She opened her arms for a hug, but despite her size, I felt as if I was holding a piece of cardboard. I pulled away. Without much decorum, she sized me up. I could tell by the look in her eyes that she didn't approve of the length of my brunette hair or my light blue sweater with the pearl beading, the one Marissa had given to me last Christmas. It had been accidentally washed and shrunk, and it probably accentuated my breasts far too much for her, but it was still the nicest thing I owned.

"Your mother couldn't make it. She's at one of her alternative women's retreats and she couldn't pull herself away," she said.

I wasn't surprised. My mother stayed away for many of the

same reasons that I usually did, mostly because of the disapproving glances and criticisms. The only one who didn't feel it was my sister, Becky, my grandmother's perfect pet.

"I'm sorry to hear that," I said.

"Well, come inside then," she said, holding the door open for me.

I stepped inside.

"You could have made it on time," she said behind me.

I glanced over my shoulder at her. She raised a critical eyebrow at me and then left me to join a group of women in the kitchen, giving one woman a very sweet smile, probably a new addition to one of her home decorating clubs. Abandoned as a punishment for being late, I looked around for a familiar face, but seeing no other, I decided to look for my sister.

Becky was in the living room, chatting with some distant cousins I barely remembered. Seeing me, she nodded but made no move to get up. Obviously, her feelings hadn't changed since the last time I'd seen her.

As always, she was immaculately dressed. She lived by the three Ps: poised, polished, and professional. She once told me she didn't even own a pair of jeans, and I believed her. She never left the house without her makeup and jewelry. You would never have guessed we shared the same freckles on our foreheads. Hers were obliterated by foundation. Every fiber of her being was committed to being the polar opposite of our mom. Becky wouldn't drink herbal tea if you paid her.

Unlike her, I frequently drank herbal tea, and I wore blue jeans, peasant blouses, and sandals to work every day at the Wisdom Bookstore, which specialized in spirituality and psychology. There was also a coffee shop, which served organic muffins and cream-cheese-frosted carrot cakes.

Everyone thought I got this love of the spiritual from my mom, but I didn't. It was from my grandfather. I loved his stories about his adventures before he met my grandmother. He'd hitchhiked all over the Far East, exploring Hindu temples, exotic cultures, and spiritualism.

My mother wasn't spiritual—she was trendy. She went to spas and retreats where they wrapped her in seaweed and gave her yogurt enemas. Before all this, she had written a best-selling cookbook, its recipes loaded with fat and calories, but she had a heart attack after it was published and she freaked out. Now, with the royalties from her cookbook, she chased after her health like a rabid bunny.

Feeling awkward standing there alone, I moved into the dining room where a buffet was set up. Avoiding the cheese plate because it reminded me of Marissa, I selected a couple deviled eggs and looked for somewhere to sit. There was an empty spot along the window seat, but an elderly woman said it was already taken, so I sat on the stairs leading up to the two guest bedrooms.

I took a bite of a deviled egg and frowned. Too much sugar in the mayonnaise, I thought. I put the egg back on the plate and studied the dining room, noticing a few new things. On the wall was a collection of antique fishing flies in a distressed frame, though I knew my grandfather hadn't liked fishing. He used to say he hated watching the fish suffer once they were out of the water.

What he had liked to do was take long walks around their property. I remembered him on one such walk, back when I was little, catching me in the woods rubbing my two naked Barbie dolls together in a fury of same-sex lust. He hadn't told on me, but I had been so ashamed that I gave my dolls a funeral in the backyard. I let them sleep in the dirt until morning, when I retrieved them, unable to part with them any longer. Their hair was heavy with dirt, and no matter how hard I tried to wash it out, it never felt like it was gone.

I hadn't really thought about the tenacity of dirt again until I met Marissa. She had been a manicurist in Paris but one day she quit, came to America, and got a job at a greenhouse. That was where I had met her. I was having trouble with bunnies eating my marigolds, and I stopped at the greenhouse to get some advice.

After we moved in together, I used to look at her short rough fingernails while she was sleeping. It was hard to believe she had been a fancy French manicurist when her nails were so rough and stained.

Even with her greenhouse nails, I'd never met anyone who stirred so much passion in me. When I was younger, I used to hold hands with girls in the backseats of cars and steal kisses in the back rows of movie theaters. I was very happy just kissing girls, not even going to second base, but when I met Marissa, she opened a whole new world for me.

Then my sister Becky found out. One day Marissa and I were having a tussle on the floor with the front door partially open when she stopped by. She saw us and fled. I didn't know what to do. I'd never told her I liked girls, and I couldn't explain this away. Grown women didn't roll around on the carpet together giggling and trying to get their hands in each other's pants.

Nothing was ever said to me, but I knew she had told the rest of the family and they didn't approve. There were fewer invitations to family functions, and birthday cards were signed *best* instead of *love*.

At the time, I told myself I didn't care. I had Marissa. She was the love of my life, but she had other things on her mind. I should have known that something more was going on. Those long distance phone calls to France hadn't been to her family. Then one morning, I woke and found she was gone.

Suddenly, there was a creak on the stairs behind me. I looked over my shoulder to see a young woman descending behind me. She was very pretty with an angular face, high cheekbones, blonde hair, creamy skin, and big blue eyes.

Moving aside to make room for her, I waited for her to pass, but she didn't.

"You're Iris?" she asked. "The granddaughter who works in the bookstore. I saw you outside."

I nodded.

"I'm Lucy. Judy's daughter," she said, as if expecting me to know who Judy was.

"It's nice to meet you," I said.

"Come upstairs with me."

Without a second thought, I left my plate on the stairs and followed her. It was better than sitting there alone, I thought.

She led me to the white bedroom where my mom used to stay when we visited for the weekend. It hadn't changed at all. There were still the full-size gabled bed, the ticking-covered armchair, and the hardwood floor with the braided rag rugs.

Lucy walked across the room and stood by the window, where the sunlight streaming in gave her skin a luminous glow. I studied her: she looked perfectly dressed in a white blouse with a black skirt. Her hair was pinned up in a make-shift French twist.

Now she smiled at me. I had no idea why she had asked

me up here. Normally, the only time my grandmother allowed anyone up here was when company stayed and I didn't see any suitcases.

"I don't think my grandmother wants anyone up here," I said.

"What she doesn't know won't hurt us."

She looked me up and down.

"I like your sweater," she said. "You've got a great sense of style."

I looked at my sweater. After I had accidentally shrunk it, I had hidden it from Marissa, not wanting her to know what had happened. She hadn't even noticed it was missing.

"I'm a fashion design student," she said. "I should know. You look great. It really goes with your eyes."

Feeling flattered, I smoothed the cuff.

"I saw you outside, sitting in your car. You didn't want to come in did you?" she asked.

I shook my head.

There was a pause. I didn't know what it was about her, but she seemed so different from the other girls I'd met before. There was a charming quirkiness in her voice.

"Is your mother friends with my grandmother?" I asked.

"Best of buds. Peas in a pod. Bridge partners for life."

Lucy sat on the bed and crossed her legs.

"Did you like the deviled eggs?" she asked.

I hesitated.

"Be truthful. Everyone raves about Judy's eggs, but what did you think?"

"I didn't like them. There was too much sugar."

"I agree, but it's her recipe."

Moving around the room, she paused by the dresser and

lifted a costume pink-pearl choker from a bowl and examined the clasp.

"Oh, my god, these are vintage early sixties. Look at the clasp."

Holding it up to her neck, she looked at herself in the cloudy mirror over the dresser.

"Most of the stuff up here is from the late fifties and early sixties," I said. "My grandmother says it was the best time her life."

Lucy put down the choker and opened the closet door. I'd always thought it was a strange closet. It connected two bedrooms, the poles running lengthwise over the empty space. My grandmother had filled it with her old clothes. Becky and I used to sneak through the closet from the other side to surprise our mom in the morning.

"Look at these clothes!" she exclaimed.

She pulled out a dress and examined it.

"This is a pink sheath dress with the matching pink jacket. Look at the rhinestone closure. We just studied this era at my school."

Digging deeper into the closet, she found an elegant ivory suit. Suddenly, she was changing into it. I averted my gaze, feeling a little flushed at the sight of her cleavage. She had a nice body, even nicer than Marissa's. Her breasts were full, her rib cage narrow, and her stomach flat. She wore a plain white slip that looked incredibly sexy next to her creamy skin.

The suit fit her perfectly. My grandmother would have had a stroke if she'd known someone was wearing it.

"Go ahead. Try something on," she said. "You'd look wonderful."

"Nothing would fit me. I'm too tall," I said.

Lucy smoothed the suit around her hips.

"Who would have guessed your grandmother was once my size?" she said.

I watched her undo her blonde hair and finger-comb it as it cascaded to her shoulders.

Without warning, Lucy pushed aside the hanging clothes, darted through the closet, and opened the opposite door. Not wanting to go through there, I joined her by way of the hall-way.

In the other bedroom, there was still the old sewing machine against the wall, the children's rocker with a needlepoint pil-low, and the full-size bed with the blue bedspread. This was the room where Becky and I had always slept as kids.

"I don't like this room," I confessed. "I've had bad dreams in here."

"Why's that?" Lucy asked.

"Becky and I used to think the attic was haunted. She used to keep her teddy bear in the rocker so nothing could come out and sit in it."

Walking over to the attic door, she opened it and stepped inside the dark room. I cringed, remembering my childhood monsters, but there was only silence. Curious, I followed her. Lucy pulled on the light string. I startled, but there were only some cardboard boxes and a dress dummy.

"Honestly, I don't think we should be in here," I said. "And if she finds out you're wearing her dress, she will blow her top."

"Okay," said Lucy.

To my amazement, she started to unbutton the suit. I didn't

mean for her take it off right here—I'd meant she should go back in the other bedroom and change back into her own clothes.

Looking me in the eyes, she inched off the jacket and lowered the skirt. Once it was off, she put the suit on the dummy.

Now she was just standing there in her slip, looking incredibly sexy. I could see the rise of her breasts as she inhaled and then let her breath out.

She crossed the floor and kissed me on the mouth. Her lips lingered against mine. There was a tentative, gentle movement. Seconds seemed to stretch out. I started feeling that whole naughty, butterfly thing in my stomach, the feeling I used to get when I kissed girls in the back of movie theaters.

Gently, she held my bottom lip between her lips. She knew how to kiss a girl, I realized. All sorts of emotions started raging through me, things I thought I'd buried with the memory of Marissa. I couldn't believe I was feeling this with someone I barely knew. I broke the kiss.

"Why did you do that?" I asked.

Lucy looked a little dazed. She bit her lower lip.

"I've had a crush on you for ages," she said, "ever since I saw your pictures in your grandmother's photo albums. Then I heard those stories about Becky finding you with your girlfriend. You broke up with her, didn't you?"

I nodded.

She cupped my face in her hands and kissed me again. This time her tongue touched mine. There was a sizzle. My knees went weak. She pulled away. I leaned toward her. I didn't want her to stop.

Kissing me on my second favorite place behind my ear, she

brushed her lips against my skin. I felt as if I was melting into her arms. She started to unbutton my sweater, the little pearl buttons letting go of the blue wool. I let her. My cleavage was exposed. She pressed her hot mouth to my skin, pushing my sweater off my shoulders with her hands.

She pulled me down onto the floor. The wood creaked. Lying on my back, I watched her lie beside me, and then her fingers were tracing the skin of my stomach while I gazed into her eyes. Sliding her fingers down between my legs, she gripped me through the fabric of my skirt. I gasped as she wiggled her middle finger around on what she wanted. A moan escaped me. Grabbing the hem of my skirt, she flipped it up and slid her hand under my panties. I couldn't believe I was so wet.

Staring up at the rafters, I felt her fingering the soft folds between my legs, working her way toward my inner crease. It felt so weird; lying here exposed only a few feet away from the bed that I had slept in as a child. Conflicting thoughts started jumping around in my brain.

"We shouldn't be doing this in here," I said.

She didn't listen to me. She pushed aside my panties and entered me. There was no in and out movement like Marissa would have used. Lucy was looking for something else, her finger wavering inside me with a *come here* motion, sending my body into waves of pleasure. I started writhing on the floor as she touched the rough, spongy spot inside me.

I giggled. I couldn't help it. What she was doing felt so good. All the tension was leaving my body. My limbs felt light as feathers, my pelvis was a radiating sun of bliss. I was being transported to a place I hadn't even known existed. I'd thought Marissa had taken me to new heights of pleasure, but she hadn't even been close compared to this.

There was a definite building of pressure inside me. I started to hold my breath. My body squirmed. My hands tried to hang on to the floor. My toes curled in my shoes. My body felt flushed. Another wave of pleasure hit me. Blood raced to my head. Colors danced in my eyes. For a second, I was blissfully unaware of my surroundings. Nothing existed but my orgasm.

Then suddenly the room rushed back in. I heard the floor creak. Twisting myself away from Lucy, I craned my neck to see who else was in the room. To my horror, it was Becky. The look on her face said everything. She turned on her heel and fled.

"Oh no," I said. "She's going to tell our grandmother."

"It doesn't matter," Lucy said.

"How can it not matter? I haven't even been here half an hour and I'm already fooling around with a woman upstairs."

"What do you think she and Judy have been getting up to?" she asked.

My mouth opened in shock. Her words were sinking in. I remembered the smile my grandmother had given the woman in the kitchen. That had to have been Judy.

"For how long?" I asked.

"A couple of months."

I frowned. I had thought my grandmother loved my grandfather. I had never imagined her with anyone else.

"It was time for her to move on," Lucy said.

I looked toward the door, imaging the scene downstairs as Becky told my grandmother what I was doing up here, and my grandmother responded.

"What about us?" Lucy asked.

I looked into her eyes, which were filled with expectation. Was it time for me to move on, too?

"Your fingers are still inside me," I said.

ONLY A WOMAN'S TOUCH

Debra Hyde

Isabel knows what I need and she sees that I get it. If I grow cranky and irritable, she'll harangue me to get my uptight butch ass to the gym. "Sweat that grumpiness away," she'll tell me. If I'm blasé and bored, I'll hear, "Leslie, you're an absolute bitch. Call your mother." And she'll pour on the guilt if I don't follow through. "Your mama might be Cocoa Beach old, but she ain't Puerto Rico poor like mine. And yours shops, too. You don't know how lucky you are, to have a rich-ass mama who shops." Yeah, Isabel's one hell of a nag, but I'm as lucky to have her ride my ass as I am to have a mother whose fawning is actually therapeutic.

Sometimes, though, I get into this certain funk, one that doesn't respond to any of the usual remedies, one that's worse than witch, bitch, and PMS combined. It's hell on earth and it requires its very own salvation.

I think it happens when I get stressed out too quickly. I get mouthy and my every observation bites with cruel sarcasm. I have absolutely no sense of how hurtful I've grown. Worst of all, I get so knotted with tension that I go stone cold and won't let Isabel kiss or caress it away. My big, mean mouth is one thing, but shrugging Isabel's touch from my body is quite another, one that she flatly refuses to accept. That's when she puts her foot down and tells me I need a dose of Aunt Sissie's miracle cure.

Of course, I'm anything but receptive to the idea when I'm in monster mode, so Isabel sets the appointment and pushes me out the door, telling me not to show my face again "until you're ready to be civil to me." Can't say I blame her. It's her way of booting my bad ass out the door without having to toss my clothes from the bedroom window. Isabel knows best.

So does Aunt Sissie.

Aunt Sissie. I don't know her real name, but she insists that everyone has a Sis somewhere in his or her family. Historically, a Sis was that eldest daughter in a large family who raised the youngest siblings as her busy working-class parents tried to make ends meet. The sibling equivalent of Mom, whatever her given name might have been before she took up the babies, Sis she became forever after, providing childcare duties when later generations needed help in a pinch. Once a Sis, always a Sis.

How Isabel found my Aunt Sissie, I don't know, but somehow my glitzed-up girl met the diva of domestic discipline, and the first time I mouthed off, I found myself rump-end up over Aunt Sissie's knee, courtesy of my dear girlfriend.

"I don't know what's gotten into her," she told Aunt Sissie that first time, "but I damn well hope you can whack it out of her."

Isabel whisked away in a dramatic huff and left me to discover release at the broad end of a wooden paddle that day. Oh, it wasn't *the* release but it was *a* release, one capable of obliterating stress and ridding me of even the most mundane nuisances.

It was also, to my surprise, a surrender I never knew I was capable of. That the hand of a woman could hurt so good and that she could so completely ignore my butch exterior and render the inner me mush, I never knew was possible. I discovered many things in my sessions with Aunt Sissie, but ultimately I learned that sometimes only a woman's touch would do. Sometimes, only *that* woman's touch would do.

So I visit Aunt Sissie's parlor roughly every three months. On a sparse wooden chair, I sit ramrod straight in my boxers and sleeveless tee, shoulders back, in a posture so proper it's antiquated. My clothes are neatly folded and set aside nearby, shoes perched on top. Only in Aunt Sissie's parlor would I take care to be so fastidious.

There I sit, waiting for her to make her entrance, and when it happens her approach is always extraordinary. The click of her heels against the wood floors sounds sure and confident, and her June Cleaver dress rustles crisply as she moves. When she comes within sight, her lipstick is immaculate and stern. Her hair is perfectly coiffed, every short strand in its place, its platinum hue complimented by a strand of delicate pearls around her neck. Her white kid gloves complete her matronly ensemble. She is breathtaking and I can't help but think that

Eddie Haskell wouldn't have dared to brown-nose this lady of the house.

Some things, like my precise presentation and her vintage domestic appearance, never change from visit to visit. She stands by the fireplace, her hand upon the mantelpiece. She gazes at a vintage English cane that hangs above it, the trophy of another era. She has yet to look at me and, denied this, I find her overwhelming.

"I understand you've been a rude, insensitive ass."

I have only one way to answer her: with an honest, embarrassed, "Yes ma'am." In her presence, it's all the confession I can muster.

"I understand you need correction." Finally, she looks at me. Her eyes are so steely that they render me impotent. Meekly, I lower my gaze to the floor.

"Yes ma'am."

She sighs. It's an unhappy sound, a weary, disappointed "here we go again" sound. The only other person in my life to ever sigh like that had long ago fulfilled her maternal duty and now prefers cheerful shopping to familial fighting. But Aunt Sissie's sigh affects me now as my mother's did then. I cannot bear to hear it and it always fills me with immediate regret.

Aunt Sissie sits down opposite me, enveloped in one of her grand upholstered chairs. Her posture is far more refined than mine, expertly natural to my poor imitation. I feel dumb in her presence.

She smooths flat the skirt of her dress and, awkward though I am in posture, I'm schooled enough to know what to do when she finally pats her lap. I rise, approach her, and place myself there. Her thighs are firm beneath me and her dress smells of starch so fresh and liberally applied that it strikes me as a terrifying and unforgiving scent. It makes me quiver.

She caresses my rump, fair fingers against my cotton boxers. I'm struck just then by what's lacking: a collar around my neck, leather accoutrement and accents, verbal insults on her part and self-abasing pleadings on mine. None of this is present; we are not mistress and slave. Punisher and the punished, certainly. Guardian and ward, perhaps. Even parent and child. Within the safety net of our adult realities, we are archetypes in action.

She pulls my underwear down, revealing my rounded ass. Lightly, she rakes her gloved fingernails over it and I gasp as a chill shoots up my spine. I can't help it but right then, my cunt threatens to grow wet. It throbs in appreciation and her first slap only drives it further into admiration.

Which amazes me, always. I never thought that I could respond to a spanking, that I could be a butch bottom, but when Aunt Sissie applied her hand to my ass, my dreams of being a stone-cold butch were dashed forever. What would my hard-body buddies at the gym say to that?

Stinging blows make for fleeting thoughts, though, and Aunt Sissie's busy hand works the sting of the slap into my skin in no time. Where others might work slowly and sensually, she works silently and businesslike, applying her hand to my flesh as if I'm little more than a chore that needs doing or a matter that needs rectifying. Perhaps, I tell myself, that's why my mother gave up disciplining me: it had become too much work, just as two decades of cooking dinner had. Why I think of my mother just now, I don't know, but the strangest realizations run through my mind when I'm under Aunt Sissie's hand.

Though the vigor of her hand is strong, it imparts more benign sensations than pain. It's the preliminary, not the pinnacle, and it feels good, so good that I can't help responding to it. But as soon as Aunt Sissie sees my bliss, she stops.

"Get off of me," she demands. "I don't want one of your puddles marring my dress."

I blush red hot as I rise from my station, embarrassed by her awareness of my arousal. I hold my underwear by the waistband to hide my wet culprit of a cleft while rubbing my ass. It is a sincere, childlike gesture, for I want neither to offend her nor to lose the burning sensation in my backside.

My chastisement, I know, has only just begun and I wonder how she'll proceed from this, the turning point where we move away from the ritualized, toward one of her many variations on this theme.

Aunt Sissie points to her desk.

"Bend over it and present yourself."

Her desk is below my waist, but I lower my torso to it as best I can and stick my backside out for her approval.

Aunt Sissie, however, isn't happy with my effort. She pushes me forward until my legs are right up against the desk—and my cunt's pressed hard against the edge. But it isn't until she pulls my underwear back over my rump and the first smack of the paddle hits that I sense just how difficult this chastisement might become.

The paddle tears into me; it lacks its usual dull thud. Its strikes bite deep and its impact lasts longer. She's using the studded side. Then, an additional element comes into play: the blows drive my cunt into the edge of the desk and its unyielding hardwood scrapes against my most hidden and vulnerable spot.

The woman, I decide, is without mercy.

Again with the stray thoughts. I should recount how the paddle creates pain that does not abate between blows. Or how I moan and cry out when an already tenderized spot takes a second blistering hit. Or how minutes feel like hours when your auntie's arm has the strength and endurance of a titan. I should tell you how, magically, every blow somehow drives the stress and moodiness from me, body and soul, how I'm left expended, empty, purged of all that's annoying to others. But all I can think of is how deliciously raw my cunt feels, crashing again and again into the abrading edge of the desk.

By the time Aunt Sissie's done giving me my due, I'm stupid with endorphins. When I rise from the desk bearing a shit-eating grin, she merely raises an eyebrow before pointing to my corner.

"Diddle but don't dally," she warns me. "And keep it in your pants, for Pete's sake."

I'm such an idiot at this point that I merrily trot over to the corner and don't even wait for her to leave the room before I start masturbating. Ah, what a rush, rubbing my clit while it still smarts from getting slammed. It throbs in my hand at first touch, ready for more sensation, and as I work it, I peek into my pants and see that it isn't really raw—any more than my ass is really blistered—but the reality doesn't negate how unbearably sensitive it is now.

I know as I stand there in the corner, I'm doing what Aunt Sissie's more typical customers do. I know her clients are mostly men—straight men who hunger for punishment and who, when they receive it, must relieve their poor, aching cocks. That Aunt Sissie treats me like the men who visit her should insult me, but it doesn't. It's deliciously humiliating, getting lumped in with all the guys, and I grow wet thinking about it as my stroking takes hold. I feel like an incorrigible boy who has one last clandestine chance at naughtiness. My stance stiffens. I straighten, as if my height is my erection. It's habit; I always do this in my corner. It helps me come.

And then a blinding strike of pain shoots across my ass. Aunt Sissie! But she's never here for this part—she never watches me wank! I turn just enough to see she has a ruler in her hand—a long, slender metal ruler. And its every blow is pure, raw sting, a pain so strong I choke on the sudden lump that's leapt into my throat.

"You liked that earlier paddling too much," she tells me. "It can't be corrective if you haven't suffered."

I abandon my clit and place both hands against the wall to brace myself.

"Did I tell you to stop masturbating?" she yells at me.

"No ma'am," I manage to mutter.

I touch myself and resume my duty. Proper posture becomes a distant memory as I slouch forward, weakened from the ruler's bite. I'm rendered dull by Aunt Sissie's severity, and that cruel, vicious implement; as it sounds against my ass, tears well in my eyes.

Pleasure rising from within, yet pain blazing from without confuses me, and I cannot focus. Though I yelp at each biting sting, though I'm slick and swollen, I discover a new threshold: I can't come. Ass aflame, cunt engorged, I rub my clit harder and faster. I grow desperate for orgasm, but I'm choking on pain that's stronger than I can bear.

I try, I try, I try...and I can't. I can't complete Aunt Sissie's final task and, finally, I admit defeat. I whimper, I sputter, I squeeze the words from my throat: "I can't come."

Abruptly, the ruler stops its assault. Except for my soft cry of regret, all is quiet.

I do not move until she tells me to.

"Get your clothes. We're done."

Tears clouding my vision, I fumble toward my clothes. I'm heartbroken that I couldn't do as commanded, that she's going to send me home, swollen, wet, and wanting. Failure shames me.

But just as I'm ready to step into my pants, Aunt Sissie pulls my boxers down one last time and inspects my ass. "Such marks! Won't your friends down at the gym love this! Be sure you don't hide it from them."

I freeze, stunned by what she's voiced. She knows this? How? Isabel! Isabel told her this! She took my most sacred routine and made it illicit. She turned it into biting gossip for Aunt Sissie to throw in my face. Conspirators, they are conspirators!

I leave, compromised and humiliated beyond compare. Just as the paddle didn't invoke the right contrition, masturbating in the "boys' corner" didn't impart the right humiliation. Neither could do its job because I enjoyed it too much. And so, the ruler and the words. Together, they shamed me. Thoroughly.

That's what I realize as my ass burns against the seat of the crosstown bus. That's what stays with me as my every step aches when I walk home from the bus stop. And when I reach our abode, I just stand there on the sidewalk, unable to move forward, void of sass and saturated with defeated.

The knowledge that Isabel gossips to my auntie makes me want to cry, and I wonder if it will prove more humiliating than I can bear. I wonder if, thus broken, I will ever see my auntie again?

Finally I move, and as I walk up the steps and into Isabel's warm arms, I pray my human foibles have not fled me. I pray my shortcomings will continue to give me reason to return to my dear Aunt Sissie. Because I want her touch. Because sometimes, only it will do.

DETENTION

Jai T.

The room reeks of used pussy. The kind of
stench that emanates from a woman's cunt in
the heat of June. Pungent and musty. She's worn
and deflated. I've left her with only my favorite tie and those menacing heels. It's the last
day of class and I've waited incessantly since
the first time I saw her swagger into the room.
To smell her pussy. To ingest the smoke of
this cigarette. Deep, greedy inhales. Slow, suspended exhales. Imitating the way my clenched fist entered and emptied her.

She's Dr. Lynn Stone, PhD. Through years
of schooling, she's mastered the study of
women. Through years of waking up in strang-
ers' beds, so have I. Philosophical Perspectives on Sex, Gender, and Love every Monday and Thursday night from 7:15 to 9:30.

She's either sitting on her desk, legs crossed and covered in black leather boots that disappear into black hip-hugging skirts or pacing around the classroom with inviting heels from the blackboard to the door, up and down the mob of wide-eyed students eagerly waving their hands with the answer, begging to impress her. My eyes are permanently fixed on her, except when she scans the swarm of us. Then I'm the androgynous boi in the back of the room, slouching down in my seat, sketching explicit thoughts of her sitting on her desk, legs uncrossed and uncovered, wearing only skin and the residue of my mouth. I know all of the answers. I could tell her everything she wants to hear but I just sit there instead, detached and isolated, pining for the fantasy.

She's the kind of teacher you think about after class, wondering what she does with herself when she's not reading a highlighted passage from an essay or discussing feminist theory. I don't think I was the first of Dr. Stone's students to get off thinking about her naked body in some compromising position with myself at the helm, and I doubt I'll be the last. Don't get me wrong, Dr. Stone was not your typical girl next door teacher turned porn star with one toss of her glasses and a sway of newly untamed hair. She's brilliant, self-assured and great at what she does. She's classy. A woman. A woman who, in my mind, however, I had no problem turning into a dirty, filthy whore insistent on being fucked. In class, she was a self-identified feminist with an arsenal of fashion magazines in her bag and a history of prom queen titles and old pom-poms from her cheerleading days—all stories that surfaced during class discussions on sex, gender, and love. Stories that always included ex-boyfriends, though that never dissuaded me. Him or her never mattered—lately it was just me and Ms. Stone. Dr. Stone. The woman crowded my mind.

It's Thursday night. I'm walking to class. I'm sweating. The air still hangs heavy at quarter past seven in the summertime. It gets trapped between the buildings piled on top of one another, brick against brick. I'm intentionally running late. I like to make an entrance. Collar up. Make her notice. When I get there and find a seat it's obvious that the air conditioner is broken. It's sweltering but I've decided I don't mind. Now, the only thing humming lies neglected between my legs. My head is teeming with thoughts of fucking her. Fisting her and sucking on her perfect, pierced nipples; gnawing on her sore, reddened clit; masticating her buzzing flesh. These are the thoughts reeling between my ears as I slowly drift back to what sounds like a conversation on masculinity. I inadvertently catch her eye, immediately sit up in my seat, open my book to the page we're apparently reading from, loosen my stifling tie and divert my eyes to my desk.

I've tolerated most of the semester this way. Not being able to get her out of my head long enough to get into the work, I've been managing to fail the class and have yet to turn in a paper, worried that if I can even sit still long enough to think about something other than that body she occupies and turn something in, she'll still be able to read right between my lines, and through them to my agenda where sex separates every letter and inhabits the spaces between my deliberate SAT words. I need to do things to her and be things to her that the authors of the essays we're reading completely and utterly condemn.

It's the last day of Sex, Gender, and Love. I had to drag myself back here, fooling myself into believing that if I didn't show, Dr. Stone would have to remain there in room 601 until I decided to pull myself together and make my final appearance. How else would I get my final back? She would have to wait for me. Standing alone in a perfect cliché, wearing painfully high heels, fishnets, and a blouse that falls accidentally off of her shoulder allowing the strap of her black bra to peek out while she impatiently watches the clock tick seconds away, vehemently inking papers in the same cherry red as the panties she has on to pass the excruciating minutes without me. However, as I make my way back to reality and inside room 601, feeling the gaze of an entire classroom that has just been rudely interrupted by some slacker who thinks it's okay to waltz in twenty minutes late, I realize Dr. Stone will wait for no one—not even her most adoring schoolboi.

Dr. Stone sits at her desk with a pile of papers in her hands, our finals—mine cleverly entitled "Ladies and Gentlemen: The Semantics of Dismantling Gender." I hope she realizes that I put my heart and soul into those pages. Studying every assignment she had given out from the first day of class in one caffeine-addicted sleepless night, I set out to put my most uncompromising thoughts to paper in eleven insomniac induced hours. I wanted her to think back on the past three months and come to the undeniable conclusion that I, the slacker who always waltzed in late and hid behind my desk, had actually been teacher's secret pet all along.

Dr. Stone calls us up to her desk one by one and I begin to realize that I'm a stranger to everyone in this class, having used my senses only to detect her alone. One after another, they approach her desk, glance at the letter adorning their papers, smile to let Dr. Stone know that this was by far the best class of their academic careers, and proceed to the door, leaving it all behind. I sit at my desk in total disbelief at how easy they make it all seem, and impatiently wait my turn. The room empties slowly, leaving only the two of us and a sea of vacant desks at last. Seconds pass, then minutes. I can see my name on the edge of her lips and mechanically begin to approach her. "Dr. Stone," I say finding my voice somewhere deep inside of my body, looking down at her behind the desk.

She plants her hands down on the desk, standing up and meeting me at eye level, and pulls me to her by my black silk tie. She bites her lip and in a raspy voice only a schoolteacher in your wildest fantasies could have, "I've decided. I'm gonna call you boy. Now get back in your seat, boy. Now." I instinctively about-face and go back to my desk. I hear the door lock and the knock of her heels against the floor, where my eyes are presently fixed. I glance from her black high heels up to her thighs and then back down again. "Don't be shy," she teases and I can't help but smile. "Do you like what you see?" She lifts one leg and lands her foot hard on my desk, confining me.

"Yes," I mutter.

"Yes, ma'am," she demands, and I submissively correct myself.

"Yes, ma'am," I repeat.

"Good boy," Dr. Stone commends me as she bends down, her blouse inappropriately unbuttoned and flaunting a sexy black bra. "Sit tight, boy," she whispers.

She goes back to her desk and returns hiding something behind her back.

"I've got a surprise for you, boy. Hold out your hands and close your eyes." I sit in silence wondering if I'll find myself

engaged in a conversation about gender roles when the room reappears, but instead her throaty voice warns, "Say please."

"Please," I appease her. "Please, ma'am," I indulge. She grabs my wrists from behind and ties them to the back of the desk. I smell her close.

"I'm gonna make you all mine. You're gonna do every damn thing I ask." She mounts me and hauls her skirt up, revealing tiny black panties that seep up her ass and barely cover her messy, wet cunt. She's rubbing her pussy between my hips, riding the cock she doesn't yet know I'm wearing. She teases me with her lips, bringing them to mine, pursed and slightly open, draped in red, seducing me. My mouth begs as she retracts. Another "Please" escapes me. This time unsolicited.

"I'll be such a good boy," I plead.

She leans in and asks, "Do you always want what you can't have?" I recklessly unfasten her blouse with my teeth and feed on her hard, rutted nipples. Her arms are strung over my neck and she's saddling my legs, riding me like a seesaw. She's unrepentant. Shameless. Greedy. She unwraps her legs from around my waist and slides off of me, leaving my eyes on her full, round ass. She bends over from her waist dragging the fold in the lips of her slick cunt. She strips off her skirt, arming herself with only a G-string and agonizing heels.

"You want to smell what you've done to me boy?" One leg at a time, her panties come off, and she tosses them at my face and struts back toward me making eyes at my tie.

I react flagrantly, "I bet you like the way I wear it." I smirk, continuing, "I bet I'd like the way you wear it better."

"Don't get fresh with me, boy," she banters, stomping her heel against the floor, insisting I play my part.

"Pretty please, Dr. Stone," I persist as the progress I've made toward untying my wrists tips in my favor.

With my hands no longer constrained I begin to disentangle my tie. She looks at me with a devious grin.

"I've been a bad boy," I confess, and feel the power shift. "Sit on my lap and I promise to make it up to you." With her bare ass up against my jeans, I trace her skin with the silk of my tie, shadowing her curves. She's restless. I run my tie up the crack of her ass, between her swollen tits and dangerously around her neck, then mask her eyes with it and she doesn't protest. I escort her over to her desk, lagging a step behind to watch the way the heels force her ass to bounce from side to side. Taking hold of her at her hips, I lift her up onto the desk, and watch her spread apart from the knees. I unzip my pants and take it out through my boi briefs and slide it between her fold. Rub it up and down between her lips to get it wet—to tease her—to show her just how long and thick it is when I finally put it inside of her, her limbs fall malleable and heavy. She's tight like a virgin so I disappear slowly inside of her. I can tell teacher's pussy is sopping wet from my cunt-soaked cock greasy with her insides when I pull out. She drags me back in so I release a little more and repeat—inside and out of her with the lips of her pussy slapping and sticking against my cock. I can tell she's close, with the end of her heel pressed into my back, her long legs circled around me. I leave her empty this time instead and help her off of the desk. With my hand on her head, I force her knees crashing to the floor until she's leaning back, sitting on her feet, her hands cradled in her lap. I drop my cock across her lips, holding it in one hand. Her tongue follows behind tasting what she's left of herself on all nine inches.

"Suck me off, Dr. Stone."

"Yes, boy," she concedes and starts to swallow it, sucking at it violently with a mouthful between her cheeks. There she is, Dr. Stone on her knees, stuffed nine inches deep—this time between the teeth—her tits knocking against me when she's full. She looks up with obedient eyes and I help her up off of the floor. She's pressed against me with the smell of rank cunt and cock emanating from our skins. I turn her around, pulling her ass toward me, her hands landing out in front of her on the desk, bending her in half. I slip it in her ass.

She grunts, "I bet you didn't know I liked it up the ass, boy. Was I always a slutty bitch in your filthy, muddy mind? Fuck me from behind, boy, isn't that what you want?" I lean forward over her, my bound tits pressed up against her back, and whisper, "I'll jerk off in your ass if that's what you want, whore. Then I'll come inside to show you how I really feel." I spread her even further, kicking out her heels with my shoes. She's stretched out over the desk throwing her ass at my cock, her tits burning from the brutal back and forth friction.

"More," she wants. One finger at a time I begin to penetrate her until her holes are filled with every extension of me. I'm making use of her, she's thrashing with pain and pleasure as I feel her body suddenly constrict around everything she has inside of her. She's silent. Expulsion. She comes, dismissing each appendage until she's empty and only herself again.

I wipe her scum off each inch and put it back in my pants. She unapologetically gathers her clothes from around the classroom.

Back in the dizzying humidity, only seconds have passed. "There's one last thing I wanted to give you, Jai," she says handing me my final paper back. I nod, weighty and unable to move. "Well aren't you going to look?" she asks.

I tell her, "It doesn't matter."

"I thought it didn't," she responds dejectedly and walks out of the room like just another one of her students would.

I strike a match to ignite the tobacco between my lips wanting the smell to be unfamiliar this time on my fingertips and the rim of the cigarette. Disappointed, I fill my lungs with smoke and nicotine and think to myself, *It feels good to be occupied.* I thumb through the pages she handed back, landing on the last one, which is adorned with a few words of wisdom, a mark penned in red and her name.

Nice job on this, you showed potential. Maybe you should have asked for a little one on one with me—it could have helped. My door was always open.

Final Grade: C-

Professor Lynn Stone, PhD.

CLINICAL TRIAL

Radclyffe

Hunger is a powerful motivator. It's amazing the things you'll do that you never would have conceived of doing if you hadn't needed money to eat. Or in my case, to eat, pay the rent, and put gas in the car. Not to mention next semester's tuition, textbooks, and the occasional new pair of shoes. All right, it's not quite that bad, but almost. I'm the typical struggling graduate student, and fortunately, in a large university there are always studies being done that pay volunteers to participate. Although I've often thought that if you're being *paid*, you probably aren't a volunteer, but something else. In terms of my newest assignment, that "something else" turned out to be pretty hard to describe.

It started yesterday when I saw an ad in the campus newspaper that said:

Study subjects needed for psychosexual imprinting analysis. Must be 18 or older. Please contact Van Adams at extension 6361 for details.

So I called, got the secretary in the experimental psych department, and scheduled an appointment for this morning at 10:15. When I arrived a little bit before the appointed time, the same secretary directed me to an office down the hall. The fluorescent lights in the cinderblock-walled, tile-floored hallway seemed overly harsh as my footsteps echoed in the hollow silence. The third door on the left was unmarked, but I knocked as I had been instructed.

"Come in," a disembodied voice called.

The room was spare, and in the few seconds I had to scan it before my attention was drawn to the woman behind the functional metal desk, I didn't notice that any attempts had been made to personalize the space. University-issue bookshelves against one wall, filled with haphazardly stacked texts, file folders, and piles of papers; no rug on the floor; two worn, armless, upholstered chairs facing a desk that sat in front of what I presumed were windows behind closed horizontal blinds. The woman who glanced up with a remote smile appeared to fit the room: late twenties, smooth pale skin, glossy dark hair pulled back from her makeup-free face, and big, dark, intelligent eyes. She wore a fitted linen blouse in a neutral shade, and although I couldn't see below the desk, I was willing to bet there were tailored trousers in a darker shade and expensive low-heeled shoes to match. Nice package in a professional, no-nonsense kind of way.

"Hello," she said in a silky, rich voice while standing to extend a hand. "I'm Dr. Vanessa Adams."

"Robbie Burns." I shook her hand, wondering how I appeared to Dr. Adams in my threadbare jeans, striped polo shirt, and sneakers. At least I'd had a haircut recently, so my collar-length chestnut waves looked fashionably shaggy as opposed to just plain old messy. At least my eyes, an unusual gray-green, were distinctive. And why that should matter, I hadn't a clue.

"You're here about seven-sixty-nine, correct?" At my confused expression, she smiled absently. "Sorry. The multivariant sexual stimulus reaction study."

I held up the page from the campus rag where I had circled the small notice in red. "Would that be this?"

"That would be the one."

I thought I saw another trace of a smile, but I couldn't be certain. She settled down behind her desk and gestured me to one of the chairs that had probably once graced a student lounge but now should have adorned a trash pile somewhere. I sat and waited while she opened a folder and took out a number of forms. The first one she turned in my direction and pushed across the desk. "This is a nondisclosure statement. I'd like you to read it, ask any questions you might have, and sign it before I begin the intake interview."

"There's an interview?"

"Yes," she replied evenly. "There are certain screening criteria which are necessary for inclusion as well as exclusion from the study. The questions I will be asking are both personal and confidential—for you *and* for the study." She paused, studying *me*. "And before we go any further, I need to see proof of age, please."

I grinned and reached into my back pocket for my wallet. After opening it to the clear window that displayed my license,

I passed it across the desk for her perusal. "Twenty-five."

"Thank you."

She passed the wallet back, and I replaced it automatically as I scanned the page before me. It was a standard non-disclosure form essentially saying that I couldn't tell anyone the details of the study, the questions I had been asked prior to engaging in the study, or the activities I might be involved in as a study participant. I signed it and handed it back. Dr. Adams took it, tucked it neatly away, and pulled out another page filled with blanks and boxes. Eventually we finished with my name and birth date and other vital statistics. The initial round of questions covered standard medical, family, and social history-type things. She dispensed with them quickly and moved on to the good stuff.

"The remaining questions will be personal ones relating to your sexual preferences, activity, and function. Is that acceptable?"

"Fire away."

"Are you single?"

"Yes."

"Heterosexual, homosexual, bisexual, and/or transgendered?"

"Lesbian." This was getting interesting. She didn't look up as she checked off boxes in various columns.

"Would you say that you have any kind of sexual dysfunction?"

I hesitated. "Does *not enough* count as a dysfunction?" I thought, but I couldn't be certain, that the corner of her mouth twitched.

She looked up and met my eyes, her face completely composed. "We're more interested in such things as anorgasmia, premature orgasm, or anything that you would define as a physical or psychological problem associated with sexual activity."

Anorgasmia. Thank god for those two years of Latin in high school. But didn't the absence of orgasm follow from my question regarding not enough? *Oh. Anorgasmia as in "the inability to have" orgasms.*

"No. Given the opportunity, I don't have any problem coming, and I generally have pretty good control." *Of course it's been so long, who can remember.*

"Good."

She made another little checkmark.

"Do you masturbate?"

I bit the inside of my cheek to prevent one of those stupid responses such as "Is The Pope Catholic?" and replied, "Yes."

"Frequency?"

"Yes. I mean…ah…three, maybe four times a week."

"You would be required to refrain from orgasm either with a partner or via masturbation for the duration of the study. Is that acceptable?"

"How long will the study last?" They were going to have to pay me a lot of money for this.

"I can't say how long your participation would be. It will really depend upon your response to the various stages. A week, possibly several."

"How will you know if I'm compliant?"

She still didn't smile, but her dark eyes twinkled. I was certain of it. "It's the honor system."

I grinned. "Agreed."

"Are you able to masturbate to orgasm while being observed?"

Her head was bent over the forms again, her pen raised above another little box. The study was getting more and more interesting by the second, and I was still only in the interview stage.

"Yes. Who's going to be observing?"

She raised her head. "I am."

I have no idea what showed in my face when my clit twitched. Hers revealed nothing.

"If you feel uncomfortable and prefer not to participate in the study," she said gently, "just say so, and we'll terminate."

"I'm okay so far." I took a breath and forced myself to relax. "Is there going to be group activity?"

"Only in the advanced stages of the study, and you may never get to that point." She leaned back in her chair and her voice took on a professorial tone. "The study is designed in levels, or tiers, and these strata are individualized depending upon the study subject's reactions to the test stimuli. Your responses to the early stages will determine the direction and nature of subsequent interactions. Although each set of study criteria is standard, not every subject will participate in the same sequence."

Somewhere out of that doctor-speak I think I got that what was going to happen would depend a lot upon how I performed in whatever it was we were going to be doing. I was curious, more than curious. Intrigued and not a little turned on. I'd always considered myself a sexual adventurer—at least I'd never said no without trying something. Okay then. Masters and Johnson, here I come.

"That sounds fine."

Another sheet of paper appeared. More blanks, columns, and boxes.

"Do you object to viewing sexually explicit images?"

"No."

"Do you find sexually explicit images arousing?"

"Sometimes."

"Do you use sexually explicit images as a tool during masturbation?"

Fortunately, I don't blush easily, and we were far beyond that point already anyway. "Sometimes."

"Literature, photographs, or videos?"

"All of the above."

Check. Check. Rustle. Rustle. I was getting wet. The interview couldn't have been more clinical. The subject, however, was getting to me. Talking about sex in any form, in any fashion, under almost any circumstance, turns me on.

"Have you ever used sexually explicit images during mutual masturbation with a partner?"

"How many people are going to read the interview form?"

Dark eyes met mine. "One. Me."

"Yes, I have."

Dr. Adams put down her pen and placed both hands on the desk, her fingers lightly clasped. She regarded me with a slight tilt of her head and a contemplative expression. "If at any time, for any reason, you want to withdraw from the study, you simply need to tell me. I will be administering all of the tests and collecting all of the data."

Well, that got me nice and hard. Administer away. The sooner the better. I nodded.

"I'd like to start tomorrow. Can you be here at eight a.m.?"

"Yes."

"It's important that you be well rested and in as relaxed

a state as possible. I know that may be difficult, but I assure you, there is nothing painful associated with any part of the study."

"I promise to go to bed early." I grinned.

"And please remember the stipulation regarding absti-nence."

How did she know that the first thing I wanted to do as soon as I was alone was jerk off?

"Got it." After all, she wouldn't know. If I did it. Or if I just happened to be thinking about her when I did.

At five minutes to eight the next morning, I knocked on the door with the small plastic nameplate that read *V. Adams, PhD.* She answered immediately. Today, she wore a moss green shell, hemp-colored linen trousers, and low-heeled brown boots. Her lustrous hair was still severely tamed and tied back with a scarf.

"Good morning, Ms. Burns."

I laughed. "Could you call me Robbie? There's no way I'm going to be able to get excited if you keep calling me Ms. Burns."

"Get excited?" she asked as we started to walk down the hallway in the direction she indicated with a raised hand.

"Well, the only reason I can figure for the questions you asked yesterday and the stipulation that I not jerk...ah, have an orgasm anytime except during the course of the study is that I'm going to need to do it here."

"Let's save this conversation for later," she replied even-ly. She removed several keys from her pocket and opened the unmarked door to a large room at the end of a hallway. Inside was a leather recliner in the center surrounded by electronic equipment on rolling carts, a bank of video monitors, and a small glassed-in booth in one corner. From what I could make out, the interior of the booth was wall-to-wall equipment. I also saw a microphone and headset resting on the counter.

Dr. Adams checked the thermostat just inside the door and turned it up. The room was already quite warm. Not overly so, but, I realized, warm enough that someone without much in the way of clothing would be comfortable. Holy shit.

"Today," she said as she gestured to the recliner, "we are just going to establish baseline values." She leaned down, opened a drawer in the bottom of the oversized chair, and withdrew two white sheets, one of which she spread out over the recliner. Turning to me, she held out the other. "Please undress completely and sit here. I have a few notes to make before we begin."

"I guess you'll tell me what I need to do when the time comes, huh?"

"Don't worry. You'll be given specific step-by-step instructions."

Under other circumstances, that sounded like it could be fun. The psychologist went into the tiny booth and she must have adjusted the lights, because the overheads in the main room dimmed and the booth went completely dark. I knew she was in there, but I couldn't see her. It's not like I didn't know what was coming. Ha ha. I took off my clothes and got as comfortable as possible, which wasn't very. Hell, my clit was the only thing that *wasn't* twitching.

It couldn't have been more than five minutes before Dr. Adams came out of the booth.

"Ready?" Her voice was soft and warm. Or maybe it was just the room.

"All set." I think I sounded pretty confident. Usually, I *am* pretty confident about most everything, particularly sex. At the moment, I was terrified I might have performance anxiety and blow the very handsome stipend she'd mentioned the day before. Besides that, I wanted to appear studly in front of her. Since she hadn't given me the slightest reason to think she had any interest in me whatsoever other than as a study subject, I couldn't say why.

"Good. I'm going to be connecting you to various monitoring devices," she said as she rolled the carts containing the electronic equipment closer to me.

Most of what she attached I recognized—EEG pads on my forehead, EKG leads on my chest, arms, and legs, and a blood pressure cuff around my left biceps. When she motioned me to lean forward so she could run a thin flexible strap around my chest just below my breasts, I asked, "What's that for?"

"Respiratory rate and excursion."

She was so matter-of-fact about everything that I relaxed without even realizing it. Until she reached for the little alligator clamp with the thin red and blue wires trailing from the tiny jaws. We're talking minuscule, maybe a half an inch long—too small to be a nipple clamp. I had an uneasy feeling about where that was going to go.

"Uh…"

"This morning," she said conversationally as she stood beside me with the tiny clamp dangling from her fingers, "we're going to take baseline measurements during unstimulated masturbation."

"Isn't that an oxymoron?" I couldn't take my eyes off the little tiny teeth along the edges of the little tiny clamp. "Where are you putting *that?*"

"First question first."

I swear to God I heard a hint of laughter in her voice.

"*Unstimulated* in the sense that we won't be using any visual aides. I'd simply like you to masturbate to orgasm unassisted by anything other than…well, whatever you ordinarily use in terms of mental encouragement."

"So fantasizing is okay?" I was struggling not to inch my way over to the far side of the chair. Escape was impossible at this point, unless I wanted to hotfoot it buck naked through the psychology building with electrodes hanging off my body.

"Absolutely. This," she said, indicating the device in her hand, "is a tonometer, designed to measure turgidity in the clitoris." She must have seen my pupils dilate. "I promise you won't even know it's there."

"Where *exactly* are you attaching it?" There was no way she was closing those little tiny serrated jaws over the head of my clit. No fucking way. Not for a *million* bucks.

"Just distal to the junction of the corpora with the clitoral body."

"Translation?" I asked through gritted teeth.

"On the shaft at the base."

"Okay. Go ahead." As I was fairly sizable, I figured that thing couldn't hurt *too* much.

"I'd let you do it," she said evenly as she drew the sheet up to my waist and leaned over, "but it needs to be precisely positioned to pick up small variations in pressure."

I tried not to tense my thighs and told myself that this was just like a visit to the gynecologist's office as she spread me open slightly with the fingers of one hand and exposed my clitoris. Oh yeah, right. I never get a hard-on in the gynecologist's office. To my acute embarrassment, the second she touched me, I got stiff. Great. Then I felt the slightest bit of pressure in my clit, which only excited it more, and she was straightening up again and adjusting the sheet. I stole a look at her face, but she had that same dispassionate expression she always wore. I was just another lab rat.

"Comfortable?"

"Oh yeah. Perfectly." I was afraid to move in case something fell off. "There's a problem, though."

One of her perfectly sculpted brows rose infinitesimally. "Oh?"

"How am I supposed to masturbate with that little thing on my clitoris?"

"It may fall off, depending upon how vigorous you need to be. But all data is information. Try not to pay any attention to it."

Right. It should be a piece of cake to jerk off while attached to a bunch of machines with a beautiful woman watching and a little probe attached to my clit. No wonder they paid a lot of money for this.

"It would probably be helpful if you closed your eyes while I check the calibrations." Then she turned and walked away.

I leaned my head back and did as she said. Behind my closed lids, I could tell that the room got a little bit darker. I can't say that I was relaxed, but part of me was enjoying this. I'd liked her touching me, even in such a distant and clinical way. Her fingertips were soft and smooth and gentle as she'd attached the electrodes, and she'd handled my clitoris like she knew what she was doing. I pictured her eyes and recalled the honeyed timbre of her voice, and my clit twitched.

"What are you thinking of?" her voice asked from a speaker

somewhere nearby. The acoustics were good, and she sounded as if she were sitting right beside me.

Something told me that the only way this would work was if I was honest. "You."

"What about me?"

"That I liked it when you touched me."

"Would you touch yourself now, please?"

"Is there a time limit?" I slid my hand under the sheet and rested my fingers on the inside of my right thigh.

"Not at all. Take as long as you need."

I kept my eyes closed as I tentatively ran my index finger between my labia and up to the undersurface of my clitoris. It was nice. It's pretty much impossible to touch an area with that many nerve endings and not feel something. Plus, my clitoris was intimately associated with my hand, and I had pretty strong conditioned responses to fondling it. Namely, I got wet after a few seconds, and if I fooled with it for much longer than that, I wouldn't be able to stop until I came. Out of habit, I carried those first droplets of thick moisture on the tip of my finger up to the head of my clitoris and circled it. I got a little harder. Intending to squeeze the head, I inadvertently brushed the alligator clamp with my thumb and caught my breath.

"Sorry."

"No problem. You're doing fine." There was a beat of silence in which all I could hear was my own rapid breathing. Then she murmured, "I'd like you to tell me on a scale of one to ten how you would rate your current level of excitement. Ten being imminent orgasm."

God, she had a great voice. And a fabulous face. And she was watching me jerk off. The sudden realization that I was going to come in front of her, *for* her, hit me in the stomach like a sledgehammer. I soaked my hand.

"Robbie?" Her voice caressed me. "On a scale of one to ten?"

"Six." Christ, how did I know? I was hard as stone and wet and every time I ran my trembling fingers over my clitoris, my hips gave a little jump. Somewhere in my increasingly addled brain I wondered what that little device clamped around my clit was measuring now. Because I certainly felt like I was going to explode. I just needed something to get me past the last bit of nerves. "Can I use two hands?"

"Of course. Do whatever makes you feel good."

I slid my other hand between my legs and toyed with the swollen labia, manipulating my clitoris faster between thumb and index finger. I was starting to get that going-to-need-to-come-soon feeling. I picked up speed with my hand and moaned quietly.

"One to ten, Robbie."

"Eight," I gasped. I curled two fingers inside and rubbed my clit harder. "Oh fuck." I hadn't meant to say anything, but I couldn't help it. I pushed my hand deeper, working the head of my clit frantically with my fingers. My stomach gave a warning clench. "Jesus. *Nine.*"

"I know you're close," the soothing voice, so much like a touch, whispered from somewhere nearby, "but if you can, talk to me as you approach orgasm. Tell me what you feel."

I whimpered, I think. I turned my head and opened my eyes, trying to see her through the glass. I imagined her watching me, then I imagined her touching me, and the fingers stroking me rapidly to orgasm became hers. "I'm so hard now, need to come so much. Almost there...close...oh yeah. Just touch me right there...a little faster, baby. Just a little harder." I arched my back as the tendrils of orgasm fluttered and curled along my spine. Blinking, I tried to focus on where I knew she must be, but my vision was tunneling as every cell in my body ignited. "Oh, god. Ten. Oh yeah, please, *ten*." I surged upright in the chair as my stomach convulsed, my hand moving so rapidly as I forced out the orgasm that the clamp flew off my pulsating clitoris. "Jesus," I groaned, "I'm coming."

Somewhere in the middle of it all, the top of my head blew off. God only knows what the EEG must've shown. I fell back, boneless, my breasts heaving under the chest band, my heart hammering. It took me a minute, maybe more, to get my breath back. When I was finally able to open my eyes, she was standing beside me. Her face, that beautiful elegant face, was still and serene. But her eyes were liquid and hot.

I smiled, a lazy sated smile. "I screwed up."

"How?" Her question was curious, her voice throaty and low. She didn't move a muscle, but I felt her fingers on my skin.

"You can't use those readings for baseline values." I was still trembling and my voice was shaky. I sucked in air and tried to calm down. "That wasn't my normal self-induced orgasm." I shivered as an aftershock gripped me. "Oh man, not at all."

"Oh?"

I nodded, still unable to lift my head, watching her face. She was smiling now, too. "I shouldn't have thought about *you* while I was doing that. It turned the ten there at the end into a hundred."

Something close to pleasure flickered across her face and then disappeared behind her composed, clinical expression.

But she couldn't hide the satisfaction in her voice.

"Well, I shouldn't worry too much about that. That's what bell curves are for."

And I couldn't wait to plot the next data point.

NAKED, RUSTED PLUMBING

Eric Maroney

Christ, I have to pee, I think to myself, looking about the train and fingering an empty
beer can in my hand. It's one of those forty-
eight-ounce cans that looks like a tiny green
keg, meant for a college party for leprechauns.
When I opened it in Milford, the guy sitting
next to me gave me one of those *you're drinking this early* looks. I tighten my hand around
the can, listening to the cracking of the alumi-
num folding beneath the pressure of my palm,
and look down silently communicating with
my crotch, before looking to the man seated
next to me. I make sure he's not listening.
Then, crossing one leg over the other, I create
a seawall against my vagina and in a silent,
Moses-like voice, command, *Not now, you
can wait.*

I tighten the muscles that clamp my labia and urethra into a quivering mass and concentrate on containment—as if it were a public epidemic, a threat to society or worse, a threat to capitalism, to wet oneself; something the surgeon general might issue warnings about. *Surgeon general says urinating in public may lead to depression, bulimia, and bouts of homoeroticism.* I close my eyes, pressing my fingers against my thighs, eroticizing the idea of letting go as I think of the summer my best friend and I took turns wading in the water fountains on the New Haven green—our jeans rolled tight and up to our knees, her thick blonde dreadlocks caught in the breeze as a stream of yellow caressed the length of her calf. There are people who are into fucking in public, why not peeing? The pressure of my bladder brimming with urine reminds me of the women who fuck me—their fingers, slender and shaking as they press against the outer wall of me.

Again, I look to the man sitting next to me. I'm afraid that one day I'm going to be silently talking to myself, and someone is going to hear me. Of course it will happen that I won't be saying anything ordinary or harmless like, *What should I have for lunch?* but something more along the lines of, *Remember to pick up the batteries for your vibrator—the new energizer platinums, only they can outlast you.* But he's not looking. His head is rolled back against the seat, eyes half closed and mouth wide open as if he is about to bite someone's nose off, and I don't mind as long as it's not mine. It might even be entertaining, something to take my mind off the dull ache cultivating itself between my legs, increasing in intensity with each moment spent in transit. I pull my bags across my lap and hide my hand beneath them as I press down on my swollen clit—an attempt to ward off the urge.

If this train doesn't stop vibrating I'm going to have to kill someone. I press my knees to the back of the maroon seat in front of me, trace the Connecticut symbols patterned on the walls of the Metro North car with my eyes, and shift around. There's not enough room to stretch, but then what could I expect for fifteen dollars? I think, scanning the train car once more. Harlem 125th Street—almost there. My eyes lock on the imitation wood swinging door of the mobile lavatory that has been taunting me since Bridgeport, with a typed out-of-order sign taped to it. This pisses me off—if someone had the time to type an out-of-order sign and hang it nicely in a little clear plastic sleeve, he probably also had the time to fix the goddamn toilet. I look down at my watch, the silver wrist-band stretching around my bronzed wrist. Fuck, I'm going to be late for this appointment and I have to piss...*now.*

I collect my bags, a khaki-colored messenger bag and a pressed suit still in the dry-cleaning sleeve, as the train enters the tunnel beneath Grand Central and everything goes dark. When I have the time I like to press my face to the window and make out the shadows of the lair, which remind me of the places dragons might sleep, curled into a hulking mass and heaving soft breaths of air through the subway system—just another one of New York City's dirty little secrets. But I have to concentrate to do this; otherwise it's only my reflection I see in the dirty windowpane, and I don't have the time.

I'm late for an audition, uptown, with a promoter who is producing a male impersonator burlesque show. Who knew that cross-dressing could be a profession? As I stand up and wait for the train doors to open, I think about how I used to steal the clip-on ties from my brother's sock drawer when I was nine. I would stand in my parents' mirror-paneled bedroom and swagger back and forth, a hand on my hip, winking at my image—something I must have seen in a black-and-white cartoon, one of those grayscale human-animal hybrids from the 1950s, who always seemed to get the girl.

The door slides open and I hurry off. *I have to pee. I have to pee,* I think while running a hand through my cropped hair. *Come on people, let's go.* I almost trip over the wheels of an older man's rolling suitcase as I tailgait him on foot past the recycling bins that read *Newspapers Only,* and toss the empty beer can inside.

Inside the station, I dodge groups of men in business suits and a cluster of nuns wearing thick-framed glasses, their cameras snapping away at pissed-off New Yorkers and the ceiling—half an empty shell of a teal Easter egg. This station's so big and yet I feel as if it's the only place where I might happen upon someone I used to know, bump into an old friend, an old lover—our packages colliding and spilling into an uneven mess all over the floor, her lips soft at my ear, *Remember me?* I jog down the stairs and round the corner. FUCK, a line, a goddamn line trailing out of the ladies' room like the back end of a Chinese dragon, and I—I *have* to pee. It almost hurts now, a soreness concentrating just below my abdomen. A tragic welling up of fluids like a beer mug spilling over after last call.

I slip into line behind a middle-aged yuppie and her daughter, whom I estimate to be around nine or ten—the age I was when I first starting slipping socks down my shorts, pleased that the bulge in my pants matched my father's, and got my first BMX, Christmas 1985. What a happy little boy I was.

"The men's room is over there." The woman in front of me cranes her neck around in my direction and points at the men's room door, which opens and closes briskly; there's no line. She looks like Linda Blair stretching this way, a large purple shawl draped over her shoulders and dull brown hair hanging loose about her neck. I imagine her fucking a crucifix or even spitting up pea soup all over the front of her shawl, as I fight to keep myself from leaning over and whispering in her ear, "The power of Christ compels you." Instead I just stare.

I hear a breathy giggle from behind, a female voice—hushed laughter, no amusement. I snap my neck around to deliver a look of disapproval, but before my eyes meet hers I feel two slender fingers nudging at the palm of my hand hanging at my side. This is odd. People just don't do this sort of thing, *this touching, this—what is this*? I shake my head and she shoots a smile at me—a coy, eyes-sweeping-downward, corner-of-mouth-tweaked-up smile—as she twists a finger around a thread of her russet hair. Oh god, oh, oh she's hot. I feel the ache between my legs turning to something else, some pleasure on the verge of release, as my eyes meet the tiled wall with a ripped sign taped to it: *Please do not defecate in any area of the train station other than the restrooms, RULES AND REGULATIONS, SECTION 1085.7—Hygiene.*

The line has moved through the door now, and when a stall opens up I dash toward it. My bag, slung over my shoulder, nudges at my left asscheek as I move and rubs the pocket where I keep my wallet, which is now digging into my flesh. I had to leave her, didn't even catch her name, but oh, I have to pee—like some tremendous force gathering up inside of me; the waves, the eddies collecting against a breakwater.

Restrooms always look the same. Regardless of where you might be in the country the stalls will be painted some hideous color—an off-yellow perhaps, that same yellow of a used cigarette filter—and the cracked tiles, various shades of dirty white. I sling my bag and suit onto the hook on the door, slam my bottle of Evian onto the tampon receptacle, and squat over the toilet, trying to aim as best I can. I am courteous this way—the type of woman who makes an effort not to mess up the seat. I'm good at it too, and this makes me proud, as if I have beat god or nature or whoever, because I can pee stand-ing up—even if it is in reverse—and I think this is the closest we will ever come to equality with men: squatting over a pub-lic toilet, peeing.

I hear the woman next to me exit the stall, her red heels clicking against the gritty floor, and another one enters and drops her Gucci bag to the tile. I reach to my left to grab a wad of toilet paper from the locked plastic dispenser and realize—midstream—there *is* no paper. "No toilet fucking paper!" I mutter aloud. I stand, knees bent and hovering over the seat, which is black in contrast with the white toilet and rusted naked plumbing. I look down at my vagina, the hair neatly trimmed in a slender strip, and I wish I were a man— wish I could take the tip of my dick in my palm and just shake it, a simple privilege, but to have a dick right now would be so convenient. I think: what if there were swap meets, a used car dealership—sparkling banners that read "We love America, Used Trade-Ins Welcome"—somewhere I could take my cunt and barter it for something with a vas deferens.

My legs are starting to hurt from squatting, a dull pain trav-eling up my thighs; my knees buckle and I fall back. Now I'm sitting on the toilet, my head hanging between my shoulders. "I wish I were a man, I wish I were a man, I wish—" I call louder with each phrase and look down at my feet, spit-pol-ished boots instead of ruby red slippers. Fuck.

There's a knock at the door. I look up and as the stall

squeaks open I see standing there, framed in the light like some heavenly gift bestowed upon a nonbeliever, the girl from the line—her arm outstretched and a roll of toilet paper resting on her open palm.

She steps forward, closes the door behind her and smiles. "Thought you could use a little help." The bottom of her mauve skirt hangs just above her knees and I reach to cup my hand around her bare thigh. I look up at her from where I sit—my pants bunched about my ankles—as she inches forward, and I press my hand higher, brushing against her warm skin; insert two fingers beneath the rim of her panties.

I make as if to get up from where I sit, locked in this quintessential position of womanhood, but she puts a hand on my shoulder, curls her fingers around the back of my neck and steps forward. The smell of her, wet and ready, reaches my nose and I lean into her, lifting her skirt above my head and yanking her panties down to the floor. My head up her skirt, I trace the sides of her labia with quick strikes of the tongue—careful not to reach her clit—as she moans low and breathy, just like her laughter. I push my face deeper into her. My bottom lip is stretched under her opening and my tongue licks, then nibbles, then sucks at her clit as if it were a tiny penis misplaced on such a delicate body. I curve my fingers up against the wall of her vagina—sliding them in and out, first slow and deliberate, then quick and rigorous, fucking her in the midst of Grand Central. Her body bucks backward, and she lets out a howl, slamming into the stall door where my suit hangs ruffled in the plastic sleeve. The door slips the lock and squeaks open as she cums in my palm and I let go of another stream of urine that splashes against the side of the toilet bowl, stained, rusted, and sweating.

Outside the stall, a crowd has gathered. The woman in the purple shawl shields her daughter's eyes and moans in disgust. I stand—my vagina still wet with piss and cum—and pull my boxer shorts and pants up, kiss the girl in the mauve skirt deeply and ferociously before grabbing my bags and exiting the stall.

Striding across the station, I think: Now I know what is better than having a roll of toilet paper, than making it to an appointment on time, than being a man—two women, alone in a bathroom stall.

BÉSAME

Gina Bern

If you've never been to Phoenix in the summer
or any time between April and even September,
take it from me: you're better off anywhere
else. I kept thinking about the heat as I made
it back to my car, parked in a treeless lot in
front of Linens 'N' Things, where my fiancé
and mother-in-law-to-be had just tried and
failed miserably to get a registry together for
our wedding. After spending more than two
hours with Abel and his mother debating the
value of this dish pattern over that, mostly in
English, but also in Spanish, which I don't
speak, I actually couldn't think of anything
more wonderful than retreating to my sweltering car. While Abel helped his mother with
her bags, I walked ahead of them, angry and
impatient. When I'd fallen in love with Abel,

I hadn't counted on his mother having so much to do with our lives. I had pulled out my keys and unlocked my car door when Abel called over to me.

"Hey! Where are you headed off to so fast?" Abel wrinkled his forehead, which he only did when he was upset or nervous.

"Sorry," I said, but I didn't mean it. "I guess I forgot to say good-bye." Abel leaned in my open window and kissed me. I'd see him later, but I needed to get to work and clear my head. We waved good-bye again, but when I looked in my rearview mirror, he was still talking to his mother and not looking at me.

I guess you could say getting married was colliding with my life with the speed and subtlety of a Mack truck. Between dress shopping, RSVPs, showers, fittings, and flowers, I was already exhausted and I still had two months to go. My latest duty was to send thank-you notes to the people who had already sent us wedding gifts, a pretty mundane task—and yet one gift we received would change everything.

In a plain, brown-wrapped package that had come from an aunt of Abel's was a *retablo* from Mexico. I'd seen *retablos* before—folk paintings that commemorate a blessing or an event in a person's life—but this one was particularly beautiful. It depicted a beach scene in the foreground, and a young woman with shoulder-length black hair, whom no one seemed to notice was being swept away to sea. Her eyes were pointed at an image of the Virgin Mary in the corner of the sky. There was writing in Spanish—probably telling the story of the near-drowning and how the woman was saved—but I couldn't read it.

I'm not sure why the *retablo* captivated me so much. There

was something in the young woman's vulnerability—and her being swept out to sea with no one to save her—that seemed more and more like my own situation. I had the sense that I had known her. I'm not much of a detective, but I wanted to find out more—about the artist, about the drowning woman—anything that might help explain the feelings the *retablo* raised in me.

A few days went by—work, family, heat—before I was able to find out anything more about the *retablo*. That weekend, Abel's family threw an engagement party for us. My parents were long dead, and I hadn't lived in the Southwest very long, so most of the guests were Abel's friends and family. In spite of my doubts and preoccupation, I snapped to attention when Abel mentioned that his Aunt Consuelo, the one who had sent us the *retablo*, would be there.

"Sera, there's Consuelo—she's the one you wanted to meet." Abel smiled and pointed to an older woman. "She's my *nina*, my godmother. I'll introduce you."

We made our way through a crowd of cousins to where Consuelo was standing. "*Nina*, I'd like to introduce you to my fiancé, Sera. She was so impressed by the *retablo* you sent, she wanted to thank you in person."

Consuelo smiled and hugged me. "It's so nice to meet you," I said, trying to hide my curiosity. "I wanted to ask you where you found our wedding gift. I've never seen a *retablo* like it."

"Oh, just on eBay. There's an artist in Mexico City...Aixa Avilar, I think her name is...she paints them. They're not real, you know. I mean, I think she makes the stories up." Consuelo had barely finished her sentence when she was called away into the kitchen.

It was after midnight when I got back to my apartment. Abel walked me to the door and kissed me on the neck. His hands were insistent, and I knew he wanted to stay over. If I let him, though, I'd have to wait another day to search for Aixa. I made up an excuse and sent him home.

With the door locked, I switched my computer monitor on and typed in Aixa's name. In a few seconds, I had a hit: she had her own website. I started breathing a little faster. As the pictures on Aixa's site slowly downloaded, I saw that it was *her* face in the *retablo:* she was the drowning woman. In the sole picture of the artist, Aixa sat in a window seat with her knees drawn up under her chin. Her head was bent forward, and she was looking past the camera. Her hair was long, wavy, and black and her eyes were a startling green against her tan skin. She wore a simple turquoise and silver crucifix around her neck and red cowboy boots. I was transfixed.

For the next hour or two, I searched for all the information I could find about Aixa, which wasn't a lot. She was twenty-six and lived in Mexico City. She had about forty of her paintings online, but none were self-portraits like the *retablo* I had, and none were as piercing. My *retablo* was unique, and I was convinced there was some reason I had received it. I had to find out why.

A week passed and I couldn't stop thinking about her. I desperately needed to get in touch with her, maybe even meet her. After five days of no sleep or bad sleep, I decided to email her. I had to find out why I was so taken with this woman I had never met.

After two glasses of pinot grigio, I finally worked up enough courage to email Aixa. "This is it," I said out loud, even though no one else was there. Trying desperately not to sound like a stalker or worse, I told her about my *retablo* and asked if she could tell me more about it. I held my breath and hit *Send*.

Waiting for Aixa's response was worse than a thousand bridal showers. I was distracted at work, distracted with Abel, and practically attached to my computer. When she finally wrote back, three days later, I was almost too nervous to read her message.

"Dear Sera," Aixa wrote, "I'm glad you liked the *retablo*. I painted it three years ago, after I almost drowned in a lake near where I grew up. As the water pulled me deeper and deeper in, I saw the color of the sun through the water, and I heard the voices of children playing on the beach. No one saw me, and I was convinced I was going to die. I never paint anything about my life—I guess it's corny—but I painted this right after. It was too personal to sell, so I kept it until now. I wanted to move on, so I sold it. Thank you for giving it a home."

I had walked to the kitchen to look at the *retablo* again when my instant messenger dinged. I thought it was probably Abel IMing me. I'd been avoiding him. I checked the monitor: it wasn't Abel IMing me, it was someone I didn't know—*La Vaquera*. Intrigued, I sat down and read the message.

<*Buena sera*, Sera. I'm sorry if I'm intruding. I just couldn't wait for a response to my email.>

I scrunched my forehead a little bit. <Hello back. Is this Aixa?>

I waited, watching my own message blink back at me. Finally, she wrote: <*Sí*—it's Aixa. Am I bothering you?>

I exhaled. My fingers could barely type as quickly as I was

thinking. <No. I just read your message and I was actually looking at the *retablo* again. You know how beautiful I think it is.>

We typed back and forth for hours. She told me about her painting and I told her about my childhood. I felt as if I had always known her—as if I were speaking to her face-to-face despite the computer between us. I was so taken by our conversation that I didn't even notice the faint line of sunlight through my window.

<Aixa, I'm so sorry, but I have to go now. I didn't go to sleep and now it's time for work!>

<When can I talk to you again?>

<Tonight. Six o'clock. Here.> I'd never felt such certainty in my life. I shut my computer down and padded off to sleep for forty-five minutes until I had to get up again and go.

Being sleep deprived makes time slow *and* fast. It was all I could do, drinking espresso all day, to make it home to talk to Aixa again at six. I poured myself a glass of wine and logged on. Aixa was already waiting.

<Where have you been all day, Sera? It's funny, but I missed you.>

<Did you sleep at all? What time did you get up?>

<I did sleep—it was full of dreams of you.>

My heart beat faster, and I read her message again. She had dreamed of me? A typist who wrote her like some silly groupie?

<What did you dream?>

<Well, first, we were together, in Old Town at night. You were wearing a peasant blouse and you had your hair down. What color is your hair?>

<It's blonde, and it's shoulder length.>

<Just like my dream! There was music, and I was holding your hand. You were warm, and I kissed you on the lips.>

<Then what happened?> I marveled at how un-shy I had become with her.

<I bought you a *mojito*, and I brought you to my house. I sat you on a chair and pushed your skirt around your waist.>

I wondered if Aixa knew how much she was turning me on. <What next?>

<Your feet are dirty from the sandals you were wearing and the dust on the street. I bring a bowl of water from my kitchen and a cloth, and I'm wiping your feet clean, moving my cloth and my fingers between your toes and over the soles of your feet. Your legs are so beautiful and so lean that I forget about your feet. I'm moving my hands up your calves and over your smooth thighs. I already know how wet you are.>

She was right. <I am wet. You know that and that gives you power over me, so I kiss you hard and pull your body into mine.>

<While you are kissing me, my tongue is in your mouth and I'm pulling your blouse over your head. You're so beautiful, I can't get enough of you. You aren't wearing a bra under your blouse and your nipples are already hard before I touch them—in spite of the heat. Your breasts are full and white and bare and I take your nipple in my mouth, sucking it, tracing it with my tongue until you gasp. You're arching your back into the chair and I can already hear you moaning.>

<When do I get to…when do I…?> It was getting hard to type how I felt. I wished she were really in front of me.

<When I'm ready. For now, though, you have to wait. I can see how hot you are, how wet you are, how much you want

me, so I pull your skirt off with my teeth. You're so impatient for me that you can't wait and you pull it off yourself.>

<Yes, I do. How do you know how impatient I am?>

<Because it's obvious, because I can see how greedy and how in need you are of this. So you're naked now—you didn't even wear underwear, dirty girl. I dip my tongue into your belly button just to frustrate you. You squirm, and I know you can't take much more. You won't come until I say so, until I let you.>

<Okay, okay, I won't.> My fictional panties and my real-life panties were now off, and I was touching myself, but I wouldn't go any further than she would let me.

<My tongue is on your belly, Sera, and it's hot and wet against your skin. I'm following your belly down to between your legs, and I'm surprised to see you're completely clean shaven. I push your thighs open with my hands: you're a pink, open flower, and I sink my tongue into your folds. When I taste you, you taste like the sea: you are salt and wet and so warm you are burning up.>

<What next? What comes next?>

<What's next is my tongue, which probes you and tastes you. I'm flicking my tongue against your center and then I'm circling it insistently. You tighten—I know you want to come—so I stop and kiss your thigh instead. You scowl at me and push yourself back in front of me.>

I plunged my fingers deep inside myself, trying to keep up with Aixa, but I almost couldn't.

<Every time you are close, Sera, I will stop. You can't come unless I tell you to, unless you understand.>

<I understand, Aixa, I do.> I was desperate for her to go on.

<How can I be sure you understand?>

<Can't you feel it? Can't you feel how much I want you to?>

<I can. I'm going to let you come, Sera, but not yet. First, I have to put my fingers into you—three of them. They're moving deep inside of you, where it's so warm and wet, and I can barely keep up with you. You're squeezing my fingers tighter and tighter—I find your G-spot—it's warm and I press against it. Finally, finally, I let you come and you do.>

Aixa had finally given me the okay, so I didn't hold back anymore. I touched myself hard and fast until I came so hard it amazed me and froze me to my chair. Stunned, I sat in a stupor for a few seconds. This was the biggest climax I'd ever had on my own or with anyone else. Aixa had done this to me and she wasn't even in the same room—or country for that matter. I was engaged, and there was Abel. I couldn't think of anything to write Aixa.

Suddenly, an abrupt message came on the screen. <When will we meet?>

I shut my computer off without writing back and went to bed, exhausted, happy, but confused.

I woke up the next morning, then the next, and the next—determined to avoid Aixa and what had happened between us. I felt so guilty about betraying Abel that I went out and bought him expensive gifts and cooked him elaborate meals. At that moment, I would've done anything to erase Aixa.

Every day and every hour, Aixa emailed me; then, having discovered my phone number, she began calling. One morning at 3:30, Abel picked up the phone and, hearing yet another silence, slammed it down. Order after order of flowers—all calla lilies, beautiful and scentless—came to my house. Abel was already so suspicious that I threw them all out. Every time I turned on my computer, at work or at home, Aixa was there, IMing me only the question, "Why?" I recklessly pushed ahead the wedding by a month, surprising Abel who confessed he had thought I was having second thoughts and that he was about to lose me.

When three weeks had passed, I felt a certain calm come over things; perhaps everything would be fine. On the Saturday before the wedding, my doorbell rang early; it was the UPS man with a package for me. The package was slender and the handwriting on the address was a woman's. Before I even opened the package or saw the postmark from Mexico City, I knew it was from Aixa. The package was a *retablo*, with a dark-haired woman looking out her window. The woman's eyes were sad and turned down; you could see the faint glow of a computer screen in the corner of the painting coming from inside the woman's house. The *retablo*'s dedication was in English: *This woman gives thanks to the Virgin of Guadalupe for revealing to her Sera, with whom she shared much passion and amistad. She asks the Virgin to send her lover back to her, before it is too late. With thanks, Aixa Avila, May 6, 2004.*

My hands were trembling as I held the *retablo*, causing the smallest flecks of paint to flutter off the tin. I couldn't look at Aixa's portrait of herself. I had begun to cry when I felt a heavy piece of paper taped to the back of the *retablo*. When I turned it over, I saw that the paper was a plane ticket for a flight from Phoenix to Mexico City. My heart seemed to stop. I pulled the ticket out of the Aero Mexico sleeve: the flight left that day, at two o'clock. The ticket was round-trip.

I remained there in my hallway for twenty minutes or more. I sat down and put my head in my hands. What was I doing with a plane ticket from a woman I'd never met, but to whom my whole body felt connected? My fiancé, who would be my husband in six days, was sleeping in the next room, unaware of everything that was unfolding in my head. As silently as I could, I pulled my smallest suitcase out of the closet and packed: a long dress, a nightgown, a hairbrush, and a bottle of perfume. I looked at my ticket again and suddenly understood how well Aixa knew me: if she had bought a one-way ticket, I would never have gone. As I closed the last dresser drawer, Abel's eyes flickered and he stirred, but did not wake up. He was a good man and I had no right to hurt him, but I did not love him. He deserved someone who would move the earth to be with him: we all do.

I drove my car to the airport and parked it in a long-term lot. I half thought, *Leave the keys in the car and leave the car unlocked. You won't be coming back*, but I didn't trust the part of myself that said that. I checked in, bought a bottle of water, and sat down. Everyone around me—mothers, businesspeople with best-sellers and cell phones, old married couples—seemed so alien. I barely heard the gate attendant announce the boarding for my flight. When I got on the plane, I found that I had a window seat: Aixa must have known how motion sick I get, or she must have thought how lonely this flight would be, or how I'd like to watch one life disappear into another.

The plane took me from a place I had been familiar with to another climate and to a lover I had never met. In a few short hours, the landscape changed from tan to green. When the plane finally stopped, I was half frozen. What would be waiting for me at the other end of this terminal? I thought of Abel, who'd woken up hours ago and by now knew I was gone. I hadn't even left him a note or an explanation. I pushed these thoughts down in my mind as I grabbed my bag and headed off the plane.

The airport was disorienting and the announcements and signs in Spanish seemed to swallow me. I stood in one place and looked around. Was this a joke? Aixa's revenge for ignoring her for so long? I felt someone touch my shoulder from behind, and I knew it was Aixa. I didn't need to turn around to know it was her, but I did. We stood there, silent, simply looking at each other for the longest time. She was shorter than I imagined, just a few inches shy of my height of five foot ten. I had memorized her face from her *retablos* and her photo, but neither did her justice. Aixa's eyes were almond shaped and green, as she had painted them, with flecks of silver and gold. Her dark hair was between black and brown, with wild waves that framed her face perfectly. Her cheekbones were strong and defined and her lips were the color of coral. Aixa's skin was mocha and gold.

"So, you made it." Aixa's comment was not a question or a declaration: simply an observation. I could tell she was still guarded toward me, but happy that I was there. Neither of us made any movement toward the other: we did not touch, which seemed so strange after how intimate we had become. Without another word, Aixa picked up the bag from where I had put it down and motioned for me to follow.

When the sliding doors of the airport slid shut behind us, the humidity was suffocating. I had never felt the weight of a place so heavily. Aixa hailed us a cab and we drove in silence.

Finally, she said, "We're going to my home, in case you're wondering...like the dream, but with no *mojito.*"

I was impressed by her grace, her self-possession, and her singular confidence. After twenty minutes, Aixa motioned for the cabbie to stop, thanked him in Spanish, and handed him a few bills. She took my bag and my hand: I felt her touch jolt all the way up my arm. I followed her over a small gravel path: her house was modest, but it suited her.

When we got inside, Aixa put my bag down on the floor. I almost expected us to rip each other's clothes off in shreds right then and there. Aixa looked me in the eyes as if she saw this, gave a half laugh, and walked to the small kitch-en, where she set a kettle of water on the stove. We sat at her table and drank coffee when it was ready. She was as brave as I had thought she would be. No matter how conflicted I was and how many people I had hurt—Aixa and Abel both— I was *with* Aixa: the beautiful drowning woman in the *retab-lo*, the painting that had brought me to her. As we continued to stare at each other in silence and silence only, not with hos-tility or even apprehension, I realized that if Aixa and I were to be anything to each other again I would have to make the first move. In her country and face-to-face, I didn't feel like I could use any words. I would have to show her.

How do you make love to a lover you've never touched before? I didn't know, and I was beyond the point of being anxious. I stood up, came around the table to where Aixa sat, and kissed her. She did not respond. My hands seemed to have their own memory of her. I kissed her again, looking into her eyes, which were open. I held her head against mine: "Aixa, this is real and I want this and I'm sorry." Something inside Aixa visibly turned on. She closed her eyes and pulled me closer to her. Her hair smelled like cinnamon. I was kissing her and my whole body was pressed against hers, the humidity making our clothes cling to our bodies and to each other. As I started to unbutton Aixa's blouse, I realized that this was not the way to make love to her. She was the drowning woman in the painting and so was I: I would make love to her in the water.

I pulled Aixa to the bathroom I had seen through an open door and turned the water on in the bathtub. Aixa stripped her clothes off in front of me—not quickly and not slowly. Her shirt came up over her head, and I could see her tan breasts, her red nipples, and the tautness of her stomach. I stood across from her and took off my own shirt; my chest was heaving and the tub continued to fill up with water. Aixa unzipped her skirt and threw it off: she was naked and the most beautiful thing I had ever seen.

Without a word, Aixa stepped into the tub and I followed her. Her hair was soaked, and clung in long strands to her chest, neck, and face as I began to kiss her again. How strange it was to touch someone you already knew so intimately and passionately. She was like I had imagined, but being with her in person was almost paralyzing. Her body responded to mine, moved against me when I touched her, kissing her neck, massaging her breasts. In the water, she looked vulnerable and sexual, like she needed to be saved and consumed. I reached into the water and felt the warmth between her legs. She gasped as my fingers entered her, plunging once, twice, and then again and again. We rocked against the rhythm of our bodies in the water: Aixa's body rose against mine, her hips and pelvis arching into my hand as she came. This was not enough. I would not let her stop and I plunged in again, quicker and faster. Her hands were between my legs: like in her dream, I was clean shaven and the water and the bare skin made me more sensitive than I had ever felt before. I nearly collapsed on top of her, but regained my balance and continued kissing her and thrusting my fingers into her. Aixa turned and switched positions with me, so that she was on top and staring me right in the eyes as we both came.

Unfazed, I stood up and got out of the tub, dripping water on the red tile floor. Aixa followed me to the bed where I began to flick my tongue against her warmth with such passion that she came again immediately. Aixa's sheets clung to our wet bodies and our drenched hair hung around our faces like we were wild women. Aixa reversed her position and then I was tasting her and she was tasting me, the water from the bath and our own wetness making us drown again and again.

After evening (*sera*), there is night (*noche*). The evening, then the night crept through Aixa's open windows, lapping at our naked skin as we lay in each other's arms and Aixa's soaked bed. I heard music from another street—something fast, sad, and pounding at the same time.

"Do you know what that is?" Aixa spoke like music, too: her accented English sweet and liquid. "That's flamenco music. It's the music I will thank the Virgin for—when I paint her a *retablo* for sending you to me."

Aixa rose from the bed and pulled her long hair up in a loose bun. She pulled on an oversized shirt and turned, saying, "I have something to show you."

I heard Aixa's footsteps leaving the hallway, then a few seconds of silence, and then her coming back. "Look. This is for you."

Aixa handed me a piece of tin. On it, a *retablo* was half finished: there were two women in bed, with the evening and
music coming in the windows. I reached across the bed to kiss
Aixa and got up to find my bag. I searched my bag for my
plane ticket and handed it to Aixa. "Tear this up or paint it—
either way, you're going to have to teach me Spanish."

Aixa took the ticket from me and looked at me like she still
wasn't sure if she wanted to keep me. She held the ticket in
her hand uncertainly and the second felt like those weeks of
avoiding her. Aixa tore the ticket in two and said, "First lesson: *bésame*. Kiss me." And I did, ecstatically. Aixa pulled
back in mock anger and said sternly, "Second lesson. Civili-
ty—you must say, 'Please,' *por favor!*" I kissed her nicely and
I never looked back again.

A CASE OF MISTAKEN IDENTITY

Lynne Jamneck

It was Jo who suggested we go to the beach. She was quite adamant that it would be a shame to spend the afternoon indoors, especially since it was officially the first day of spring.

We trucked along a heavy picnic basket and, once at the beach, spread our towels down on a secluded spot behind the sloping rocks. Yes, I'll admit—I had underhanded motives. I'd been planning a covert surprise for Jo, and I made sure we were some way from the nearest beachcombers.

I took my shoes off, which is about as far as I'll go where public undressing is concerned. I keep my armor on most of the time, 'cause it's a fucked-up world and you never know when you're going to have to look presentable. Jo teased me for keeping my jeans on, and said the bulge in my crotch must be starting to ache with constraint.

Clever bitch—she'd known all along. I took two bottles of chilled beer from the picnic basket, gave one to Jo and dug ravenously into the rye bread sandwiches she'd prepared. She'd slathered them with strong mustard—just the way I like it. It made my mouth burn. Jo noticed and laughed. I gulped beer until it ran down my chin.

"Chris...shit...hey Chris—check this out!" Mike waved the binoculars at his fratboy-friend who was busy packing fresh ice on the beer in his cooler.

"Looks like some son-of-a-bitch is about to get lucky," Mike smirked. The girl sure was a hot little number, he thought. Lying there with her tight white bikini, sand sprinkled on her tanned body, only a couple hundred yards away, half hidden by an outcropping of rock.... He sure as shit wished he could be the one giving her some. She licked something from her lip and laughed, looking down at her boyfriend's head. If only the bastard would move out of the way so he could get a good look at her tits.

"Oh, my god...," he muttered distractedly.

"What?" Chris tried to snag the binoculars from his buddy. "What the fuck's happening? Mike—you bastard, give that here!"

"Ohhh..." was all Mike replied, relinquishing the binoculars to his friend reluctantly. "Take a look—I think she's gonna go down on him."

It was when Jo started to lick that chili-mustard from her own lip that I started getting really fucking horny. Plus, the fact that she was staring at my crotch and saying things like "I know what Daddy wants" didn't make it any easier. I tried to ignore her and eat my sandwich instead but then she started fiddling with the buttons of my fly.

"Now there's an idea," I muttered as she drew herself up to my thighs. Small patches of sand clung to her skin, mixing with the coconut-scented oil she'd made me rub all over her body earlier.

Jo didn't waste any time in attending to my needs. We were both infinitely aware that, deserted as our little spot might seem, anyone could come strolling into view at any moment. She said, "Now don't get greedy or I'll stop." Then she took my seven inches into her gorgeous mouth and slowly, gradually swallowed me whole.

"Yeah, baby...," Chris groaned as he held on to the binoculars with one trembling hand, the other working inside his Rip Curl shorts. He sure wasn't going to pass up the free show.

"What's she doing?" Mike salivated from the side.

Now it was Chris's turn to smirk. "Looks like a good old-fashioned deep throat to me, buddy. Fuck...aw shit—that girl knows how to give head. Wish I could walk over there and tell her to suck my dick...."

"Why don't you? She might like it."

"You fucking nuts?" Chris muttered without putting the binoculars down. "Her boyfriend would kick the living shit out of me. Jesus, look at the muscles on that guy. No thanks— I'll just stay here and appreciate the view along with some DIY. Sure wish he'd move his back though so I can see better.... Oh yeah, buddy—give it to her...give it to her good...."

Mike opened another ice-cold beer. Chris's grunts were becoming more pronounced by the second.

I'm not sure whether it's because Jo has the aura of a virginal saint, but ever since day one she's had the knack for bringing out the roughneck in me. As she kept blowing me with that teasing, innocent expression in her eyes, tendons in her sleek neck straining, she made me want to push her flat onto her back and fuck the innocence from her.

Instead—for now—I placed one hand firmly at the back of her head and told her to hold still. I started plying the inside of her mouth with long, drawn-out strokes, rapidly moving on to short stabs as the enjoyment on her face urged me on.

"Hold still, baby," I grunted down above her dirty-blonde head. "Daddy's gonna be real good to you...."

Mike exchanged a beer for the binoculars in his friend's sweaty grasp. His dick was hard, and who the fuck could blame him? He wasn't entirely sure whether it was the sight of the girl and her buff boyfriend fucking or that of his mate jacking off next to him that had given him such a raging hard-on.

The entrées seemed to be at an end now. Bikini's boyfriend motioned for her to lie back while he felt his pockets, presumably for a condom. Mike wondered whether they had any idea that they were being watched—wondered whether they would be the type to get off on it if in fact they did. Also, he wondered why it was that the tough-guy bikers got all the hot girls. Was it the tight vests? The close crew cuts? The arms blackened with tattoos?

Then he wasn't wondering anymore, because Bikini Girl's back arched silently in his view, partly blocked by her heaving boyfriend's jean-clad ass as he started screwing her right there. In broad daylight.

Mike's hand moved down of its own free will, past the

elastic border of his colorful Hawaiian swimming trunks. His crotch was tenting at an alarming but satisfactory rate. As he took himself in hand he heard Chris swallow hard and say: "Now all we need is some good old-fashioned Cock Rock to round this picture off."

The thought that someone might be looking at us passed through my mind vaguely as my one hand pinned Jo's hips down, the other got lost somewhere in her tangled hair. To tell the honest-to-god truth, at this point I really didn't care. I was having a marvelous time watching the reaction on Jo's face as I continued to fuck her adorable behind into the hot sand. I bent down and took each of her nipples between my teeth, the taste of coconut on my tongue perversely edging me on. In between the rush of blood and noise in my brain I heard Jo's now not-so-innocent remarks, ranging from the question-ing *You like that, don't you?* to the not-so-sublime *Daddy's dyke cock hurts so good....*

I leaned back and told her to roll over onto her stomach. The sand stuck to her cheeks like two little bull's-eyes. With practiced ease I took hold of her hips with both hands and slipped into her.

"Let Daddy show you how hard he really can hurt, baby...."

I started laying into her, fingertips poised on the tight-ly stretched skin between her thighs, slamming into her at a rate that made her gasp for air and eliciting short "ah... ah..." sounds. One of her hands flailed at me viciously, but I grabbed it and held it behind her back.

"Quiet sweetheart," I sneered in her neck, "before the neighbors hear you and I have to stop."

Chris lay on his back, staring into the sky, cold beer can against his face to cool his raging hormones, inspired by the free show he and Mike had been fortunate enough to observe. Jacking off with a buddy under the summer sun—what could be more perfect? They'd been taking turns watching, both manipulating their hard-ons inside their trunks, till the distant approach of a beach patrol put an end to their surveillance.

"You know," Mike said smilingly as he popped open another beer. "Only one thing could have possibly made that an even better experience to witness. Imagine that had been two chicks digging into one another."

Chris nodded in agreement. "Now that would be worth getting arrested for."

"I'm going to have to start taking you to the beach much more often," Jo mused, smiling as she navigated traffic.

"Oh, believe me," I observed as I adjusted my crotch, "it's got nothing to do with the beach. Absolutely nothing."

RIDING THE WAVES

Rose William

I wasn't sure that I would like it. In fact, the
thought of it made me nauseous. I couldn't
imagine allowing a man to touch her, his
cock growing hard and pressing against her.
I couldn't stomach the thought of *watching*.
Watching her kissing him, touching his chest,
stroking his dick. And worst of all, she wanted
him to fuck her, something I would give anything to do, if only I really could. But I loved
her, and was willing to try it. For her.

So I let her choose the guy. I told her that I
didn't care who it was or what he looked like,
didn't care what she told him. I went along
with what she wanted, gave her free rein, and
removed myself from the planning.

Two months went by, and Elly didn't mention it again. I thought that she had changed

her mind. Perhaps she had realized that I only agreed to it for her. Our lives went on as usual. She taught and worked on her thesis; I worked at the hospital. We rented movies and had big weekend breakfasts and cleaned the house and went for walks and had sex. We settled into our lives as if she had never brought it up.

Then one day, on the way home from work, I stopped at the store and bought her mangos and frozen pizza. When I arrived home, there was a man sitting on the couch, drinking a Coke. I knew instantly why he was there.

"Hi," I said cautiously, appraising him. I could tell he was tallish: several inches taller than me, and markedly taller than Elly. He had on jeans, worn thin but not holey. His hair was messy and sandy blond, and he wore a surf T-shirt. He wasn't anything like the guy I would have expected her to pick, and I wondered where she had even found him.

"Hey." He smiled, annoyingly relaxed about the whole thing. He was casually settled into the red cushions, legs slightly apart, one hand at his side, the other holding the Coke and resting on his knee.

It was then, as I stood in the living room staring at a strange man, that she came into the room and we both looked at her. I wanted to cover his eyes—she was too beautiful for me to share, too beautiful to give to him. Elly is always beautiful, but sometimes she sparkles. She wore a clingy red tank top without a bra, and I could see her nipples sticking out slightly. Usually she thought her nipples were a nuisance. They were almost always slightly hard, and she bought padded bras to conceal them. But she also knew that their presence made her instantly sexual: she was inviting me—us—to look at them. Below the tank top she wore a white skirt with embroidered flowers, and a layer of tulle peaking out. Her feet were bare, her toenails polished the same red as the flowers on the skirt.

But her sparkle didn't come from her clothes. It came from her attitude. She was at home in her skin. She wore no make-up but lip gloss and she probably hadn't brushed her wavy hair after that morning's shower. But she knew that she would be able to drive anyone wild. Especially me. I wanted so badly to touch her then, to feel her skin, to hold her close and wrap my arms all the way around her small frame. I wanted to lead her to our bed and pull her tank top over her head, to run my hands over her and take her nipples into my mouth. I wanted to hear her breath in my ear, and feel her respond to me. Instead, I just looked at her. She came to where I was standing, grocery bag still hanging from my hand. She looked into my eyes, and then flicked her gaze across my face, as if she were making a final assessment.

"Hi," she said, and kissed my lips lightly. It was a casual kiss, the kind she'd give me if she were running to the post office. She took the plastic grocery bag from my hand and set it on the floor. She took my jacket and laid that on the floor as well.

And then she turned from me and walked to the couch. She took the boy's Coke and set it on the coffee table. She took his hand and led him to the bedroom, turning once to look at me. She wanted me to follow. At first I couldn't do it. I could only watch them disappear into our room. Our place. When I had forced my feet to move, and arrived in the doorway of our room, they were standing near the bed. She looked up at him and pulled his face toward hers.

And she kissed him. Ran her fingers through his messy hair and held on to the back of his head. My Elly kissed a stranger

in our bedroom as my chin trembled. I blinked slowly, stoic-
ally, willing the tears not to come.

He wrapped his arms around her, running his hands over
her shoulders and down her back, grazing her ass, pulling
her hips toward him. Her hands went under his shirt and
she touched his chest. When he took his shirt off, I saw how
smooth and well-developed he was. I imagined the hours in
the surf had left him chiseled and lean. She touched her lips to
his chest as he stroked the waves of her hair. She waved me to
the chair and quickly glanced at me while she kissed her way
down his chest and abs, and pushed him into a sitting position
at the edge of the bed. I mutely moved to the chair, which had
been moved slightly. I realized that it was in the perfect position for me to watch her blow him.

He was already hard, and when she unbuttoned his jeans,
I saw that he was wearing nothing beneath them. They had
planned this. Elly had ambushed me, not even warned me that
today would be the day. My face felt hot.

Elly pulled her shirt off and I watched her full breasts sway
as she leaned into his lap. She started with slow licks, from his
balls up to his head, the way she had so many times with me.
But he could *feel* her—his cock wasn't made of silicone. He
could feel every lick, every flick of her tongue. As I watched,
I thought of all the times she had laid me back and teased my
thighs and belly with her tongue before finally sucking me.
How I could almost, but not quite, feel her. How just watching her and pushing her head down, I could *almost* come in
her face.

She finally stopped teasing him and took his cock into her
mouth. He moaned, and I shifted slightly in the chair, realizing for the first time that I was wet. I looked at his swollen

cock, watched her perfect mouth as she bobbed up and down on it. And watching his face, the way his hips moved and his hand in her hair, I could feel her too. My pussy throbbed as she sucked him.

And when I knew that she could feel his cock throbbing, when she knew that it wouldn't be much longer before he came, she stopped and got to her feet. He groaned, turning up his head, looking at her. She slipped out of her skirt and when she picked up her foot to step out of it, I could see how wet she was. So could he. She tugged on his arm, pulling him to his feet.

"Take off your pants," she told him, and while he obliged, she crawled onto the bed. She positioned herself on her hands and knees and my pussy flooded onto my scrubs. She was facing me, her brown eyes looking intently at me as he got on the bed behind her. And I knew. It had all been for me. Because she knew me better than I did. I had been right: the surfer wasn't really her type. He was *mine*—the kind of guy I'd fuck, the kind of guy I would want to *be*. She had known how wet I'd get, how I'd be able to feel what he was feeling, how watching him fuck her in my favorite position would put together the last puzzle pieces of my fantasies.

He pressed his head up against her wetness and gasped. I knew the feeling. I knew how wet she got, how she made my fingers slick, how she dripped down my wrist. As he slid into her, I thrust my hand into my pants and rubbed my clit. I moaned, that feeling welling up in me too soon. I wanted to come with him. I wanted to come inside her. I pulled my fingers away and squirmed in the chair. I realized that I was mimicking his rhythm, grinding in my seat. She reached for her clit, and I felt my eyes get hot and wet. She made quick circles while he held on to her hips and thrust into her.

I could tell she was close from the way her jaw slackened and her breathing changed. I started touching myself again, hoping he would come when I wanted him to. Her eyes didn't leave me until she started to come. As she squeezed them shut, I knew that her pussy was clenching around his cock. He cried out and held on to her, and as Elly rode out the last waves of her orgasm, he exploded inside her and I let myself go. I could feel it, feel myself coming. Not by myself on a chair, but in her. My cock jerked and throbbed as I filled her up with my cum. It was what I had wanted since the first time I laid eyes on her. I felt tears on my cheeks.

Like the perfect guest, he didn't overstay his welcome. Elly pulled a nightie out from under a pillow and slipped it on as he got dressed. She gave him a quick hug and kiss on the cheek, and he let himself out, waving at me with a sheepish grin.

Elly came and sat on my lap, pulling my head to her chest and kissing my hair. My damp eyes left wet spots on her nightie as I pulled away and looked up at her.

"It was just what I wanted."

PUPPY SLUT

Michelle Brennan

It was my first time cruising in a men's room, first time pissing in one too. The odor caught me off guard, strong and musky, heat-producing sweat, or maybe that was just my own adrenaline causing this surge. I sauntered up to the urinal, unzipped, and pulled out my cock. I'd played this moment over in my head a hundred times in the past hour, beer warming up in front of me at the bar. I knew if I didn't do this whole thing right, I'd piss all over myself and have to pass it off as some kind of golden shower fantasy to cover my ass. I had an extra pair of black Carhartts in the car, just in case I needed them.

He was tall and clean cut, with porcelain skin and sculpted dark sideburns, and his steel-toed boots looked as if they'd been freshly licked clean by some lucky boy. Damn, did I want to be down by his boots right then. I didn't care that he'd yet to notice me or, if he had, was waiting for me to come to him. Maybe he knew I'd be waiting for him in the bathroom, whacking off, and that's why he sauntered in after me not a minute after I disappeared from my stool.

I glanced over at him, making sure he caught me looking, wide eyed and holding my shit right out in the open, wanting to kiss his boots and swallow his cock whole.

"Evening, Sir," I muttered, caught off guard by his hungry stare, his eyes telling me, not asking, that my ass was his that night. I tried not to lose my confidence when he approached, and suddenly I realized where I was and what I had just gotten myself into: a men's bathroom, being picked up by this leather daddy, holding onto a hard cock attached to a sparkly blue harness. Mama always said stranger danger, but I was never one to take the advice of an elder, unless he was clad in chaps and smothering my face in his crotch. Which is exactly where I ended up. On my knees in a dank bathroom where musky sweat, cum, and leather overloaded my senses, and the adrenaline pumped through my veins as if hot lava had just flooded through my body. I could have suffocated and gone to heaven just then.

I grabbed at him with my paws, groping and working at his zipper. His hands, big workingman's hands that smelled of trucks and gas, grabbed my neck; petting my hair like a potential owner sizing up a new puppy. He gathered the back of my shirt into his fist and yanked me away.

"Where are your manners? You need a training leash, boy. Get the fuck up." One quick slap across my left cheek told me to keep my mouth shut. I scrambled quickly to my feet, a bit wobbly and disoriented, the hunger in my cunt consuming me, threatening to lash out impulsively.

One man, who'd apparently been watching the encounter, laughed out, "Got yourself a rabid one there, huh, daddy-o?" Then this guy was suddenly being taken care of by two other men who'd been lurking in the shadows while this encounter was unraveling.

"Fucking tourist bullshit faggots," Daddy muttered as he dragged me out of the bathroom, his grip now tightening around my neck. "You think you can just give me those puppy eyes, paw at me a little, act completely disgusting back there, and expect that I'm just going to fuck a piece of trash like you?" he grunted into my ear as he pushed me past the other bar stools, and out into the late night air. It was cold on my face and the mark his hand had left on my cheek stung. The parking lot was quiet and scattered with bikes, trucks, and a few cars. He led me to his truck, reached in and grabbed a choke collar from the dashboard and slipped it over my head, then pulled his hanky out of his back pocket to tie over my eyes.

"Get in," he commanded as he pushed me onto the truck bed. I remembered then that in my flurry of hunger I had completely forgotten to piss. I didn't know how this daddy would feel when he felt my wet cunt crying out for him to fuck me, fill me, break me.

But that thought was only entertained for a second before I was on my knees in the truck bed. There was a blanket laid out below. It was soft and smelled of big dogs and sex and woods. His grip was now on my pants as he slipped my belt off and pulled my jeans down to just above my knees. His hand moved up along my back, pushing down in spots, as if testing my strength to see where I might break if hit too hard. Suddenly, I felt the worn leather of my belt come down swiftly over my ass, causing me to squeal in a mixture of fear, ecstasy, and pain.

"Pay attention puppy slut," he said as he imprinted all five fingers on my asscheek over the spot where he'd inflicted the first blow. I whimpered a bit and tried to keep my composure. His force was even stronger than I'd anticipated.

"I like my boys red and shiny, and you need to be quiet or else we can't do this here and I'll just have to leave your horny red ass out in the cold," he growled.

My body froze. He told me to shine and I was going to gleam. He shoved a gag into my mouth, but what I really wanted was to take his bulging dick out of his tight pants and let him fuck my mouth hard with it. There was no time for requests; I felt a small, solid object pressed into my hand.

"Puppy slut, if you can't handle Daddy you just throw this; otherwise, I better not catch your slimy paws letting go of any present I give to you."

It got quiet then, except for the sound of crickets and frogs. He had planned ahead by parking his truck in the far end of the lot, below a lamp with a burnt-out bulb. I listened hard, trying to follow his movements and feeling disorientation creeping up my nerves. Fear raced through my veins.

He's just getting me riled up, I reminded myself. I needed the fuck, ached from the thirst of wanting him to rip me open. I was worried he was planning on leaving me there for the vultures; maybe he didn't like faggot riot grrls like me hiding out in boys' bars; but then he was up behind me again and this time a heavier belt with metal loops along it came down on my ass, one blow after another cutting the air quicker each time. The gag in my mouth grew moist with my squeals as my ass felt warmer and redder, the night air adding sting to each moment I wasn't in contact with the belt. I could not help but thrust my ass toward his belt, and ultimately, his cock. I wanted to hear his zipper slide down, wanted to hear him stroking himself, wanted it all so badly. I was trying hard not to be a greedy bottom.

And then, just as quickly as the blows started, they stopped. He took hold of the collar he'd placed on me and yanked me up onto my knees. Whatever I had been wanting slipped from my memory as his fingers coiled around my neck, then moved slowly down onto my shoulders, pushing me down further, then removing the gag.

"Puppy slut, are you hungry yet? I bet you'd like Daddy to feed you, you drooling little faggot."

I still couldn't see, but I knew he had a boner about an inch away from my mouth.

"Uh-huh," was all I could whimper, trying hard not to break.

"It would be nice if we could get everything we wanted. I know I'm getting what I want tonight. Who would have thought I'd sniff out the one cunt-wielding gem hidden in that bar. My beast's sense of smell does me well most nights," he barked, and pushed my head down on the blanket, roughly pulling my ass up in the air. The lube was cold and came out of nowhere; suddenly his fingers were carving through my cunt, exploring my innards with ease and precision. I was right there, ready to explode as more of this hand shoved its way into me, fucking all the way in, while with his other hand he strapped a condom over his cock and dribbled more lube onto my ass.

I was rocking with Daddy's hand, trying to remember to keep quiet. My cunt muscles tightened, locking his hand in. I was more than ready to shoot my load all over him when he pulled out and smacked my ass, my cum making each blow that hit the red welts from his belt sting. He lifted my ass up higher, his cock tracing the smooth crack of my rear. I bucked and whimpered, needing it so bad. The tease was too much now; keeping silent was impossible.

"Please, Daddy," I whimpered. "Please fuck me! I'll be your good puppy slut and take it all. I'm so hungry, Daddy. I can't take it anymore. Please, please fuck me!"

He yanked me up and slapped my face hard to shut me up before I could finish my pleading. I was right where he wanted me, nothing more than a whimpering pathetic dribbling puddle of a pup slut; dying for his meat in me, fucking the piss right out of me. My body shook and wailed as he slid his cock into my ass. It was hot and solid and I yelped again as he slammed deeper into me.

He coiled his hands around my hips, holding me in place and helpless beneath his body towering above me. He rode my ass like a cowboy, like he'd done my shit a hundred times before and was coming back for more. As each thrust dug deeper into me, the pressure from his cock made the familiar warmth of piss spray all over my thighs and pool in small puddles by my knees. He grunted and fucked harder. Just as I felt his boner throbbing and hoped for him to come in my ass, he reached down, stroked my cock, slid his hand back behind the balls and rested it on my clit and began jerking me off— and I came instantly into his hand several times, body bucking with spasms and pushing even harder against his cock. Daddy receded from my ass and let go of my hips as I fell back onto my rubbery legs. I could hear him removing the condom, and I wanted to see his dick, throbbing and wet. "Let me—" His hand was behind my head as he spun me around roughly and slapped my face.

"I thought I told you to be silent, puppy slut. You can't listen to Daddy? Well, then I'll just have to shut you up." He tore the blindfold off and got a good grip on my choke, keeping it tight while he guided my mouth to his dick. I took it eagerly, desperately, a starved puppy finally getting a bone to gnaw on. I swallowed his cock like a good fag as he twitched and yanked out and came on my face, slapping cum against my cheeks with his cock. Sweat and quick breaths came as he let me collapse by his feet, curled up and licking his boots.

"Thank you, Daddy," I whispered, content with my first night of cruising.

PLANET 10

Catherine Lundoff

I had a thing for Altarans ever since I saw my
first one. Unfortunately for me, they didn't
leave their home world of Hana-altair much.
But every now and then one of them went off-
world to sow some wild oats, then went back
"to serve her people" as the Xenasciens put it.
Oh, didn't I mention that part? Yep, they're all
females. My kind of alien, if you get my drift.

Good thing for me that humanoids and
Altarans got some crucial things in common.
Couple of Xenasciens even say that we're all
from the same original species. It'd kinda
suck to have a thing for critters that could
only live in methane or were all slimy. Good
thing for any Altaran I managed to get lucky
with too, I hoped. Especially if she liked them
short and furry.

My extra fingers and toes and the layer of body fur are a souvenir of growing up on Knossos. That's my home world, a nifty place that started out as an old Earth penal colony. And just like our ancestors, Knossans like to ship their troubles into space. It's a mean place to grow old, all ice and Canoboshi bearcats. The bearcats are named after the scientist who discovered them. Just before they ate her.

I got shipped out a few turns back when it became obvious that breeding for the state or joining the merc forces wasn't in my future. Just as well. I'm more of a lover than a fighter anyway, and the wrong kind of lover for Knossos Prime for sure.

But back to my thing for Altarans. I saw my first one a Standard year or two back when I was wandering around Qiang Shx Spaceport on Deben acting like your average hick. It wasn't hard to do since Qiang Shx is bigger than any city on Knossos. The place is set up in overlapping circles with a big market in the center, all sealed under a big dome to keep out the poisonous Deben atmosphere. Or to keep the miners on the planet, depending on who you talk to. Point is, it's a helluva big port.

There was every kind of being and machine you could think of including things I'd never heard of, let alone seen before. I was pretty much breaking every rule in the *Guide for Interplanetary Etiquette*. My crew buddies, Shango and Irxq, had to keep hold of my belt to keep me from wandering off.

So I was gaping even before I saw her. She was a little taller than me with huge gold eyes, no pupils. The gills around her long jaws were fluttering, all shiny under the spaceport lights. I didn't know it then, but it meant she was laughing.

She had her tail tucked up into her elbow, and she was talking to some Deltans who were trying to sell her something. There was something so dainty, but really strong about her, you know? I gaped even more, especially while I looked from the curves of her breasts down to her powerful legs with their clawed feet.

I elbowed Shango and pointed, "What's she?"

What I was thinking must have showed in my voice 'cause he rolled his eyes and sighed. "Oh, honey! You do not need to become a lizard chaser. The chances of her saying yes are a million to one. Plus you'd have to find one that was a total anomaly to do the kinds of stuff you were talking about last night." He and Irxq chortled, or snorted in Irxq's case, not having a voice box to speak of. I had been a little too forthcoming in my cups the night before, apparently.

I drew myself up and fell back on my sore pride. "I was asking from a Xenascien perspective." Shango grinned at me till I grinned back. He's a Deneban humanoid who only likes male humanoids from New Afric and Jazzville, and only the ones with the old Earth Brit accents to boot. To each his fetish, I guess. Pal that he is, he told me what he knew about Altarans, which wasn't much. Afterward, I went and trailed after her all over the spaceport like a lovesick pup till she got back on her ship and it took off.

From then on, I was hooked. I couldn't tell you exactly what it was, but I just had to be with an Altaran. There was something so incredibly alien about them, but really beautiful too. Plus I'm always fascinated by what I think I can't have, especially if it's female. Bad habit. I looked up everything I could find on them in the holofiles, the *Encyclopedia Intergalactica*, you name it. That's how I know about their home world.

I also found out that Shango was right. The chance of me finding one who'd even think about getting sexual with me was pretty damn slim. They generally stuck with their own kind and exceptions were rare. I had a hell of a time even gleaning that much, and I spent many a sleepless night wondering just how I'd *mate* (their word) with a lizard anyway.

I decided to keep hope alive by staying in practice. With that in mind, I did things I hadn't even dreamed of back on Knossos. I dreamed a hell of lot, so that's saying something. None of it got me any closer to an Altaran but it was fun. I never lost my thing for them though: all that time, all those females, and I still wanted one of *them*.

So the long and short of it was that I ended up back on Qiang Shx again since that was part of our long run through a couple of solar systems. The bar I chose catered to those with preferences like mine, female to female contact, lots of different species. That meant that it had to be big enough for sealed spaces with different air and climate control for the clientele. Pretty damn pricey too, but I had just gotten paid so my credit was good.

Shango had told me about the place, with lots of motherly warnings about not wanting what I couldn't have. He dropped me off then went to hang out with his latest conquest. I found myself an empty booth and settled in to look around. There was plenty to look at. Lots of females from different planets, all colors, shapes, and sizes. I was checking out a cute Deneban with long braids twisted together with shells and bits of metal, when *she* walked in.

I could have sworn it was the same Altaran I had seen on my last trip through here. She had the same look but a little tougher, if you could say that about her species. Since she was alone, I figured I was in luck, especially since by now I'd read everything I could find about their mating rituals. I got up and approached slowly while she was still looking around.

I bowed low. "Does this one require a companion?" The big gold eyes turned on me and she cocked her head to one side. I had to try not to whine. She continued to look at me and I looked down, so as not to seem too eager. It was like wanting a vidstar: they looked hot, but maybe they were duller than servodrones when you got too close. I stood there hoping that my wondering was about to come to a screeching halt, but ready for the worst.

"Perhaps. What does that one have to offer?" I could see her gills flutter in the lights, ever so slightly.

"Whatever that one requires," I responded, praying to my patron goddess Yonasha that the Xenascien tape was right about how they did it. If not, I'd blown it.

She wandered around me, looking me over. I could hear her claws ticking on the tile floor and I started to shake with nerves. She walked around to face me, then gestured at me with one long, thin claw. Heart ready to jump out of my mouth or out of my leggings, I wasn't sure which, I followed her.

Her shirt plunged in the back, giving me a nice view of rainbow-hued skin. Just below the shirt, her long, slender, incredibly supple-looking tail came down to a delicate point. My imagination ran wild thinking about what it would be like to be with her, hoping till it hurt that she was my "anomaly." No surprise that I damn near stepped on her tail when she stopped at one of the booths.

Stumbling around her, I slid suavely into the seat across from her and wondered what to say to get off on the right foot, so to speak. I needn't have bothered. She took a long look at me with those big golden eyes. I'm not bad looking by Knossan standards, but if you don't like them short, plump, and fuzzy, that's not saying much.

Her gills fluttered slightly. "What does that one want?" I could see the slits of her nostrils flaring just a little. Could she smell me? Knossans are known for the smells that we give off when we're interested in being more than casual pals, kinda like freshly turned soil on one of the Proxima farm worlds. How the hell would she interpret it? I didn't know what, if anything, it would mean to her.

Nerves and want increased my scent till it surrounded me like a cloud. Through it all, I mumbled, "You."

She ordered a drink, something I'd never heard of before. Maybe this Altaran was different. Then, "Will that one do anything that this one desires? Anything at all?" I looked into those golden eyes and whispered my yes. Much as I wanted to find out what she could possibly want, I was scared shitless to find out for certain. But I said yes anyway. Points for my side.

"Unfasten that one's upper garment." Here? My eyes darted around the crowded bar. Sure, it was dark, but not that dark. Very slowly, I unfastened the top of my uniform. "Keep going," she commanded from the other side of the table, seeming farther away every minute. I did.

"Open it all the way. Let this one see that one." I spread the edges of my uniform open, exposing my breasts. They're not quite the erogenous zone that Earth women have, but they do the trick. I sat there feeling multiple eyes on our booth, until the manager hissed in mild annoyance as she passed and pressed the button that lowered the semiprivate shield. It blocked the view a little, but we would have had to cloud it to completely seal it off. She didn't move toward the mist button and neither did I.

"Let this one see what that one does for self-pleasuring." Dammit, I wanted to touch her not me! My frustration must have showed on my face because she stuck her delicate forked tongue out and licked her drink slowly and sensuously while she looked at me. That made me decide to put on a hell of a show. I'd make her want closer contact with me if it was the last thing I did.

I ran my six-fingered hands over my nipples, then pinched them, rolling each of them in turn until my breathing sounded heavy even to me. I glanced away from her at the bar's other patrons, still visible through the shield. Several watched, eyes moving eagerly over my body. I cupped my breasts and held them out toward her and the other watchers. My scent filled the sealed cube and she began to look vaguely interested. I could get used to this.

Still rolling one of my nipples between my fingers, I slid one hand down to my pants. "Remove them." I shuddered. I didn't like being this vulnerable in public, especially not to someone I didn't know shit about. But all those watching eyes made me hot and scared, all mixed together, and after choking off the voice inside that asked if I'd lost all memorysense, I dropped my uniform and stood, my cute and fuzzy body exposed to the world.

"Sit," she ordered. I did. I just loved taking orders. "Spread that one's lower limbs." I stretched my legs out to their widest, almost keeling over from my own smell. "Continue." I slid my fingers, one at a time, into myself. I was nice and slick, what with checking out a whole new side of myself.

Not to mention letting the rest of the bar do the same.

I slipped two, three, then five fingers inside and started moving them in and out. The walls of my 'gina got slicker and started clenching around my fingers. I watched her under my half-closed lids while she sat there and watched me. Those gills were sure moving. Over her shoulder, I caught the eyes of the Deneban female I'd been checking out earlier and held them. She watched like I was an after-dinner sweet and she just couldn't get enough.

It's hard to get a good angle when you're trying to stick your own fist inside yourself, but I was giving it my best shot. The Altaran just kept watching. Damned if I could tell if I was having any effect on her, but I was having fun at least. I got wetter and wetter, making space inside me for all of my six fingers. All that attention was like shooting starshine and I was flying higher than the dome on the port. I looked into those golden eyes and pumped harder. I couldn't tell how many fingers I had inside me any more. Hell, maybe I was growing more.

I 'gasmed hard, the best ever. Maybe it was the thrill, but it felt like something that wasn't my hand pulled out, too. Did she fuck me? How? Thinking about her tail made me shake, made me want more. I came back down, still looking into her eyes. What was she going to do now?

It surprised me as much as it did our watching audience. She popped her credit piece into the slot, clouded the windows and tossed me my uniform. "That one has entertained this one ably. This one does not wish to be unappreciative." With that, she slapped some credit pieces on the table, unsealed the door and walked out. Just like that. Leaving me sitting in a sealed cube in a she bar clutching my uniform like it was the only familiar thing in the world. Shit.

There was a slight rap on the security shield while I was still sitting there like part of the bench. I buzzed the lock. Maybe it was her, coming back. I could always hope. The tall Deneban I'd been watching earlier slipped inside, resetting the mist shield behind her. "I thought you could use some company."

I thought about my beautiful lizard walking out of the bar and out of my life and I looked at this tall, sturdy female, curves spilling out of her uniform. I looked at the pile of credits the Altaran had left. Grabbing my uniform, I pulled it on. I leaned over to the Deneban and kissed her, long and slow, on her full lips.

"Thank you. You're beautiful and any other night I'd love to be with you, but I gotta go after her. It's just this thing I have to do. Have a night on me." I pushed the credits toward her and jumped out of the cube while the walls were still coming down.

I couldn't see her in the bar so I headed for the door. A big Ctepar stepped in my way like a living boulder. "Hey pretty pretty..." I shoved past with an effort. Tonight was not the night I would have picked to be popular with this crowd. I was running now, out the door and into the alley that passed for an Old Port street. It was the only spaceport I'd seen big enough for its own slums. What a place. She wasn't in sight so I headed for a fancy boy waiting at the street's end.

Flipping him a credit, I demanded, "Altaran. Which way did she go?"

"You too, honey? You're the second one tonight, including the Sekurcops. Last I saw she was headed that way." He pointed down into a maze of alleys. I kept running. I didn't want to think about the Sekurcops, Qiang Shx's police force/army. Must be big-time stuff if they were chasing her. But I was going to get there first. I had to.

I shot down a couple more alleys. No sign of her. I collapsed against a wall. Planetary gravs always wipe me out. Of course, that was when she rounded the corner. It was fate, I just knew it. She stopped and looked at me, tail twitching from side to side, skin flaring bright with more colors than I'd seen her show before.

What little sense I had kicked in and I dropped into a defensive pose. It's something that we learn as cubs in the crèches back on Knossos till it becomes like breathing. I didn't want to be on the receiving end of those back claws in a less than affectionate mood.

"This one paid for that one's services. What more does that one want?"

Where to begin? "I didn't want payment. I wanted to be with you," I said, with all the words tumbling out on top of each other. Then I scared myself by starting to cry. I hadn't cried since they beat it out of me in basic training. Shit. So much for handling disappointment like a big fuzzy.

She studied me for a long minute. "This one did not mean to cause distress, but wonders why that one is reacting with such emotion. Has this one violated etiquette?"

I ran my hand over my eyes. "No, not exactly. It's just that I've dreamed of having a lover from your people." I paused, realizing that I sounded like she was interchangeable with a million other Altarans. For that matter, as far as my fantasy went, she was. Oops. Maybe not the best impression I could be making if I wanted this conversation to go anywhere.

"Why choose this one?" she asked, putting her proverbial claw on the very thing that I hoped would slip by. Shit. Well, at least I had stopped crying.

"You picked me, remember?" I mumbled, pulling the shreds of my pride together. Her gills fluttered in amusement. "Come with me to my room tonight," I pleaded.

"There is only one way that these two can be together as that one desires. It will require a great transition."

Her voice rang like a bell against the stone. I shivered, but I asked anyway. "Why?"

"This one feels the pleasure that comes with power, but only seeks to mate with others of the clan or those undergoing the transition."

"And what if I was willing to undergo the transition?'

"It is permanent. That one would be as this one is."

Definitely an unlooked-for obstacle to my fantasy. "This one has stayed too long and must go. The Sekurcops seek this one because of the very thing that one seeks. It is forbidden to transform Guild operatives, but the change is this one's service to the clan. Unless those willing to be changed come to Hana-altair, the clan cannot grow." It sounded almost like a ritual formula. My uncertainty about that kind of choice must've showed in my face because she didn't press the point.

"This one cannot risk being caught." She started to move away. Without thinking, I reached out and grabbed her front claw, "I know a faster way." I pulled her down the maze of alleyways and backstreets that made up the Old Port. She moved faster than me, but slowed down to keep pace with me anyway. I started to hope again. If she stayed with me, maybe I still had a chance. Maybe she didn't mean what she'd just said.

I took her down some back ways that Shango had told me about, and we hid behind recyc containers and whatever else we could find when anyone passed. I had some crazy idea about smuggling her out as freight on the ship I worked on, and I whispered it to her 'cause I thought it sounded good. She just looked at me with those big golden eyes and said, "This one is grateful, but has made other plans."

Damn. My bad luck again, I figured. But since we were there and she was right nearby anyway, I couldn't resist running a hand down her arm scales. I just had to find out what that skin felt like. It was kind of like handling wires in the freighter drive compartment, all dry and crackling feeling somehow, almost like you weren't really touching it. The tingling in my fingers made me pull away, but not before that little gesture of mine was interpreted as an invitation.

Suddenly, she pulled me down a more secluded alley, not that any of them were well populated this time of night. One claw pressed me faceup against the clay brick wall. "Decide. Does that one desire the transition?" she hissed in my ear.

"Why now?" I mumbled into the brick of the wall I was facing.

"Because it is this one's duty to the clan. This one will not fail her duty. There should be time to start that one's transition before this one must go."

Great. I loved the idea of being a work-related hazard. Then I started to think. I braced my hands against the wall and thought about my friends, my job, my life. What did I have to lose? Old freight hands didn't have much of a future. I would get enough age pay to settle planetside somewhere cheap and that was it. Being turned into a lizard started to look like one big adventure. Hell, it even started to look like more than sex. Shango would understand that, I thought hopefully. The word was out of my mouth before I could think any more about it. "Yes."

"The transition requires mating, much as that one desires. It will be painful." I nodded, starting to feel all warm and wet like I had in the bar. It sounded like my kind of event. "Then that one must go to Hana-altair and meet with the elders. Tell the elders what has happened here. They will initiate that one." I nodded again, closing my eyes for a long moment to say good-bye to what I knew.

With a single swipe of her claws, she ripped the uniform off my back. The cool air hit me at the same moment that her tail did. I howled and scraped my face on the wall. Quickly, I shuffled my feet back into place. I'd be ready on the next one, I thought. I wasn't. Ten swipes later and I was on all fours in front of her. Another slash of those claws and most of my leggings bit the dust. I groaned.

This was all I'd thought about for hours. Hell, years. I wanted to feel those claws on me, feel the thick electric thrust of that tail, give up everything to someone so alien I could barely understand the way she thought. I threw back my head and howled, not giving a damn about the Sekurcops.

One of those long hands with their sharp claws slapped over my mouth, closing it against my groans. The pain was making me float, high as a satellite and damn near ready to pass out. I hadn't had this much fun since basic training.

She ran one claw down my back and over my ass. I could feel a thin line of blood follow it. Then I felt the end of her tail between my legs and I spread as wide as I could. She shoved it inside me, so hard I could feel it bend. Then she clawed another stripe from my shoulders down to my ass. This time I was whimpering and begging. I wanted more of her, wanted to feel that tail and tongue inside me driving faster and faster.

I could feel her run her tongue down my back, over the

stripes of blood that she had drawn, lapping my blood from my short matted fur. Then she started licking her way down between my legs so I could feel the forks of her tongue stroking from one end of my slit to the other.

Her tail was sliding in and out of my wet 'gina at the same time.

This time, we didn't have an audience, but it wasn't changing my reaction. Another cut followed her claw down my back. Her forked tongue darted in and out of me, working around her tail. It hurt like hell, but having wanted it for so long kept me going now. I could feel the scales of her tail rubbing along my 'gina walls. It was like being laid open. I was having a hell of a time deciding whether to pass out or come.

"May I have permission to come?" I whispered. For an answer, she whipped her tail out of my 'gina and slid it as far as it would go into my ass. I 'gasmed hard and sudden, shuddering all over. I'd given up any willpower that I'd had long before this. She could do damn near anything to me and I'd come.

I collapsed onto the dried clay pavement, just barely saving my face with my hands. My back end was still up in the air receiving her tender ministrations. Her tail slid in and out a few more times, then got yanked out and smacked across my ass. That got a reaction. Again. Yow! Then she went back to fucking me with it. By then, I was growling as my scent filled the alleyway. My 'gina juices ran through the coarse hair on my legs and I could see my blood trickling down onto the clay. I smelled so strong it made my eyes water.

I shuddered all over as I came again, then I blacked out for a minute as I hit the pavement. When I came around, she was gone. Shit. Just when we were getting to know each other.

There was something on my back, along with the claw marks she'd put there. It hurt worse than anything else. I knew I'd have to get back to my quarters before I could find out what it was, so I staggered up, grabbing the wall for support, figuring to get home before I passed out. Thank Yonasha for combat training or I never would've been able to stand.

My fur burned where the blood was matted into it, pulling my skin every which way. At least she'd left me the robe that she was wearing to replace what she shredded. I pulled it on, cringing as it went over my back. I felt like something a bearcat dragged home.

It was still night, so I didn't get a look at myself until I had limped through the alleyways back to my planetside quarters. Shango woke up and wandered out of his quarters when I rolled in, so he got the first look. "By the sacred flames!" he whistled. "Oh honey, you did it, didn't you?" He hauled me into the bathing area and cleaned me up, then left me to soak while he got food like the pal he is. I hoped he would want to visit me on Hana-altair, after I broke the news.

I was still lying in the bath when I saw a light sheen of rainbow scales appear under the short fur on my arms. Hauling myself to my feet, grumbling and groaning the whole time, I looked at my back in the mirror. In the center was a bloody claw mark that looked branded into my skin. Scales shone under that, too. The news was going to break itself once he got a good look at me.

I stared at my hands, waiting for claws to sprout like little seedlings. They didn't, but they would soon. I could feel it. Soon I would be going home. Home. The tenth planet from the sun, Hana-altair. I rolled it around my mouth, liking the way it sounded. I wondered what it would be like having a tail.

PHOEBE'S UNDERCOVER
BON VOYAGE

Skian McGuire

It wasn't hard to take Phoebe down. I had my knee in the small of her back and was slapping the cuffs on before she knew what hit her. Of course, she wasn't really resisting yet. It wasn't any fun until the cuffs were on.

For a moment we just sat there—or lay there, in Phoebe's case, with her face pressed against the pavement—and I looked around. I don't know if any movies were ever actually shot at the Bijou's warehouse annex, but the rich man who built the theater spared no expense in creating this celluloid fantasyland next door. All under one high ceiling is the perfect little city scene, three row houses and an alley with plenty of room for the squad car my boss Verlaine got from a junkyard. The row houses were no mere false fronts, either.

It didn't take much to turn one of them into a station house, right down to an old-fashioned *POLICE* lamp outside.

The doors from the club were closed to the regular Sunday evening traffic. This was a private party, to give Phoebe a good send-off. I hoped she would have something to remember us by.

I managed to get the locks set while we caught our breath, Phoebe and I. Just. Then she went wild, trying to buck me off, swearing and kicking and grinding her head against the asphalt, trying to brace and get her feet under her while her hands were cuffed against her back. Phoebe was a fighter, all right. After she elbowed me in the gut and knocked the wind out of me, I was ready to call in backup. The other uniforms were standing by, grinning on the sidelines and more than ready to mix it up with our little blonde hellion. I called them over as soon as I could suck in air.

Anybody who didn't know Phoebe would see nothing but a sweet, helpless little thing, all pink and pretty. She'd be cute in camouflage, from the halo of pale gold curls and blue eyes down to some size four combat boots. Just five feet tall, she looks like something you could toss over your shoulder and carry away, while her tiny, perfectly manicured hands beat on your big strong back. You can almost imagine her squealing, "Oh, put me down, you brute," now, can't you?

Nope. No way.

In a short, tight little dress, with bright red lips à la Courtney Love, she can kick off her strappy high-heeled sandals and send two grown men to the hospital with only her bare hands and feet. I've seen it. If Phoebe didn't want to be subdued, I would be missing some teeth before ending up in the cuffs myself. It's a good thing Phoebe likes cops. I mean, she *really* likes cops. Hell, I guess that's why she *is* one.

Between the four of us, we got a grip on her and hoisted her up. She sure as hell wasn't going to walk.

We manhandled the jerking, heaving, spitting, biting one-woman riot up the station house steps, cursing, and struggling to hold on. There was one last thing to make sure of.

"You remember your safeword, don't you, baby?" I asked her, panting.

"Of course I remember my fuckin' safeword, you stupid shithead," she screamed at me, trying to twist around so she could sink her teeth into my arm. "If I want to use my fucking safeword, I'll use my fucking safeword, you motherfucking asshole. Arrgh!" At this, she kicked one leg free and booted the Sergeant right in the tit. I whistled through my teeth. Phoebe would pay for that later.

We hustled her straight past the desk into the holding pen, where Caine and Walters held her upright against the chain-link while the Sergeant and I messed with the cuffs. It took some doing, but eventually we got her strung up facing us, with a set of bracelets locking each wrist to the mesh, crucifix-style. She never stopped struggling, and she never stopped calling us every vile, filthy, ridiculous thing she could think of. Phoebe has a wonderful imagination.

Caine and Walters backed off her fast; her legs were thrashing out at them the minute they let her go. I surveyed the scene while we regrouped.

Nobody would have mistaken us for real cops, or if they had, they wouldn't have figured us all from the same department. The Sergeant favored a midnight blue uniform, with a cross strap over the shoulder to her basket weave Sam Browne belt. Caine was gaudier, with a broad navy stripe up the legs of her sky blue trousers, and navy blue epaulets and pocket flaps adorning her sky blue shirt. Did I mention sewn-in creases? Clarino duty belt and chukkas, too. The glare could blind you. Walters and I went for the traditional look, with navy blue trousers and light blue shirts; Walters spiffed hers up with a real NYPD shield. I've got my Bijou Security patches and the badge that Lainey got me. Not very salty, maybe, but I'm the one with the keys.

The Sergeant dusted off her hands. "All right, Officers," she said. "Let's get this prisoner strip-searched."

Phoebe blew a wet raspberry at us and brayed a loud, mean laugh.

"You fucking bunch of thumb-twiddling pig-assed twats think you're gonna lay a finger on me, you got another thing coming, you stupid blue-face cuntsuckers!" She kicked one foot out after the other and ended up hanging herself up on the cuffs.

"Grab her legs." The Sergeant shot a look at Caine and Walters, and they dove in before Phoebe had a chance to recover. I got some Flex-Cufs around her ankles. As Caine and Walters panted and wiped the sweat from their eyes, I doubled the plastic straps, just to make sure.

The prisoner rested against the bonds for a moment and delivered a few desultory epithets, conserving her strength. The Sergeant was unfolding her drop-point blade from its pearl handle. I pointed to the leg of Phoebe's jeans just above the Flex-Cuf.

"Poke a hole there for me, will you?" She knelt to oblige, then started working on the other jeans leg herself, sawing away slowly with that cold shank of steel. My handy-dandy EMT knife was nowhere near as sexy, but it made short work of the denim, all the way to Phoebe's crotch in one clean swipe.

Phoebe thrashed as best she could to keep me from unbuttoning her fly and yanking down the zipper, but it was no use. I cut through either side of Phoebe's cotton panties and yanked them off her. Then I straightened up and looked her in the eye.

The girl was still spewing insults as fast as she could think them up: full-auto, that is. I waited until she paused for breath, then I stuffed the wadded-up panties into her open mouth.

I'd have sworn that the look on Phoebe's face was nothing short of triumphant. Caine was on the job with a roll of adhesive tape before she could spit out the gag, and we got the thing secured. It was strapped on well enough to hold, but loose enough that she could breathe around it if she had to. She could still make plenty of noise, too. I didn't want to take away all of Phoebe's fun.

"Well, now," I said. I grabbed a handful of tit and squeezed, none too gently. "Got anything hidden in that bra? Besides a nice pair of hooters, I mean." The other officers started snickering and snorting. Phoebe's eyebrows shot up. "Let's find out."

My knife made short work of the T-shirt she was filling out; a shame, because it was a beauty, sporting a cartoon of a cop waving a long-barreled revolver and the legend *It's not how big it is... it's what you can do with it.* The Sergeant finished slashing off Phoebe's formerly skintight jeans and pulled them free of the Flex-Cufs just as I zipped through her bra straps. I had already released the front hook; I tossed the flimsy scraps and put my knife away.

After Caine thoughtfully removed the prisoner's child-sized Nikes, the little blonde stood gloriously naked, except, of course, for the bracelets and the wadded-up panties stuffed into her mouth, which hardly counted as clothing anymore. There was nothing childlike about her figure: full, round breasts; a small waist on womanly hips; and a thatch of pale hair that attested to the authenticity of the curly golden locks above. Phoebe was a beautiful woman, even wearing a gag. Perhaps especially wearing a gag. Without the threat of the Sergeant's well-honed edge against her tender flesh, the prisoner had resumed her struggles, issuing unintelligible but loud vocalizations I was glad not to understand. She'd have been spitting, if she'd had the chance.

I stared her down as I took her nipples between each thumb and forefinger, twisting and squeezing until tears came to her eyes. Still, she didn't drop her gaze. I grabbed a curl of blonde hair close to her temple. She winced, shut her eyes and whimpered.

I pretended to look closely. "I think the sleazy whore has lice!"

Phoebe's eyes snapped open, in spite of the pain, and she jerked her head away from my hand. Redoubling her efforts to pull a foot free of the Flex-Cufs, she almost succeeded before Walters dove into the fray and yanked on one more loop.

"Caine, you go get the shaving gear. We'll have to move her again, but let's check those body cavities for contraband first." I nodded to the Sergeant. "Would you like to do the honors, sir?"

She didn't need to be asked twice. With a self-satisfied smile, the Sergeant pulled a latex glove from the pouch on her belt and snapped it on. I passed the lube to her and she dropped to one knee between the prisoner's legs. Phoebe wasn't in the best position for a thorough search, but as she wouldn't bend over and spread her own cheeks, this would have to do.

The Sergeant's fingers disappeared between Phoebe's thighs, and I watched the prisoner's face while a diligent probe was made. Her chin tilted up and her eyes closed; her breasts rose and fell.

"Don't need any grease for this hole; the slut is dripping wet," the Sergeant said, working her fingers in and out. "She doesn't care how she gets fucked." Phoebe sagged against the handcuffs. For the first time since I stuffed the gag in her mouth, she was actually quiet. "I bet she'd like a nice hard nightstick up her snatch, right about now," the Sergeant purred.

Phoebe squinched her eyes shut even tighter, then her face went slack and her eyes opened slightly. Her skin glowed with a light sheen of sweat. Her lower body swayed a little, as if moved by a gentle breeze.

I glanced over at Walters, who was stroking the bulge in her pants. "Later," I told her. I was feeling a little sweaty myself. "Let's wrap this up."

The Sergeant pulled her hand back out from between Phoebe's thighs and squirted a generous dollop of lube on the end of her gloved forefinger. Then she hooked her other arm around the prisoner's hips. Phoebe bounced a little as the Sergeant's groping hand goosed her cheeks apart. She let out a muffled squeak as the Sergeant's finger plunged past her tight sphincter up to the last knuckle.

"Nothing in here," the Sergeant announced as her finger probed up, down, and all around. "Nothing but shit, anyway. I think this one needs a good enema to clean her out. Make sure she hasn't swallowed any dope balloons."

Phoebe had shut her eyes again, and her brows knit in a look of concentration. I was starting to wonder what was up when her expression changed to blissful serenity.

"Hey!" The Sergeant bellowed and jerked her arms back, nearly losing her balance. "Hey! The bitch is *pissing* on me!"

A dark stain spread from the cuff to the elbow of the Sergeant's midnight blue shirt, and she held her arm as far away from herself as she could. Drops fell from the fold that clung to her forearm and she tried to shake the liquid out. Caine and Walters stepped back in a hurry.

Phoebe was laughing into her gag as a puddle formed at her feet.

Avoiding it carefully, I stooped to push my face right up next to hers. She was still laughing. I grabbed her nose and pressed my hand over her gagged mouth. That took the smile out of her eyes pretty quick; when she started to look panicky, I let go.

"Don't begin to think you're gonna get away with that. You're going to lick that floor clean before we're done with you." I grinned my most evil grin. "But remember what they say: revenge is a dish best eaten cold."

Out of the corner of my eye I thought I saw a look of revulsion cross Walters's face. Phoebe just cocked an eyebrow at me, mumbling something through the gag that might have been, "Make me."

Stripped down to her white T-shirt, the Sergeant came back from the washroom, drying her hands with a wad of institutional brown paper towels. She tossed them in a corner and put her fists on her hips, glaring at the prisoner.

"Whore's gonna pay big-time," she growled.

"Sounds good." I motioned to Caine and Walters. "Take her down."

Actually, it took all four of us to uncuff the cute little thing and secure her again on a vinyl-covered prison cot, face up with her thighs doubled up over her. It was no mean feat, getting her legs pinioned that way. I got a kick in the ear for my part. God knows why, after all that, I took pity on her, but I knew it couldn't be easy to breathe. When we finished, I knelt by her head, panting a little.

"Now, if you'll keep that sewer mouth of yours shut voluntarily, I'll take the gag off you," I told her. "You will speak only when you are directed to speak. You will address the officers respectfully unless you want to get that filthy yap washed out with soap. And if I have to put that gag back on you, I'll clean out the other end of you, too, with that nice enema you love so much. Is that understood?" I picked at an edge of the adhesive tape. Phoebe grunted. A couple of quick yanks and the gag was off. She yelped as the tape took some of the down from her face with it. I poked a finger into her ribs.

"I said, *is that understood?*"

She had turned her face away from me after I pulled off the gag. I got a handful of hair and twisted her face back in my direction. She winced and replied grudgingly.

"Yes, ma'am."

"Didn't your mother teach you any manners, fuckhead? What do you say?" I knuckled her hard in the ribs.

Sullenly, she answered, "Thank you, ma'am."

"Isn't that nice, now." I smiled. This girl was about to have an attitude adjustment. I got to my feet. "This piss-ant little tramp is all yours, Sergeant."

Maybe muscles don't make a butch, but they sure don't hurt. In her white T-shirt and well-fitted uniform trousers, the Sergeant was a vision of bulldyke splendor. She had the build that makes girls swoon, and she had the swagger, too. Self-

doubt had never been her bête noire. Many large and impos-
ing girls had quivered before the Sergeant's steely gaze, never
realizing that she was several inches shorter than themselves.
She had what you'd call a commanding presence. Not that
Phoebe was impressed.

The Sergeant walked slowly around the cot, twitching a bou-
quet of Flex-Cufs against her thigh. When she reached her prisoner's head, she bent and grabbed a fistful of blonde curls.

"Wipe that smirk off your face, cunt," she ordered, pressing Phoebe's head back into the cot and making her arch her
back to accommodate the awkward angle of her neck. Winc-
ing, Phoebe tried to school her features, but she was clearly
enjoying this. The corners of her mouth persisted in curling
upward. The Sergeant stared at her coldly, then abruptly let
go of Phoebe's hair. The prisoner's body relaxed only a little;
I could see her bracing herself for what was coming next.

The first blow of the narrow plastic straps fell solidly across
Phoebe's exposed thigh. It had not been a very forceful blow,
but Phoebe yelped and jerked her lower legs down, flailing
them sideways. Caine or Walters—I'm not sure which—snorted; Phoebe did resemble poor Gregor Samsa, on her back like
that and waving her legs in the air. One of her little pink feet
just grazed the Sergeant, unintentionally, I'm reasonably sure.
But still, the Sergeant frowned menacingly.

"This won't do," she said. "Give me some more rope."

There was just enough left to truss Phoebe's ankles to the
cot over her head, with a rolled-up towel under the small of
her back to take off some of the strain. The Sergeant went
back to work, laying another careful stroke across each of the
prisoner's cheeks. Her thigh was now sporting a blazing red
stripe where the first blow had landed. Phoebe jerked but did

not cry out again, even after four more broad, ragged imprints had been scorched onto her soft pink skin. The Sergeant took her time, placing each stroke carefully as she walked around the cot, scrupulously avoiding the furry trough of Phoebe's splayed cunt.

Phoebe's face was screwed up in a knot of pain, and tears were leaking from her squeezed-shut eyes, but she made no sound. She held her whole body rigid as she waited for the next blow to land; when it came, she writhed in silence, then braced herself again, gasping for breath. Stroke after stroke fell across her quivering thighs and ass, until they glowed a livid red. Sweat beaded up on Phoebe's brow as she panted and strained against her bonds. Finally, when the purple weal of a blood blister crossed one fiery cheek, the Sergeant tossed the handful of plastic straps across the cell. She was breathing hard and her own face was flushed, but not from effort. With a low groan, she bent to run her hand across Phoebe's hot flesh. Phoebe shivered. The Sergeant slipped her other hand between the prisoner's spread legs; Phoebe moaned and raised her hips to meet the probing fingers.

"Christ, she's wet," the Sergeant muttered, fucking her rough and sloppy so we could all hear the moist sucking noise of her fingers moving in and out. Phoebe went wild, humping up against the ropes in time to the Sergeant's crude pumping. I took a step forward, and the Sergeant got control of herself, pulling her hand reluctantly away. She straightened up, and Phoebe let out a low wail of dismay. I chuckled.

"Plenty of time for everybody to get some of that," I said, raising a warning eyebrow at Walters, who was watching the scene slack-jawed. "Later," I added pointedly. It was just not possible that that thing in her trousers was any bigger than it had been before; it must have been the way she was squeezing it.

"Let's get rolling here." I barked out some more orders, and pretty soon the hum of electric clippers was the only sound in that small space. Phoebe went rigid as soon as I reached for her. Oh, how tenderly I stroked those golden curls, waiting for her to relax and open her eyes. She wasn't expecting tenderness: as I leaned over her, watching, her eyes shut even tighter and her lip trembled. She was trying not to cry. I grabbed a handful of hair and held it gently. Finally, she got herself under control and opened her eyes.

"It's what you wanted, baby," I whispered at her, leaving room for it to be a question.

After a second she nodded, biting her lip, and closed her eyes again.

I brought the blade guard up to her hairline, just touching her brow. Phoebe flinched.

Handfuls of yellow curls tumbled to the floor, leaving a pale fuzz that I hated to shave off, it felt so good to my hand. No going back now. I handed the clippers off to the Sergeant who was already in position, ready to start on Phoebe's pussy. Caine passed me the shaving gel and a disposable razor. Walters stepped over and held Phoebe's head well up from the cot, but it was awkward. I nicked her, in spite of my efforts, and she jerked away from the blade.

"I didn't think I had to tell you not to move, fuckface."

Phoebe strangled a rejoinder and stared daggers at me. She obviously hadn't forgotten my earlier threat. Suddenly, her eyes went wide and her mouth formed a cartoon O. We'd both forgotten about the Sergeant's activities down south, and I hadn't noticed when the buzzing stopped. It was the cool tingle of the gel that got Phoebe's attention, I'd bet. I finished scraping the fuzz from the back of Phoebe's skull and straightened up to watch.

The Sergeant could have been an Italian barber. Shaving is not just another one of her many areas of expertise; you could say it was her calling. I'd seen her shave a very hairy man's entire body to baby-bottom smoothness without so much as a nick anywhere. And it was not just the garden-variety Bic or safety razor that she wielded with consummate skill. She could lather up a toy balloon and scrape it clean with a straight blade, the classic test of mastery. That's what Phoebe had asked for, but the Sergeant wasn't sure what light we'd have. She wouldn't do it.

Four quick swipes and Phoebe's mound was as smooth and pink as the day she was born. With a frown of concentration, the Sergeant pulled Phoebe's labia together and drew the razor in short, precise strokes from the tops of Phoebe's inner thighs to the edges of her slit until nothing was left but a fringe of stubble. The Sergeant paused to dunk the razor in the water basin, and we crowded in a little closer.

Probing and pulling, the Sergeant rolled the edges of Phoebe's labia under her fingers and held them flat as she scraped off the remaining fuzz. Then, with the handle in a dainty two-fingered grasp, she maneuvered the blade carefully around the notch where the mound and labia meet. It wasn't until the shaver clunked against the metal basin that I realized we'd all been holding our breath. Phoebe let out a huge sigh. But it wasn't over yet.

With an evil grin, the Sergeant smeared another dollop of gel down the crack of Phoebe's ass. Phoebe squealed in surprise and jerked against her bonds.

"You'd better not do that again, slut." The Sergeant's voice was stern but her face clearly showed amusement. Phoebe clamped her eyes shut and grimaced; as she forced her lower body to relax, her face went slack again.

Deliberately, the Sergeant made stroke after painstaking stroke toward the tight rosebud of Phoebe's asshole, then repeated the process even more slowly on the other side. At last, there was nothing left but a ring of stubble around the sphincter itself, and Phoebe was trembling with tension.

The Sergeant reached down to rinse the razor and paused, her face clouded with displeasure.

"Stop moving!" she roared.

"Jesus!" Phoebe yelped. Her visible effort to still herself only made her involuntary movements bigger and more spastic.

"Shit," the Sergeant muttered. "Do something to take her mind off this, will you?"

Walters looked at me and stroked her fly. I nodded.

"No, hang on," I told her a moment later, realizing there was no way for Walters to get at her prey. We got Phoebe's ankles back to where they were before, in the dying cockroach position, and hooked her bracelets together underneath the cot. Now that her arms and legs had more free play, Phoebe would just have to hold still. The Sergeant waited patiently at the foot of the cot until we were ready.

Walters swung a leg over the narrow bed. With a wide-legged straddle, she rested her butt lightly on Phoebe's chest. "Suck on this candy, baby doll." Walters licked her lips and started to work the big dick out of her pants.

Phoebe wasn't going to make it easy: her lips pressed shut in a thin white line before the rose-dark cockhead that bounced impatiently on her chin. Even with Walter's thumb and forefinger firmly pinching her nose, she seemed ready to hold her breath until she turned blue rather than let that monster in her mouth.

I leaned in and whispered in Phoebe's ear, "Maybe it's time for that enema after all."

Phoebe's lips parted. Walters guided the big knob into our captive's mouth.

"Hold...still...*now*," came the Sergeant's muffled voice. The entire tableau froze, Walters straddling the cot and pressing her hard-on down into Phoebe's candy-glossed piehole, me and Caine at either side like altar boys, steadying Phoebe's winglike knees, and Sergeant Greenvale in full genuflection, ready to administer the sacrament.

Four precise strokes, and the razor landed in the basin with a clang.

"All right, boys," the Sergeant sang out, "as you were!"

Phoebe gave a little cough as Walters pressed the big dildo home. The Sergeant and I stood back to watch while Caine unzipped her own rod and worked it into Phoebe's well-lubed cunt.

"That girl sure is a piece of work," the Sergeant told me, shaking her head in admiration. Phoebe's eyes were closed; so were Caine's. Walters bent over to gently cradle Phoebe's hairless head while fucking her mouth. We could hear little grunts and moans of pleasure from all three of them.

"She sure is," I agreed. "We're gonna miss her."

Phoebe's excitement was building. Walters swung off so she could kneel by the cot, stroking and squeezing Phoebe's breasts, kissing her ears and cheeks and head and eyelids while Caine moved rhythmically in and out.

"Did she tell you what kind of detail she's going on?"

I shook my head. "Just something undercover."

Phoebe was getting louder. "Oh, god, oh, yeah, oh," she called, while Caine murmured, "Oh, baby, come for me, yeah, honey, that's right, that's right," and Walters kissed and nibbled and sucked everything she could reach.

"And that the shave is part of her cover," I added.

"Or it doesn't matter." The Sergeant shrugged. "She was pretty coy about it. All I know for sure is that a little roughing up was good to go."

The legs of the cot were beating a tattoo on the cell floor as Phoebe bucked under Caine's onslaught, and she was yelling obscenities full blast. Caine herself was bellowing like a calf, and Walters was squatting bare-assed beside them, grunting, having unstrapped her piece to bring herself off, one hand pistoning the big dildo in and out while the other worked furiously at her clit.

"That's so undignified." I nodded toward Walters, reflecting on the number of times I would have liked to do just the same thing myself.

"I hope she put a fresh rubber on it," the Sergeant remarked gravely.

At last the sweaty threesome was quiet, draped on the cot and each other like a heap of puppies. Phoebe didn't look half bad with a bare knob. I guess you have to have the right shape skull.

"Okay, let's go, let's go," the Sergeant waded in, clapping her hands. "Let's break this up and let the lady get some circulation back." Caine groaned and heaved herself off Phoebe. "Get those cuffs off her. And put that thing away, for god's sake," she pointed at Walters's discarded dildo.

"You know, I thought I'd take Phoebe home myself for the last..." I pulled out my pocket watch, "...ten hours before she has to report." Phoebe was straightening her legs and working the kinks out of her shoulders. "But it looks like she still owes you for that shirt."

"Go out and get that bag of clothes, will you? And you can dump the basin and swab down that cot." The Sergeant handed out her orders and turned back to me. "What are you saying? You want to turn the prisoner over to my custody, Officer?"

"Let's ask Phoebe." I called to her, "Hey, Phoebe! You and the Sergeant have some unfinished business. You want to choose your poison for the rest of the night, or do you want us to flip for you?"

Phoebe's sleepy eyes opened wide. "Flip for me?" She hooted. "You, maybe, Sam. But the Sergeant?" She howled.

The Sergeant grinned.

"All right, all right," I said, smiling. "Some other time, maybe." I waved at Caine and Walters, now busying themselves with laying out a fresh set of jeans and T-shirt for our guest of honor. "I'll just send those guys..."

Phoebe ignored the clothes and made her careful way to me. "Thanks for a great time." She put her arms around my neck and kissed me, deep and lingering. Her beautiful breasts pressed into my shirtfront as she molded herself to me and set my heart to racing all over again.

"Do you want to catch some z's? Or keep going?"

She threw a mischievous look toward the Sergeant. "Sorry about the shirt, Em."

I caught sight of Walters and Caine from the corner of one eye. "What in hell is going on here?" Walters had strapped her rod back on; Caine seemed to be helping her adjust the fit. Her mouth was millimeters away from touchdown. "Clean that thing up and put a rubber on it, for god's sake." I excused myself from Phoebe's embrace. "Have you maggots forgotten your drill?" They bounced to their feet. I eyed the half-masted stiffie poking out of Walters's fly and shook my head sadly.

"These jokers are in need of training, Sergeant. Would you be so kind as to take charge of the prisoner for the rest of the night?"

"With pleasure, Officer." She turned to Phoebe, who was now dressed and seating herself gingerly, sneakers in hand. "Shall we, darlin'?"

Phoebe lifted an eyebrow and gave Em a look that would've turned my knees to water. I sighed. I saw them out and bolted the door behind them, with one last kiss for Phoebe and a wink for my lucky friend. Back at the pen, Caine and Walters were disassembling each other's uniforms, too busy to notice my return.

I cleared my throat. They threw me startled, guilty looks. Caine giggled. Walters hurried to button her shirt, getting them wrong.

"Jesus Christ." I rubbed my weary eyes. "Didn't one of you baboons even think of cleaning that up?" I pointed at the puddle Phoebe had left on the linoleum. They looked at each other with identical expressions of horror. "No, no, with the mop, you morons."

I thought longingly of Phoebe and the Sergeant, the good time they were undoubtedly having without me. When Phoebe came back, I'd take it out on her hide. If she came back, I corrected myself soberly, with more than a little worry. I hoped we'd given her a good send-off, at least. In the meantime, I'd just have to make the best of it.

"Straighten up! Caine, put that dick away. Walters, you're still out of uniform. Undo it and try again, then DROP and GIVE ME TWENTY!"

It was going to be a long night.

Phoebe, bon voyage.

TAKING STEPS

Thea Hutcheson

"I won't eat dog food again for you."

I looked at Misty in surprise. "Why not?"

She looked up at me. "Because I give up everything." I wasn't sure what to say. That's what subs do—at least what they negotiate.

A month or so after we met, we were comparing notes about a leather convention and discovered we'd both been at the same humiliation demo. The top had gotten the slut to eat dog food for sex treats in front of the audience. We talked about it and thought it was cool for different reasons. She liked the idea of giving up so much for a top and I liked the idea of coercing someone past ordinary boundaries. I had worked her up to it, in slow steps, exploring humiliation play during our few months of interacting.

Misty was a wonderful slut, small and delicate with curly brunette hair, an elfin face, a major sex drive. She wanted to be made to do all kinds of outrageous things, which made her perfect for this kind of scene and my kind of play.

I enjoyed planning the steps that led to her acquiescing; pressing her to see what she would do for me, the lengths to which she would let me take her. Those humiliation scenes always created tension between us. I would urge her to do something, she would acquiesce, and there was this pull, like a rubber band, between us.

I was excited thinking about it now. The new vibrator and its remote were lying on the kitchen table when she came home Sunday. After dinner I put it on her really slowly and showed off the remote and both speeds with a quick demo that didn't get her off, but showed her what it would do. Then I removed it. I watched her face when she realized I was really done. It was all I could do not to smile.

"Did you like that, Misty?"

"Oh, yes, Jean."

"What did you like about it?"

She didn't even hesitate. "I like the way it straps right to my clit and you adjust it to fit me. And I like the way it buzz-es really fast like a big bee. But most of all, I like the way it feels." She was blushing now.

"The big bee does the trick, huh?"

"It would if you left it on," she said in her poutiest voice.

"You want me to put it back on?"

She brightened, but by now, she knew me well enough not to get her hopes too high. "Yes."

"What would you do for it?"

This was fun to watch. She knew she had to be reasonably

honest or I wouldn't accept it. But, of course, she didn't want to humiliate herself any more than was necessary, so it was a seesaw. She was so transparent that I could almost read her mind as she reviewed all the conversations and scenes we had had recently.

"I would go back to the corn maze again."

That had been fun. "Nah, you already did that."

"You could do me in the backyard while there's a game at the stadium."

She really liked that vibrator.

"Nah, I think since you really like it so much, it ought to be something really big."

I watched her as all the really big ones went through her mind. I let her off the hook. "How about you eat dog food for me, the wet kind," I said, knowing she had eaten kibble as a kid with her Barbie gang.

That was unexpected and I watched as she worked through it. Say no versus be pollinated by a big bee, humiliation versus pleasure, crossing the ravine versus staying on the comfy side. I could feel that pull between us.

"Do I have to answer now?"

I shook my head. "Tomorrow at dinner."

She waited until we were nearly finished eating. "One bite. Just one, that's all and I get the vibrator until I say I'm done."

It was what I had figured and all I actually wanted. I paused, pretending to think it over, then nodded. "Okay. One bite and I'll give you the big bee until you say, 'Enough.' How about Saturday night?" There was a nice steady pull coming from the center of my chest.

That gave her all week to think about it.

Come Saturday night, I told her to take off her clothes and stand in front of me. I strapped the big bee securely to her clit and hit the remote. "How's that?"

"A smidge down and a bit snugger, please." I made the adjustments and buzzed her again. It was amazing what a vibrator pressed to her clit would do. Her whole body sank into her center as all her attention centered on her clit.

"Go get your chair and bring it here."

I pulled the toy bag out from behind my lounger and got out her favorite purple rope, some lavender cord, her purple anodized nipple clamps with the matching chain and my favorite toy, a dick on a stick.

"Take your position," I said when she came back. She sat and spread her legs with her hands resting on the back of the seat so her tits poked out. I paid extra attention to binding her arms behind her to the chair back, letting her wiggle for comfort adjustment. Each leg was a separate event, slow and deliberate. Finally, I went to work on her tits with the cord, crowning them with the clamps.

"Comfy?" I asked when I stood back to look her over.

"Yes, Jean."

"Ready?"

"Yes, Jean."

"Let me make sure we're together on this. The purpose of this scene is for you to eat dog food so you can win the attention of the big bee until you're finished. Is that right?"

She put her head down, shaking it and blushing furiously. I gave her time to work through it.

"Yes, Jean. That's the purpose."

"Say it so we're both clear." I had to fight the tension and not lean toward her.

She shook her head again, sighed and smiled lopsided. "The purpose of this scene is for me to eat dog food so I can get the vibrator until I say I'm done."

I smiled. "Okay, then. Let me reacquaint you with what you can look forward to."

I gave her a nice hit from the remote then slipped her the dick on a stick, just enough to get her excited, and stood back to watch her think about it.

"Please, Jean, please give me the dick on the stick."

"You like that?" I did. "You want a buzz from the big bee too?"

"Yes, please, Jean."

"Please Jean, what?"

"Please turn on the vibrator."

"Bzzz," I said as I gave it to her. I smiled as she squirmed, trying to suck the dick in. I pulled it out.

"You like that?"

"Yes, Jean, I like that a lot."

I started torturing her tits and after awhile I asked, "Do you want some more of that big bee?"

"Yes, Jean."

"What would you do to get that big bee buzzing again, Misty?"

She knew what she was supposed to say and I knew she knew so I smiled broadly.

"What would you do?"

"Whatever you asked." I was enjoying it hugely so I let her off the hook for the moment.

"Do you like it enough to eat some dog food, a little Mighty Dog?"

She blushed then. Here it was. Put up or cry red. I watched

as she weighed shame versus pleasure, humiliation and reward, everything up on the scale. The tension was pulling good now and I swayed a little.

"Yes, Jean."

I wasn't going to let her off that hook.

"Yes, what?"

She sighed hugely. "Yes, I want the vibrator so much I will eat one bite of dog food."

I smiled. "Well, then, let me get you out of this chair."

I slowly untied her tits. She sucked breath as they came free. I massaged them gently, removed the clamps and smiled as she hissed when the blood came back into them.

I put a place mat on the carpet and put down the new dish I had bought. It even said *Misty* on it. "I'll bet you're thirsty after all that. Have a drink, my little slut."

For a moment I thought she would refuse to get on all fours since that hadn't been in the negotiation. But she scrunched down so she could get a decent drink.

"That's my good Misty. I know this is hard and I think you deserve a reward." I gave her the dick on a stick and hit the remote control for a few seconds. She arched her back to take them in and I could feel her pussy tightening up, pushing the dick out. I removed it before she could fall over the edge of an orgasm.

"Did you like that? Do you want some more?"

I watched her think about me and her, doing versus not doing, the pleasure of that vibrator versus all the distaste and social disgrace of eating dog food. She might cry red. At that moment, I thought she wasn't going to play. Then she whispered, "Yes, Jean."

I felt cocky. "I didn't hear that."

"Yes, yes, Jean," she said again, angry. Who was she angry at? I made a note to ask her.

"Okay then, let me fix you some." I opened the can of Mighty Dog, shook my head at the odor, and spooned it onto the plate.

Nudging the water bowl to the side, I laid the plate on the place mat. "Good slut, Misty. Eat and I will give you the big bee as long as you like."

She looked to the plate and then me. "Now, Misty, don't you want the bee?" I gave her another buzz, just to remind her what the choices were.

She looked at me for a moment as if she hated me. "Just one bite. I never said I would do more than that."

I couldn't read the look in her eye so I didn't push it. "One bite and you can have the big bee for as long as you like," I agreed.

She looked at me long and hard, weighing me, and I found my gaze sliding away first. She sighed and turned to the plate. "Ugh," she said as she bent down, paused and delicately took one decent bite, gagged and then gamely chewed and swallowed. She lifted the bowl and drank the rest of it. I added more and she drank that too.

She had done it. "That was great, Misty. You are the best slut, the most wonderful slut I have ever seen," I said as I picked her up and carried her to the bed where I petted her and kissed her, heedless of the lingering Mighty Dog flavor.

I undid my pants and took out my cock. I saw her pleasure because I hadn't said I would, but I knew how much she liked my cock and a vibrator together, and she really did deserve it. She got up on all fours and I put it up to her and leaned in.

She sighed and let everything go loose as she pushed back.

I slid in. Her hands slid out in front of her so her tits mashed into the bed. I hit the continuous button.

I took hold of her hips and started at her and her cunt tightened up like it was trying to push me out. *Oh, no,* I thought. *No you don't, you take every bit.* She always thinks she can pace herself against the vibrator, but not before the first orgasm and never against my dick seated against her G-spot and the vibrator going full tilt.

She started wailing, "I'm coming," and our legs and the bed were soaked in a flood while that rubber band in my chest pulled tighter and tighter and I was coming great guns. She had several more, smaller but longer lasting, and finally said, "Okay, I'm done now."

I flicked off the remote and after a moment we rolled over on our sides. I held her and we fell asleep. I woke when she got up and took a shower. I meant to get up but somehow fell back asleep.

When I got up, we had breakfast and I was going to start the debriefing after the dishes, but she said, "I won't eat dog food for you again."

"Why? I know it was bad, but that was the best scene we ever had."

She didn't look at me. That was a bad sign. Slut remorse?

"Because I give everything up for you, and you give me back nothing."

I was confused and angry. "Nothing? I work hard to get you off, to give you good scenes."

"But you don't give anything back, Jean."

"You call that whole thing nothing?"

"Pleasure is easy to give. I'm not talking about sex."

"What are you talking about?"

"I'm talking about the way that I humiliate myself for you."

"I don't ask you to do that. I just take you where you want to go."

"And that's all there is for you?"

"What else do you want there to be?"

"I want you to give something back. I want reciprocity."

"If our sex is not reciprocal, I don't know what is."

She smacked the table. "This is not about sex. This is about making yourself vulnerable. I've made myself very vulnerable for you, over and over. I trust you to not take advantage of that."

"And I haven't taken advantage of it. I've been honorable."

"But you haven't been reciprocal. There's no real intimacy between us."

"What we do is pretty damn intimate."

She shook her head. "What we do is just acts. I'm talking about sharing. We don't share anything that's important. And that's what I want. If I'm going to trust you with my vulnerability, I want you to do the same for me."

I stared at her for a moment. "Then you're doomed to disappointment."

"But why? What are you afraid of?"

"I'm not going to do it, so there's no chance for you to find out."

"Then I guess that's all there is."

"I guess so."

She got up and went into the bedroom. I cleaned up the kitchen. When I came out she was carrying her bag and some hangers. I stood, shocked. I hadn't realized she meant she was finished with me.

"Where are you going?"

"I am not going to open up like that for somebody who can't give it back to me." Tears formed in her eyes.

"I'm not eating dog food for you."

"I'm not asking you to. I'm just asking for you to show me the same side I've shown you. That's what couples do."

"Is that what you thought we were?" I hadn't really thought about it before.

"I guess I was wrong."

She left and I just stood there. After awhile I threw my ropes in the washing machine. I rinsed off the vibrator, shoved it in the toy bag and tossed it into the closet. The chair went into the corner; the dog bowl went into the wastebasket.

"I guess that's all there is," I said, imitating her. "Well, I guess this is all there is of you now." I took the trash out and marched back in the house and slammed the back door and then opened it and slammed it again, over and over.

During the day I moped around, telling myself I was angry at her. "She was the one who wanted to be made to do stuff. I have no desire to eat dog food for her or anyone."

But a few nights later I started wondering about why she wanted to be made to do things, which led me to that pull I felt when we played.

It was easier to bury it than think about it. I went to the dungeon the next weekend, picked up a sweet little thing, tied her up and whaled on her like she asked. But it wasn't fun. I just kept wondering what made them put themselves out there like that, ask for it, thank me for it? What else was I supposed to do with it?

I untied her, got her to a couch and made sure she had a

snack and some water. When I turned to go, there was Misty. I don't know how long she'd been there. I was mad because I felt guilty.

She smiled at me. I wanted to smile back, but that would be admitting…something.

"Poor Jean."

"I'm not poor." I walked on out the door. She followed.

"Then why are you taking it out on that poor little sub?"

"She asked for it."

"I don't think that was what she was asking for."

"She asked me to flog her."

"She asked you for a scene."

"Same thing."

She paused, shook her head, confused. "Isn't there anything else but the scenes? I admit I never considered you might think so. Now I have. Poor Jean, I did it too fast. I should have worked up to it, but I was mad."

"Worked up to what?"

"To telling you. I know you work up to asking me for big things. Little steps, sometimes baby steps, depending. You worked up to the dog food ever since we first talked about it, didn't you, getting me ready, breaking the walls down, getting me there step by step." She looked at me again.

"I should have done baby steps with you. I was just so mad at eating dog food for you and you not giving anything back that I stormed out. Then you didn't call."

"I was supposed to call? You say that's all there is, and I'm supposed to call?"

She made a face. "I was mad. I gave you everything you asked for and you didn't give me anything back."

I turned. "Why do you keep saying I never gave anything

back? I gave you toys, clothes, the scenes you asked for, all kinds of things."

"Yes, exactly. Things. You never gave me anything from here." She touched the center of my chest, where that pull was anchored. I stared at her.

"I never give anybody anything from there."

"But why? What are you so afraid of?" She waited but I didn't say anything.

"I trust you, Jean," Misty said. "I play with you because you use it for our mutual pleasure; you aren't going to misuse it. What do you think I'd do with anything you gave to me? I'm not going to hurt you. I'm not going to use it against you. I love you."

She loved me? I couldn't answer because that confused me and, besides, I never showed any weakness. Ever.

"I have to go." I turned and walked away. She just stood there. She was still standing outside the club when I drove past her.

I went home, made a drink, drank it, poured another one, and walked around the house. I ended up in the laundry room, kicking a clothesbasket. It had the sheets from our last night together in it. I put the drink down and lifted them up to my face. I could smell her, us, in them.

She loved me. She went everywhere I took her, did everything I asked, always came back for more, no matter what. I just couldn't go where she wanted. My chest was so tight I could hardly breathe. That place in the center of my chest felt like it was being crushed. The first tears burned my eyes. Then they were streaming and I was sobbing.

I didn't understand why and I couldn't stop. I finally rolled over on the floor and wrapped the sheet around me and just cried. I woke in the morning and got up, stiff and sore and cursing. Curiously, my body was hurt but my head was clear and my chest felt light, although it ached right there in the center when I thought about Misty.

She loved me. And I had bawled like a baby smelling her on the sheets. When my mom was alive, she used to tell me I had to pay attention to my body, because it never lied. After she died, I hated what it told me. Life after that wasn't so good and it became easier, safer to bury what I felt.

So what was my body saying that I would cry so hard from smelling sheets? Keeping everything hidden away was such a habit, I didn't know if I could figure it out.

But the one thing I knew was that I didn't want that ache in my chest when I thought about Misty. I wanted the pull that I felt when I asked her to step over a line. I wanted it to pull us together so I wouldn't ever have to wrap myself up in a sheet alone on the floor again.

I called her. She was awake. "Will you meet me at Nash's?"

"Sure, in an hour?"

I was hoping for sooner, but beggars can't be choosers.

She was there, at our favorite table hidden behind the palms.

"You look like shit," she said.

"I don't feel much better."

We sipped coffee for a while. I kept looking at her, remembering how transparent she had been as she'd worked through the decision to eat the dog food. Why was it so easy for her?

"How can you do them?"

"What?"

"The things I ask you."

She sat thinking for a moment. "Because I know I'll learn things about myself and because you are such wicked fun."

"I thought you didn't like the dog food."

She smiled. "It was awful. But I really liked that vibrator. And I liked the way you understood how I got there. At least I thought you did."

I looked down at my coffee. "I understand that my chest hurts when I think about you being gone. I understand that I hate it and I want it to go away."

"You understand what I am asking for?"

"Yes, no, maybe. I don't know if I can do that."

She smiled and patted my hand. "But you just did."

"Huh?"

"Honesty is its own kind of vulnerability, Jean. Thank you." She curled her fingers into my hand. "My chest hurts too. And I want it to go away too."

That spot ached as it tightened up and my eyes burned. I wanted her with me. No matter whether I could give or show or have, I wanted her with me. She lifted my hand, held it to her mouth and kissed it. The tension in the center of my chest tugged and I realized it would pull us together if I just let it.

I wondered what that would be like, her tied to the chair, me with my hand on the remote and that rubber band pulling tighter and tighter. She kept watching me. How different was this from eating dog food and how many steps were there between where I was and what she wanted?

"Hey, let's go home," I said suddenly. "I just thought of a really interesting game."

"There's no dog food, is there?"

"No, but it'll take several steps and probably lots of tries."

PHONE CORROSION

Julian Tirhma

A gray screen's readout tells how long I've
been on the line. I move the handset away
from my ear to check the duration—21:27.
While the phone's away, Mei says something
I don't quite catch.

"Yeah." My standard response. Everything
she says is more or less interchangeable. I light
a cigarette and inhale right at the receiver so
she hears the sucking sound.

"Are you smoking again?" she deadpans.

"It got hot. Smoking makes me feel less
sweaty." Dusk overtakes the sky. From
the roof, I see clouds spread thin as butter
smeared on a pan to let the cake slip out. Satellite dishes decorate the roofs of other apartment buildings. Twinkly lights litter the top
floor windows with flashing epileptic rhythms.

Red, white, and blue. I want to bend coat hangers into an extended hook and pull them down.

"But cigs make you sweat *more*," Mei says.

"Not me." I wish I wasn't so sarcastic.

"Do you want to get off the phone?"

"No. Why? Do you?" The thing is I kind of *do*. I'm on my last cigarette, but I still want to get her off. Otherwise, why bother calling?

"I want my girl to be spick and span before she has her snack," I begin.

"I *am* clean. I took a bath." Her voice goes up an octave. She captures the perfect mix of trepidation and defiance of the spoiled child who doesn't know she's spoiled.

"Hold out your hands. Let me look under your nails." They have a bit of grime. And the bow in her hair has slid down, bangs falling in front of her eyes. "You're as disheveled as the poodle. What gave you the idea you'd eat your snack looking like that?"

Her favorite part's coming up. I hear her breathing change. I say, "Little Miss needs to be hosed off. You're filthy! You'll bring germs. Go to the porch and turn the spout on this instant." I always wish I had a spigot on the roof to make the right sound effect.

"Yes, ma'am. Is that enough water?" She's become even more timid.

"Now stand still. Take off your dress and put it on the bench. This will be just a tad bit cold, all right?" I can't tell if my voice deepens, but I soothe her. She isn't being punished, just made to feel bad for lying.

"Eeeeeehhhhhhhh," she screeches. "It's cold! Turn it off! I'm washed now. I am." Even after I turn off the hose, she whimpers. "It's not fair. I'm dripping wet and freezing." Her teeth chatter in feigned shivers.

"You may have your snack now. Do you want me to feed you the cookie so you don't get it soggy?"

"Yes, please. Can I have a peanut butter cream?"

"*May* you have a peanut butter cream," I taunt. I'm sure she jerks when she hears her name's homonym, infused with all the governess authority I can muster. Her fingers are probably crowding in her cunt, but she's standing, so her arm aches. She's made herself wait to touch her clit until the first bite from the cookie.

"May I?"

"Of course you may. You are the *best* little girl." I hold the cookie so she has to stretch her neck to bite it. She spills crumbles all over her chin. I use her undershirt to wipe it off.

"Goodness, it's delicious. Mmmmmm. Thank you, ma'am," Mei manages to gasp. Now she's probably stumbled to her knees, bracing her arm against a wall so she can thrust into her hand as it earnestly fiddles. I can't believe the things she does without dropping the phone.

"That's a good girl." I usually improvise at this point, which as often as not backfires. Tonight, I just pant and moan, giving her the idea my hand is doing something other than unraveling the vinyl strips on my rusty lawn chair. No matter how cheesy I sound, I always hear her whimpering on the line like a puppy who's heard her master's car in the garage.

"Thanks, Tea. That felt good." Mei's back to her butchy, deep voice.

"What about taking Honey and Burdock to the dog park tomorrow?"

"Sure. I'll meet you there." It's easy to get Mei to commit.

Well, to things involving me.

I obeyed Rule Number One: I was on the phone less than an hour, so I definitely hadn't cheated on my other lover.

When I embark on a visit to Adam in Boston, we're not on the best terms. They say if you're always fighting about little things, you don't want to see the big things. I don't mind admitting I won't hand-hold him through the so-called identity crisis he's having over dating a dyke that doesn't dig men.

I made the mistake of waiting too long to buy my ticket. Besides getting ripped off, I wasn't even guaranteed a seat. Adam wasn't pleased to hear the plan when he called me on my mobile, doubting that I truly wanted to see him. I was *going*, wasn't I?

"I'm ruled by Mercury. What do you expect?" I said. I hate when other people shine it on, but I do it all the time.

"That's right. I forgot to check if it's going retrograde before I called." Adam's enamored of sarcasm, too.

"Look, I'll get there eventually, okay?" Our phone fights are never the kind that turn heads in airport terminals. They aren't so loud that they'll be followed by even louder make-up sex.

Our fighting is like one moment in normal people's fights, all drawn out and frozen. We have to say each other's name every minute to make sure we're still there. I'm doodling on the back of my itinerary so when the page is filled, I have a reason to hang up. The way he says "Tea" gently is a relief, and then they announce my flight.

The hotel is so plush. I feel scummy. When I arrive, someone *escorts* me to his room. In his presence now, I know we're still fighting because we're polite like someone's listening. I haven't seen Adam in a month, so I study him for changes. He's wearing eyeliner, brown not black; it suits him. His fingernails are very short. His lace-up boots, sitting in the closet, have new red laces. I'm too stubborn to apologize and he has no reason to.

I start it innocently enough, with a long, swaying hug that shows him how much he missed me. I bury my nose in his neck. He's an inch shorter than I am, so it's easy. He smells like lotion: not a manufactured scent, like peach, but olive oil or lanolin or whatever they stick in unscented lotion. I hate being polite. I want to be second-marriage nonchalant. We only have two days.

I don't want to admit sex is always the same with him, but it is. Adam puts on music. We tongue kiss, 'cause we have little tongues that don't choke each other. We sort of dance. We grope under clothing. When I'm wet enough, he fucks me.

I think the glamorous hotel has put him in a strange mood. He smiles a lot while he watches himself touching my tits shyly, like he forgot how. I flew out here for a weekend of shy and forgetful?

He takes my hands and puts them on his chest, hesitantly. "*My* tits want some attention."

I tweak his left nipple playfully, but lower my hand to his pants to feel if he's hard. "Your tits?! I want what's in here." Tugging his fly, I pull his hips to me.

"You want what's in there? Nothing that great is in there."

"It feels like something. Something that wants out." I start unzipping his pants.

"What kind of dyke are you, Tea?" He pulls away and looks me in the eye.

"Uh, the kind of dyke that doesn't like that question! The kind of dyke that doesn't turn away hard cock when it's right in front of her."

"Oh right, I forgot." He rolls his eyes. "Then I'm gonna take a shower." Adam shuts the door behind him. What the fuck is his problem? Does he really want to rehash all the bullshit of dykes loving cock, the semiotics of it, for the millionth time?

Hearing the water splashing convinces me he's really taking a shower and not just hiding out. I unlatch my suitcase on the bed. Rummaging through all the smut-related accoutrements I brought, I find a green mermaid dildo. Turning up the music louder to block his shower noise, I hop on the bed and go to it.

My face smashes to the pillow so that my glasses dig at my face while I hump a folded blanket. I replay the mornings when he woke me up by rubbing it against my thigh, when I was too sleepy to tell if it was attached or silicone. I roll the dildo between my hands until it warms up, then flip over and hold it against my cunt. As I jerk it, imagining what Adam would do if he caught me makes me wetter than the actual movements.

Everything surges around and I want it inside. I match a green condom to the mermaid's seaweed skin and encase her shimmering scales in pretty latex. Mushing her around, I smear the wet into my bristling hair and up around my clit to make my cunt open. I squeeze my eyes shut and try to block out the smell of the hotel sheets, the romantic lighthouse paintings, the dirt under my fingernails. I feel desperate and don't mind a bit.

After flopping around a while, the mermaid flicks her fin against my huge clit like she's beckoning a sailor from her rock perch. Then she combs out her hair with a piece of coral and flips her fin faster, showing him how she's so lonely with no one but squid and pelicans for company. When she thinks the sailor might follow her, she dives from the rock and plunges into the salty froth. In her native element, she slips through the heavy water that presses in on her from all sides, like she's been slicked up with oil. On and on she drives, her thick tail propelling her, with swirling hair following in tendrils.

If I angle the mermaid right, my cunt balloons, making room for her to dive deeper. My breath forces its way out through my nose, noisy from allergies. I leave my clit alone until I'm closer to coming. The mermaid's as deep as she can go, skimming her stomach along the sand, tickling the anemones and making them squeeze their pink mouths shut.

When I'm ready, and suspecting that Adam will discover me if I wait much longer, I grab my clit with my thumb and index finger like it's a tiny dick. I pull the hood up as far as it goes, until it stings, and then push the fleshy fold all the way back down. The first few jerks make me forget to keep fucking myself, and it hurts in the best way. My poor, tiny, purple dick, with such low confidence; it still likes being yanked. I tug to feel it lengthening and finally twitching. That sweet, ocean-current heat surges, and I come like a tiny sailboat getting crushed against the rocks.

Adam opens the door to the bathroom. I can see him in the mirror, but he ignores me. He comes out wearing a big, white towel around his waist, and surveys the room.

"Jesus, it smells like sex in here, Tea."

"So?" I can't stand the way I sound like a teenager.

"I was going to apologize for what I said about you being, or not being, a real dyke."

"Thanks." I drop my used latex in the toilet. "Is that it? Are you over your fit?"

"I don't think I'm the one having a fit." He sits on one of the stuffed chairs. "I think things are freaking you out that you don't want to talk about."

"I *want* to talk about it." Oh boy, here we go.

"Okay. We went to that benefit event...the one raising money for queer immigration..."

I put my hands on my hips, but drop them when I realize I look like my older sister. "You want a prize for giving money to queers, bucko?"

"That's not what I mean. Sasha's friend Kate was hitting on me, so Sasha said, 'No dice. *She's* taken.' "

"Sasha's a new-agey dork. She probably didn't want to embarrass Kate by telling her she got faked out by a little bit of eyeliner."

"Well, the way I see it, Sasha and Kate get it."

"Get what?" Sometimes I like annoying Adam by playing dumb.

"Will you *please* not... You're a smart cookie, Tea, so why don't you just accept it: I'm a dyke." Adam stares at the fancy lamp on the side table, avoiding my eyes.

"Okay, and is this where I embrace you and tell you that I love you no matter what?" I try a laugh, but it doesn't come out so good.

"Fuck you, Tea. You'd pop me in the head if I said that. Don't give me that."

Adam is right. I can't bigot my way out of it. I've been too loud-mouthed about transphobic lesbians to convince Adam that I qualified as one.

"You're a dyke." I try not to say it like, "You're a toaster oven," but it comes out a little shaky. I sit on the bed and say it again with conviction, if not celebration. "You're a dyke."

I'm not supposed to cry. I'm not supposed to act like Adam just told me of a terminal illness. I'm not supposed to make it all about me. How many times had I repeated that same advice to rooms full of selfish queers? I start crying anyway. Adam moves to the bed to comfort me, even though I don't deserve it. "Are you shocked?"

"You know I'm not shocked. You love horses and thick-soled boots. You love all my friends. I mean..." I hug Adam really tightly. I wanted to tell Adam that even though it isn't about me, it is about me—how I like the novelty of being the only dyke in our circle with a boy lover, how I like pushing people's essentialist buttons.

"So...I'm boring now, huh?" Adam asks.

"I'm not sure." As crappy as I am at communication, I never lie. Instead I muster, "Adam, I am sincerely proud of you." I thought Adam might shrug off my warmth as a joke. Instead, Adam stands up with arms held out.

"Will you do the honors?" Adam looks down at the towel hanging at waist level. I carefully loosen the tucked edge without undoing the whole thing and pull it up above her tits, under her arms. Then I tightly fold over the corner of that luxurious hotel towel and smooth it to her hips.

"Will *you* do the honors?" I offer my tear-streaked cheek to get a good smack upside the head, but instead she gives me a kiss.

GONE

ViolyntFemme

She's gone. I am sitting here alone, alone in the house, alone in the room, alone inside myself. I can still catch traces of her...a stray scent of perfume, one of her hairs on the floor, a coffee cup with her lipstick seemingly tattooed onto it. Jez? I call; half hoping, half expecting, and all needing an answer. None comes. I curl up on the bed, wrap myself in the scent of her and sleep.

She's here. I feel her tits against my back, her hot cunt against my ass. She is murmuring how much she has missed me, needed me and thought about me. Her hands come up around my breasts, kneading and pinching. I feel her teeth on my neck and earlobes; I twist my head back and our mouths meet in a clash of lips, teeth, and tongues. One hand snakes down between my thighs, pressing against my clit, rubbing slow circles until I am humping it like some sort of naughty dog with its favorite pillow. Wordless cries escape my mouth as she enters me with her fingers. She rolls me onto my back, her fingers never leaving my cunt. With one hand on my breast, constantly tormenting my nipple, she uses the other one like a piston, fucking me into the bed, adding more of herself until her entire fist is in me. I am coming, bucking, and screaming her name. Jez! Jez!

Jez!! The sound of my own voice wakes me up. My own fingers in my cunt, still moving frantically, my dream orgasm slowly subsiding. I get out of bed, groggy but aware enough to know that I am still alone. I go to the shower, hoping to wash her scent off of me, anger now taking the place of sorrow. Last week we were fine, laughing over breakfast, talking about plans for the weekend, fucking in the shower...

I walk into the bathroom; I can see her washing, her outline slightly distorted by the glass. I snap the buttons on my harness and feel the weight of my cock in my hands. As she turns her back to the door, I silently enter, step behind her, and run my finger down the cleft of her ass. She stifles a moan and presses that luscious ass back against my hand. I tell her she is a naughty little slut while reaching around and testing her cunt. She is already open and waiting for me. I slide into her, inch by inch, pushing her up against the wall. I grab a handful of her hair and fuck her slowly until she starts pushing back, begging for it harder. I oblige, her moans fill the room.

I go on with my day, eating, breathing, moving, and just going through the motions. Twice I see a glimpse of red hair coupled with a heart-shaped ass. I chase after her, scaring the bejesus out of two women who think I am crazy. Maybe I am. Friends come by to check on me, invite me places, joke about "getting me out in the land of the living." I respond that I would rather walk with the dead. I go to her grave, stroke the outline of her name carved into the stone. Just last week she was lying next to me in bed, six days later, thanks to an out-of-control Impala, I am lying on top of her as she lies in the ground.

I leave the cemetery, tears still coming, and go home. When I get there the rage that had started this morning over what happened finally overtakes me. I tear through the house, ripping pictures off the wall, throwing clothes in trash bags, making inarticulate sounds of grief as I go. I find the bottle of champagne we were saving for our upcoming five-year anniversary and drink it all. I pass out and sleep dreamlessly.

I awake to find the house in shambles, I had forgotten about my tirade the night before. As I walk through the house, surveying the mess, I see something peculiar. In the middle of our bed there is a pile of ripped photos. However, the center one is untouched. It is the picture of us on our wedding day, me in a tasteful suit and her in a gorgeous white slip dress. Lying on the picture is her wedding ring, the ring I could have sworn was on her finger when we—a new wave of hurt washes over me—buried her. I take the ring and slip it over my finger, nestling it next to mine. I try not to wonder why it is there, telling myself that she must not have been wearing it, and during my fugue last night, I created this weird shrine. I spend the rest of my day cleaning up the house, crying over the mementos

I so haphazardly destroyed and finding grim joy in the ones that survived.

I wait a few more days before visiting her again. I try and take my friends' advice and join the land of the living, albeit halfheartedly, for a short time. My well-meaning friends make this harder though, with their well-intentioned condolences and all the talk about her being in a better place. How can I join the living when all anyone wants to talk about is her? I smile, nod my head, and murmur all the things the bereaved spouse is supposed to say.

I find myself back at her grave, the living driving me back toward the comfort of the dead. Somewhere in the recesses of my brain, a sane part of me says that this is fucked up, that this is not the way things should be. I, however, don't care. I lie there on the ground, knowing that the woman I love is silently moldering beneath me. Knowing the corpse below me bears no resemblance to the cherished body I once held in my arms, with its crushed back and shattered face. At some point I fall asleep, arms around the gravestone.

She is here, only this time I don't think I am dreaming. I can feel her weight settle on top of me, her lips kiss my face; and I hear her voice in my ears. She is naked, and I suddenly realize that I am too. I roll over, placing myself on top of her, rubbing my thigh into her cunt. The warmth from it is shocking compared to the coolness of the rest of her.

Where have you been? I ask. Why did you leave me? She places her finger against my lips, hushing me. I realize I don't care; all that matters is that she is here, under me, holding me in her arms. We kiss frantically; my hands explore her like it's our first time all over again. She moans as I suck on her breasts, pulling her stiff nipples into my mouth. My hand replaces my thigh as I place it over her cunt. I always loved the feeling of it in my hand, the smooth skin, the heat and wetness leaking out. I reach down further, one finger gently tickling her ass, while she bucks against me trying to get something inside her. I'm beginning to lower my head to her cunt when she stops me. She twirls her finger in the air, motioning for me to turn around so she can get to me while I eat her. I happily comply, settling my cunt over her mouth. I reenter her with my hand, two fingers in her ass, while my thumb nestles in her cunt. I suddenly feel her do the same to me. Feeling her fuck me the same way I am fucking her sends me over the edge. I bury my face in her cunt, licking her clit, daring her to make me come before she does. We become one being straining at each other, melding together until our cunts begin to twitch at the same time. My orgasm hits me like a truck, lights swirling before my eyes, the brightness overtaking me, her answering wetness flowing over my face. All I see is white...

I am sure someone will find me, my cold body still clinging to the headstone, a peaceful smile on my face. They will say, "We should have watched over her better. We should have known something was wrong." Or, "The poor dear, she died of a broken heart/exposure/grief. Blah, blah." Or a million other equally clichéd things. They will blame themselves, blame others, and blame me. Then they will go home, maybe hug their loved ones and maybe even fuck, proving their life and virility in the face of death. But none of that matters now. You see, my love, my Jez, was gone. And now I am gone too.

VIRGO INTACTA

Anna Bishop

The little nun is seventeen.

Her name is Maddalena, and she's beautiful in a way that owes all its appeal to the freshness of its bloom. She reminds Andrea of those tiny red plums that grow wild on the scrubby trees circling the villa they've rented for the month, the ones that show the prints of her fingers in purple against their ruby skins. When broken open, their flesh is dark gold with a hint of rose-blush rising in veins to the surface. The little nun's skin is like that, too, plump and golden with youth between her collar and the white band of her novice's headdress. And like the plums, she's native to these sleepy hills, born out of their dusty soil and raised among their goats and grapevines. Andrea looks at her and feels like she's been taken back in time.

Ro says she'll bruise just as easily as the fruit, and spins elaborate fantasies about Maddalena when she and Andrea are alone together. Andrea's own skin testifies to the violence of their mutual ardor; she's long grown used to the garden of violets that blooms and fades and blooms again on her body when Ro is sublimating a ferocious new passion.

Maddalena is a player in Andrea's personal fantasies, too, but they're gentler encounters than Ro's gleefully imagined bacchanals. Hot afternoons, white cotton sheets, mosquito netting checkerboarding sunlight into tiny square dapples on their skins. Her face between Maddalena's olive thighs. Her own fingers reaching up to link with those small, capable, calloused hands, fluttering against her grip like frightened sparrows. Andrea can't remember her own first orgasm, and would rather not relive the loss of her virginity, so easing the little nun over that fragile bridge between innocence and carnality seems like the perfect way to redeem her misspent youth.

Not that this is likely to happen. The girl is the niece of old Elisabeta, the live-in housekeeper, and she's only here working in the villa because of Elisabeta's recent hip surgery. She arrives an hour after the convent's clock tower rings for morning prayers, half a mile down the road, and departs for evening Mass as soon as dinner is on the table. Elisabeta, the reluctant invalid, hobbles after her in the interim, leaning hard on her cane and scolding her in thickly accented Italian.

That the rich Americans vacationing here until the end of the month are both women seems to have played a role in securing the convent's approval of this arrangement. What the Mother Superior would say if she knew the details of their relationship (to say nothing of Ro's suspiciously deep voice and five o'clock shadow) Andrea can only speculate. If

Elisabeta knows anything, she appears to have kept the news to herself.

Certainly Maddalena has noticed. She cleans their bedroom, after all, and is as openly curious as she can be under her aunt's careful scrutiny. Andrea has looked up more than once from Ro's casual embrace to catch a flash of fascinated dark eyes, quickly averted. Later, passing Maddalena in the upstairs hall, Andrea is intrigued when the little nun blushes but doesn't look away.

She reports this to Ro, who promptly incorporates Maddalena's innocent show of interest into the ongoing fantasy that's encompassed their lovemaking for the last week and a half. An hour or so into it, Andrea is bowed back against the pillows, cunt skewered on three of Ro's fingers, clit being savaged by an expert thumbnail. She's juicing all over Ro's hand and biting her own fist to keep from screaming out loud.

"She's kissing your feet," Ro says. "Crying. She's got nipples like cherries. You know that noise a newborn kitten makes? That's what she sounds like when I twist them."

Andrea imagines that small round golden body arched in agony and pulsing with need, ruby-nippled, plum-cunted; imagines Maddalena in her place, impaled and squirming on Ro's fingers and crying with the need to come again, to stop coming, to be touched, to be left alone; imagines covering her mouth in a kiss and drinking those baby-howls like some sweet sticky elixir of youth. She comes, and comes, and comes again, Ro folding in her fourth finger and her thumb and shoving hard while she gasps obscenities into the sweating hollow between Andrea's breasts. When Ro finally fucks her, it's even better. *Everything's so pretty when it's new*, Ro whispers into her ear, *don't you just want to open her up and see how she works? Put your fingers in; it's like kitten fur, like pink satin, like velvet that's never been touched. She's all blank in there, waiting for you to tell her what sex is. She's all new. She's all yours.*

She's all yours and you're all mine. That means I get... everything.

Fair enough, Andrea thinks, and manages to say as much before she can't talk or think anymore.

Later, they turn on the ceiling fan and collapse back on the big white bed, letting the cool night air from the open window dry their bodies. Andrea drifts her fingertips over Ro's nipples lightly enough that they don't even harden, but just lie pink and quiescent like sleeping lips waiting to be kissed awake, and pretends she's touching Maddalena. A long inside quiver runs through her, interior walls clamping down on themselves in a delicious twist of pressure that grabs her by surprise.

"Ow," Ro says without opening her eyes. "Easy, tiger."

Andrea realizes she's pinching. "Sorry," she says. "Got carried away."

On Friday afternoon, Elisabeta tells them in halting English that she'll be gone to the big hospital in Grasseto from Sunday evening all the way through to Tuesday afternoon. Signora Abruzzi, their nearest neighbor, has agreed to cook for them in her absence, she says. As for the cleaning...well... Maddalena...?

Here she hesitates, small black eyes darting between them, anxious fingers twisted in the front of her apron. Ro, resplendent and unreadable behind dark glasses and a paperback novel, says nothing.

It's up to Andrea, then, to resolve the tension. She smiles

and sips Elisabeta's homemade lemonade, tart and thick and syrupy, like melted sorbet, squeezed from the tiny sweetish lemons that grow in aromatic groves all along the nearby coast. It's difficult to imagine a response that's going to please both the old woman and Ro, too.

"Ah," she says finally, shrugging. "But of course there's no problem. It's perfect timing, really." They've been contemplating a weekend of shopping in Siena. Signora Abruzzi needn't worry herself about the cooking. As for Sorella Maddalena, if she'd just be so kind as to turn down the linens on Monday afternoon in anticipation of their return and perhaps lay out a cold supper, they won't require anything more of her.

Ro shifts slightly behind her novel at this, though her expression doesn't change. Elisabeta breaks into smiles and relieved chatter. *Certo, certo, molto giusto, molto bene.* If the Signora and the...ah, *Signora*...are to be away...ah, then, everything is solved. Elisabeta can go to her appointment without worrying; Signora Abruzzi will not be overtaxed with work; Maddalena can observe Sunday services and be back on Monday morning to ready the villa for their arrival.

Grazie. Grazie. Molto, molto bene.

Ro is less voluble, but equally pleased. "You're a better liar than you used to be," she murmurs later, against Andrea's cheek. "It's hot."

They're in the pool. Ro's lips are cool and wet, curled up just now in a knowing little half smile. The upper curves of her small high breasts, pushed up and out of her bathing suit by its built-in padded bra, are beginning to show a tinge of pink; she's always been more likely to burn than to tan. *I ought to make her put on more sunblock*, Andrea thinks, but Ro moves in closer, one hand pulling aside the wet spandex that separates them, and it's far easier to succumb to the decadent zero-gravity delights of underwater fucking than to force herself to move away.

Ro turns her to face the villa. She grabs the pool's slippery tile edge with both hands to steady herself.

"Look at the windows," Ro directs from behind her, holding her by the hips and navigating past her swimsuit bottom with one practiced, determined thrust. Andrea was expecting that, but it's still a thrill; something about the dichotomy of lapping water and sun on her shoulders and Ro inside her makes her helpless and liquid from the neck down, as if her brain turns off the minute her sex engages. "She's watching us, isn't she?"

It's true; the sheer white curtain on the French doors leading off the terrace into the cool interior of the villa has been tugged slightly askew. The sun glinting off the water makes it difficult to tell, but if Andrea squints hard she thinks she can make out a shadowy figure behind the curtain. The possibility that it's Maddalena sends a throb of longing through her that rides the border between pain and pleasure. She bites her lip.

"Isn't she?" Ro prompts again, low voiced and pleased with herself. She slides her hands up to cover Andrea's breasts, finds her nipples through the wet fabric of the suit, and pinches hard.

Andrea groans, nods, groans again.

Ro half-lifts her until her upper torso kisses the hot terrazzo tiles at the side of the pool and moves in close. She braces herself against the side of the pool, finds a better angle, fucks harder.

"Well, what are you waiting for?" she pants, pulling Andrea's head back by a handful of her wet hair so she can't look away from the window. "If I'm going to do all the work, you can at least show her what she's missing, can't you?"

Andrea—humiliated, uncomfortable, unspeakably and astronomically aroused—is happy to comply.

"So we're not really going into Siena, then?" she ventures that night after dinner. She's just finished brushing her teeth. Ro's sitting up in bed with her laptop open on her knees.

"Oh, we're going," she says, hitting the enter button with a flourish. "Too much relaxing in the country is bad for the soul. Or the digestion. Or something." She closes the Power-Book, pushes it off her lap, and gives the comforter beside her an invitatory pat. "How long we'll *stay*, now..." She strokes Andrea's hair, her eyes gleaming and far away. "*That's* another question entirely."

They leave Siena directly after breakfast on Monday morning. The drive back is silent and tense with expectation—so charged, in fact, that Andrea starts to backpedal.

Maddalena won't be there, she tells herself. She'll be gone already. Or prudently out of sight. Or she'll scuttle out the door the moment their car pulls up.

She'll be afraid. She'll be indifferent, or righteously indignant, or disgusted.

It'll never happen.

But when Andrea, laden with shopping bags and the smaller of their suitcases, gets to the top of the stairs and opens the door to the master suite, Maddalena's bent over making the bed. She looks up and spins around with a gasp. She's holding a pillow that's half-in and half-out of a freshly ironed pillowcase.

"*Signora*," she says, catching her lower lip with her teeth.

It's too perfect, like a porn movie, or a *Penthouse* letter. Andrea can't help but think that it isn't really happening, even as Ro comes in with the big suitcase and puts it down inside the door, even as she's caught up in an embrace that's at once frankly sensual and bone-meltingly tender.

Ro's at her best when she's kissing for an audience. By the time she comes up for air and pushes Andrea gently to the side, they're both breathing hard and trembling with excitement. Maddalena hasn't moved; she's watching them wide eyed from the other side of the bed, still clutching her pillow. Ro sinks down sideways on the bed, takes the pillow away, and reaches for the girl's hand. Maddalena flinches and lets out her breath in a little huff, but doesn't pull away.

It's that easy, that surreal. Andrea blinks at the pair of them, at the virgin in sensible navy blue now held swooning in the cradle of Ro's arms. She watches Ro unpin the white-linen headdress, watches Maddalena's hair tumble down her back in a pair of heavy dark braids. Ro wraps the braids around one fist and tugs with more tenderness than force, just enough to make Maddalena's head fall back against her shoulder. Her throat bends into a line as pure and golden as an Italian sunset. Ro kisses it, and the little nun makes her first sound, a moan that's far more capitulation than protest.

For Andrea, who has expected at the most to be the one holding Maddalena still, the one offering kisses and comfort as a foil to Ro's ferocity, this tableau on the bed is at least as perplexing as it is arousing. Even before she looks, she knows there's a challenge in Ro's eyes: *Well, what now?* she seems to be asking. Andrea remembers those words from the middle of some other, earlier night, and shudders.

She's all yours. You're all mine.

She kicks off her shoes, sits down on the foot of the bed, and puts her hand on Maddalena's ankle. There's something building in her that she can't identify for a moment; it's her sun-dappled fantasy from a week ago, she realizes, the one she'd thought lost in the aftermath of Ro's more colorful speculations.

Sunlight. White sheets. Two women in a quiet bedroom.

Well, okay. Make that three.

She looks up and meets Maddalena's frightened, fascinated eyes. "Shhhh," she says, one finger on her lips, and smiles. *"Sta bene."*

Her hands slide up under the navy blue cotton of the habit to rest on Maddalena's knees. Far above her, Ro whispers something meaningless and comforting as she strokes the small round face. Maddalena's knees part on a little sigh, and Andrea's hands move higher, leading from the balls of her thumbs, tracing tiny circles. She skims one thumbnail in a light vertical line over the cotton barrier covering Maddalena's mons, then down over where the fabric stretches tight and damp. Andrea can feel the flesh underneath it straining toward her touch. A shudder, another sigh, more whispers from Ro. Andrea lifts the navy blue skirt in both hands and settles its folds just below Maddalena's navel.

She looks up. They're kissing now, a pretty Italian girl in braids and a fiercely beautiful woman who can make Andrea come just by looking at her the right way. Maddalena's hips have begun a slow instinctive roll that's only too familiar to Andrea. *This is what I must look like*, she thinks, blushing. She watches the kiss deepen for just another moment before she hooks her fingers under the waistband of Maddalena's panties and draws them down and away.

She wants pictures, she wants video, she wants to freeze this moment in amber forever, but that little patch of ebony curls is lifting off the bed in mute entreaty and Andrea plunges recklessly ahead, too fast really, two fingers drawn down the slit and between the lips, fiddling them up and apart until Maddalena's clit is caught between them and the girl arches toward her with a yelp of such surprised, half-panicked pleasure that she slips off Ro's lap. Ro laughs and drags her back up again, away from Andrea's fingers, and to their delight she starts to fight, whimpering protests in time with the fast pulse in her throat.

Maddalena's head tosses and her trapped hands beat ineffectually against the white chenille bedspread. Andrea holds her cupped palm half an inch away, just close enough to brush the black curls, and watches Maddalena struggle and thrash until she's tired herself out and has to collapse back against Ro's chest. She's gleaming with a fine film of perspiration. Her habit is rucked around her waist now, all modesty forgotten.

"Don't tease her any more," Ro says in low tones. "Show her what it's all about."

Andrea nods, drags the ball of her thumb through all that syrupy wetness around the girl's desperately clenching cunt, and rolls it over her clit. It feels grape sized and twice as thin skinned, like it'll burst if it grows any bigger. Andrea starts a slow circle, and has to throw her free arm over one of Maddalena's thighs as the clit hood slips back and her wet thumb grazes the surface underneath it. She does another circuit, and another, and another. Ro has the girl's hands pinned above her head and one arm clamped around her waist. Maddalena is panting and shaking her head and talking a blue streak in Italian.

It's like the beginning of a joke, Andrea thinks: *How do you make a nun curse?*

But it's not funny, really. Just...amazing.

She pauses to let Maddalena catch her breath, just for a second, and slides her middle and index fingers south, buzzing on those breathy little pleading sounds and the way Maddalena's cunt flutters against her fingertips and the intense, half-feral satisfaction that flashes across Ro's face just before she lowers her mouth to Maddalena's throat.

Maddalena convulses. Andrea slides two fingers inside her.

Like kitten fur, she remembers Ro saying. *Like pink satin.*

She's never been touched here, Andrea thinks, and feels her own clit pulse. *By anyone. Ever.*

Virgin skin.

And it's easy, it's wet, it's tight but it's yielding and altogether wonderful and then Maddalena gives a little gasp just as it gets not...*quite*...so easy.

Andrea stops pressing. Their eyes meet.

"*Per favore*," Maddalena says, in a broken whisper that makes the hair on Andrea's arms stand to attention. "*Per favore...no.*"

Has she ever felt so powerful? Ever?

She hesitates, just for a moment, then washes her thumb once again over Maddalena's engorged clit. The little nun's eyes well up and spill over, two big tears that make tracks all the way into her hairline. Andrea half expects to see them drip off the ends of her braids. Maddalena's body shudders; her head lolls; she quivers and clenches under Andrea's hands. Andrea pulls out her glistening fingers and fiddles them ruthlessly north again.

Virgo intacta, she thinks, sending Maddalena over another

edge. *But let's make no mistake, little nun. No one's ever going to touch you again, without you wishing they were me.*

It is the sexiest thought she's ever had.

They are halfway home on the airplane, sipping lime tonics and arguing amiably about whether or not to take a taxi back from the airport, when Andrea realizes that that last little bit of arrogance that had come to her as she touched the little nun was exactly like something Ro would have said. Of course, Ro would have said it *aloud.*

First, she's shocked. Then she laughs.

Ro arches an eyebrow. "Something's funny. Care to share?"

Andrea thinks about it, then shakes her head.

"No," she says, and links her fingers through Ro's. It feels good. Familiar, like a little homecoming. She squeezes. Ro squeezes back.

"No?"

"No," Andrea says, and smiles. "I don't think so. Not this time."

INTO THE BAPTISMAL

Peggy Munson

Kay was the one who broke my virginity pledge, when I was just fifteen.

Barreling through the country in a bus, I stroke myself as I think about seeing her again. My pussy is a glistening night-light beneath my old brown coat, guiding my frantically rubbing hand. Across the aisle, a curdled man chews his floppy lip in sleep. Through the windows, the taffy of headlights stretches between mile marker signs. We near a leaning, eavesdropping barn as I jiggle my clit to come. *Oh God,* I moan into the travel pillow fluff. The barn listens to a clothesline of flapping shirts that flirt with midnight sylphs.

We were naïve at fifteen, grappling for our own religion. A pair of plaster prayer hands sat on the dresser, as small as elm leaves. Midway through a languid summer, we bull rode the old propane tank on sunny days, hot metal against our cotton underwear, trying to feel sensations down there. Kay's dad had been a rodeo clown, and we still pretended to be cowgirls. Some nights we threw Kay's sister's Barbie clothes in gas-can-fueled fires and made "polyester pyrotechnics," as Kay liked to say. She had flint eyes that promised a hot meal on a shipwreck island.

Our hormones were starting to rise. "Dare you to moon the moon," she said one night, when the moon—as my aunt used to say—was in estrus. So full you want to jab it with a stick.

"You're on," I replied, and dropped my pants to my knees. I thrust my butt up and shook it. That's when Kay ran her finger up my crack and said, "Check out your furry caterpillar crack," and made my asshole shiver.

It was my first inkling that I liked my cousin Kay. I had never felt that kind of want—the kind that leaves you trembling.

But we had signed virginity pledges with Faith Baptist Church, and we were also big recruiters. We used to troll through school and find some limp-haired Mary and wax hellfire and brimstone until she contracted her body to Christ. Still, things had shifted in Davis City, and our best recruiting happened before the paper screens came to town—before the car plant rose amongst the cornfields and Japanese business-men demanded restaurants with Shoji screens. The first time I tasted raw fish, I watched a boy punch his fist through the Shoji paper and saw how much disdain boys have for flimsy white contracts. The sushi chefs circled the boy with chop-py words but what did they expect? The puppetry of shad-ows made boys stiff with rage. Boys spent hours *tocking* lampshades, wishing they could punch their way through skirts. Girls needed more armor than pulp and ink.

"Feel mine," said Kay. "Seriously. It's a wooly caterpillar." She took my hand and thrust it down her back end. "Tell me if you think I'm revoltingly hairy."

It was a sinful invitation. There were too many potential butterflies down there. Then, my hand slipped down her crack to her wettest spot. "It's not worth pissing yourself over," I teased, yanking out my fingers. I pushed her away with so much freaked-out force she fell against the clothesline and grabbed a pair of shirtsleeves to steady her body. I dove after her, giggling. Before I knew it, we were wrestling the phantasmal shirt on the ground, playing sumo with thread ghosts instead of shoving the men of the cloth from our minds. At one point, Kay slipped her hand under my waistband. She tickled my badlands. Her finger flitted against a nerve that shot through me like a diamond blade, and I couldn't help but gasp—her hand down there felt amazing. The sun surrounded her molasses skin and tight braids. I leaned close like I was going to kiss her.

Then the screen door banged. "Kay? Ally? What are you two goofing about?" It was her dad. He still resembled a rodeo clown. He knew there were bulls that needed the distraction of hyperbole. He squinted at us on the lawn, the shirt and our bodies all akimbo. "The shirt attacked us," said Kay. "It was an ambush, Dad."

"Stop your tomboy roughhousing and run it through the wash," he chided. "I need that shirt for church tomorrow." Then his eyes crossed from Kay to me, and I saw his shoulders buckle, the invisible oxbow of insight bearing down on him. I hated watching men go limp. It was easier to see their rage, the way they punched their hands through the veneering of thin signatures, goading girls along. That night I curled up next to Kay in Grandma's spare bed, rubbing on a pillow between my legs as she slept. I felt the heavenly spirit light up my groin. I wanted Kay to watch me.

In the morning, Kay and I zipped up our desire in Sunday clothes. Church was a reminder that we didn't believe in the literal body and literal blood. We didn't think Jesus inhabited stale crackers the way Catholics did. Instead, we put our faith in symbolism. In the hard pews, our bodies were sterile Mason jars of seductive fruit, in cellars for times of famine. We let hunger build in us until tornadoes pushed us down into places of relief. We waited until the funnel clouds unleashed their angry cunts on tiny houses that fell like paper screens. Then we still ate bland casseroles.

In spite of our lawn wrestling—and whatever he thought he saw—Kay's dad was kind to us. Kay had washed and ironed and starched his shirt and laid it out that morning. She made him Sunday breakfast of sausage and eggs and orange juice and milk. She put triangles of toast on four points of the plate, like black tabs that hold yellowed photographs. A sweet man, he knew the world was made of bulls and cowboys, and one could only stave off the bulls for so long. He sensed the way things were moving, and he directed the flow then scurried over fences, so as not to be gored. He let Kay go her own way. After church, he wiped his brow and said, "This is some lunatic heat. You girls ought to head to the swimming hole."

"You think?" Kay said giddily. On Sunday, we always helped our aunts with chores—sorting Amway goods, mashing potatoes, snapping the ends off of beans. Although the city was sprawling, and our church had a brochure in Japanese, life on the farms hadn't changed much. Kay and I liked the routine, the old houses dotting the landscape and the mores that held us safe and still.

"When your folks were young, it was a veritable tradition," he said to me. "Swimming after service. They called it 'into the baptismal.' I used to go with them too, before I ran off with the rodeo."

I found it peculiar that Kay and I were still modest enough to turn our backs when we changed into swimsuits. Hadn't I touched her wet spot the day before? Thinking of how I touched Kay made me feel a psychotic hunger in my crotch. I turned my back and stuck my legs through my swimsuit, looking at the prayer hands. When I straightened up and spun around, Kay was gawking. She looked flustered. She gathered her clothes and towel and said, "Your boobs look huge in that, you know."

I hadn't noticed but she was right. Our bodies were filling out. I couldn't remember a time in life when I didn't feel watched, and yet, the awareness that Kay had ogled me made me unduly shy. We walked on the grass beside the road to avoid hot asphalt but then got scratched by weeds and a few disorderly cornstalks. At the swimming hole, Kay grabbed the rope and swung into the water with a splash. "Come on, cowgirl," she said, grinning. It was too early for the gossipy crickets, and the pond was as smooth as a rolled crust. I was self-conscious about the way my boobs jiggled as I flew through the air and splashed in next to her.

"You'd better be careful at the city pool," said Kay. "If you dive in that suit, those melons will pop out." She wouldn't stop talking about tits. She was leading me into a corral of wild horses with her. "How come yours are so much bigger, anyway? It's not fair." She grabbed one of her own while she spun her legs underwater like an eggbeater being slowly hand-cranked.

"No, yours are nicer," I said, a little too rhapsodically. "They're so even. They're like halves of a whole."

"A whole what? A whole Ping-Pong ball?" she replied. She created a fury of water, pushing it up into high feathers with her hollow palm. "Water fight!" I yelled. I lunged for her swimsuit to pull her under. And then one of her perky tits popped right out, and my hand accidentally scooped around it. Buoyancy directed everything, and I felt out of control, like I hadn't even guided my own hand until it was feeling her up. Kay looked stunned, staring at my fingers. I felt her nipple harden and I rubbed some friction against it with my palm. "Are you crazy?" she said angrily, and shoved me away.

But it was obvious that my hand and her breast belonged together, the way certain eggshells once held hardboiled eggs. She was my cousin but was adopted, so the fit did not feel familial. Her skin was as black as night-burned country asphalt, and mine was pale as flour: nobody mistook us for blood kin. I wasn't hurt by her rebuff. I felt calm right then. Kay was kicking to the side of the pond, her tits tucked properly back in her suit. Until that contact, I had felt the uneasiness of being lost. It was what I often felt when I rode my bike along unmarked roads through the uniformity of cornfields, and then suddenly, saw the sun pass the crest of the sky and fall west, so that west was a definite direction. I always knew to turn west then, even if I didn't know which road I was on, and the turning made the journey more enjoyable, better than one without the scramble and fear.

On the bank, the weeping willow did not look sad anymore.

It was a cabaret wig of leaves. I wanted to touch Kay's hair but she looked delicate and mad. She was carving roughly into the dirt with a stick. Her suit clung to the rounds of her stomach. The sun flitted through the leaves to cover her in confetti of dappled light. I knew I shouldn't talk or comfort her but the silence was awkward. Normally, I would have put an arm around her shoulder but now, I stood several feet away and yanked leaves off of branches, making them bow backward and snap. "Did you hate it?" she finally asked.

"Hate what?" I answered dumbly, ready to blame it on buoyancy.

"Did you hate my breast? Is anyone ever going to want to touch it?" She looked anguished.

"I told you it was nice," I said, distantly. I didn't want to squabble.

"Nice is not much of a word," she answered. "Sometimes I don't want to be the obedient Christian. Sometimes I don't want to recruit virgins. I mean, what if I'm boring, down to the boobs?"

"You certainly aren't that," I said, softening my tone. Kay was staring at her chest. "Close your eyes for a second."

Skeptically, she sank into my instructions. Her lids shut. I grabbed her hand and smoothed her palm around my boob. I lifted my hand and put it on her breast. Kay squeezed her eyes at that moment, and her breathing changed. Aside from that, we were completely quiet, like deer that trance hunters with their eyes. I worked her nipple with my thumb the way I might work the edge of dough, then just held my palm there and breathed. Touching her tit was like holding my hand over a globe as it was spinning and taking me to new hemispheres. Kay made whimpering noises that sent a tingle down my spine. "You see?" I said knowingly. "They're both nice and not boring at all." I didn't dare move her hand anywhere else, even though her touch was too light. My boob filled it out completely. I felt naïve for not knowing how much I had wanted it there. We'd talked a lot about the evidentiary, such as broken hymen and blood on a sheet, but we couldn't pretend that this was meaningless.

Her eyes popped open. "Ally," she said seriously. "This is not what nice girls do." She yanked her hand away and started putting her clothes back on over her suit, even though it was still wet. It left two ovals where her butt was and it was soaking through her shirt. She looked ridiculous. I followed her lead and put my clothes on, and we headed quietly back to the house. I moved a stick along cornstalks as if they were pickets. "You think it's going to storm?" I asked, if this was the reason for her hurry. "I'm not a meteorologist," she replied tersely. The clouds were so unfettered that they grew to celestial proportions, casting huge shadows. I began to shiver, and Kay sped up so fast I could barely keep up. Right before we got to the house, she spun around. I almost slammed into her. "If this is what you are, I want to know," she said. "If you're some kind of a dyke, you better tell me now."

"Come on, Kay." I dodged and tried to weave around her but she stuck her arm out, stopping me. She raised one finger up and pointed it at me. She was really pissed off now.

"You said you'd only give it up for God," she said. "You *signed.*" Her voice was trying to squeeze itself into a fevered whisper.

"Nothing is broken yet," I answered sharply. "We're still intact. Good lord!" Before we could go further, the sky broke open and it rained. I smelled the scent of rain on new cement because her dad had poured a patio last month. We bolted for the house. The screen door slammed behind our dripping bodies as we hurried in.

What we did seemed innocent enough, nothing a doctor wouldn't do. I closed my eyes and rubbed my lower lip against my palm, to feel its strange pink texture. Even that made me feel so amazing, especially if I thought of kissing Kay. The days were like notes held too long by a soprano in a house of clear glass.

Grandma loved hawking Amway in the rain, because more people were home, and they were grateful for any company. Plus, being industrious in poor weather earned good standing with God. "You poor girls are rained in and reined in," she said cheerfully as she bustled out the door. We should have been miserable to be cooped up in the trailer but we weren't. Kay had softened toward me, though we avoided talking about our outburst of lust while we read magazines on the bed. Kay methodically studied an article on how to pluck eyebrows. "The family's chicken pluckers from way back," I assured her. "It's our legacy." Every time one of our legs got lazy, our calves or feet banged together, and then we pulled away, electrified. I imagined myself stroking the cocoa skin of her thighs and kissing her elegant collarbone. Kay sprung up and paced around the room nervously. She held Grandma's costume necklaces to her neck and put them down. She fiddled with some decorative bells. Finally, she picked up the prayer hands.

"Maybe we should test your faith," said Kay, mischievously. "Do some kind of trial by fire."

"Like what?" I answered neutrally, my body stiffening. I

hoped her game was some spin-the-prayer-hands that involved groping and tongues.

She smacked the prayer hands into her palm. "These are small enough, and one of us should know how it feels," she said.

"How what feels?"

"It, Ally. *It*," Kay said patronizingly. "How many *its* are there? Don't make me spell it out."

"As previously noted, I've got meeself two big 'its," I said, trying to break her with a stupid joke. But Kay wasn't having it.

"Be serious," she said. "I am."

She shoved the magazine to the ground so it was flapping like a bird held by its feet. Chickens are slaughtered that way: inverted and desperate. Minutes earlier, Kay and I had been savoring girl talk about makeup and celebrities, chattering in a parlor of easy commonality. Now, she had assumed a different posture, slinking low toward the chicken coop. She got right up on top of me. "We'll just see if you like it," she said. "Okay?" She tucked the prayer hands into the elastic of my shorts, so they pressed cool and firm on my waist. "It's better to try these things with someone you know, so you'll be ready when the big day comes. Who do you know better than me?"

"Not even myself," I replied, terrified of her sudden assertiveness. Kay began rubbing the prayer hands lightly against my skin, which made me tingly. Then she set them on the bed.

"Come on, Ally," she soothed. "Don't be chickenshit. You're the brave one. Someone's got to try it. They say not to sign a contract unless you understand the terms. How can we be good virgins if we know nothing of the alternatives?"

"That doesn't make sense," I answered. I felt a powerful convection heat cooking me from the inside out. I wanted her so bad.

Then she kissed me on the cheek and assumed the pragmatic planting and sowing tone we'd learned from our family. "I know what to do," she whispered authoritatively. "I've been reading magazines all day." One hand reached down and opened up my shorts. I couldn't believe what was happening. My brain floated on top of me like a doomed dirigible. Her fingers slid beneath my underpants, into the gasping canyon that had formed slowly from an unheralded stream. "Does this feel good?" she asked timidly, as she was tracing patterns with her fingers, looking for a place to put them in.

God, it felt incredible. I didn't want her to stop. I thought about my stretched-out, cheap underwear that had come in a three-pack. We always bought it in quantity, the way one might send bundles of dry goods to Africa, and I loved its pragmatic and distant spiritual insurance. Kay wore the exact same kind, and there was something seductive and sexy-librarian-like about its plainness. She acted like she had swerved around that familiar stitching a thousand times. Kay's lips were parted and swollen with red, hungry. I felt one finger slip inside of me and I gasped. "Oh wow," I said.

"Don't you ever masturbate?" she asked. Clearly, *she* did.

"Where would I do it? In the shed? I'm never alone." I didn't tell her about my pillow grinding.

Kay moved her finger in and out, then started widening my hole with it by circling right inside the opening. "Concentric circles, nesting rings," she said. "Just look at it—you're beautiful. And why not in the shed?" I wished that I could kiss her but I knew I might break the spell if I moved. Kay had more sense than this usually. "I guess you must like boys a little bit," she commented. "You like having something inside." I didn't point out the flaw in her reasoning, that the thing inside of me wasn't a dick, but *her,* and nothing else could feel so good. She pulled my shorts down off my feet. She yanked my matronly underpants away. "Let's get on with it," she said feverishly, and I thought *Hallelujah, yes.* I looked at my coils of pubic hair and then, above, her saintly face. The scent of me wafted through the room, an aromatic telegram, and I was scared the trailer doors would not contain the news. We panted in the tentative stillness. "Now spread your legs," said Kay. "Relax."

We'd never done the Passion Play or Stations of the Cross, but Kay seemed to know something about sacrificing virgins. My toes grazed the footboard as I spread my legs apart. Spreading them so wide felt amazing, and my thighs grew hot. I felt a teasing breeze from somewhere but the windows were all closed. Kay ran one finger up and down my wet pussy, parting the seas. "Okay, it will hurt at first and then feel good," said Kay. "If the sex books are correct. I think I'm competent. Try to relax." She slid the diminutive fingers of the prayer hands into me. Their coolness made my muscles clench. I felt the sweetest pleasure bubbling through my groin as she eased the hands in.

"Oh, Kay," I exclaimed, despite myself. "That's nice. Please don't stop."

"Don't worry, Ally Cat," she said. "I've got to find your soul in here to save it."

She slid the plaster further into me until I crawled backward a little bit. Then her slender fingers stroked my body, coax-

ing me, letting me know it was okay. I felt myself spreading
for her. She tweaked the spot above my hole, so she could
slide the hands further in. "I found your magic button," she
grinned. She massaged around my opening, while I let out little moans. "That's it, relax for me," she said. My saggy underwear hung on the foot post of the bed. She rocked the prayer
hands in, and suddenly, I felt a rapturous explosion, right
from the plaster fingertips. "Oh!" I said, and Kay slammed
one hand over my mouth.

"Be quiet," she said. "People will kill us. Did you come?"

"I think I did," I said. She looked angelic with her hair
glowing in the lamplight. It was my first orgasm.

It kept pulsing in me, like the glow of a star, while Kay set
the prayer hands back on the dresser.

I wonder if that star guides her now, as it does me.

Kay's kin are the only ones who want to see me since I came
out as a dyke. They are serpent handlers, or Sign Followers—
as queer to my other scripture-strict relatives as I am. They
split off with the Indiana family after taking up with snakes,
and it has been six years since I last saw Kay. At twenty-five, I
feel like an awkward teenager when I walk toward the house.
The serpent handlers haul metal chairs for tomorrow's service. Aunt May shucks corn by the round hood of my uncle's
truck. Like the others, Kay wears nondescript garb, her hair
smoothed back, but her arms are buffed out and sexy from the
Army. She Frisbee-tosses a paper plate my way and squeals,
"You made it!" Aunt May strides up and kisses me right on
the lips, and I back away, surprised. "It's our faith tradition,"
explains Kay. "Second Corinthians tells us to greet those of
our own sex with a 'Holy kiss.'" The landscape is lush with

suggestive underbrush. I am tense about what slithers beneath the obvious. How could they accept me when they believe the Bible asks them to drink poison and wrestle deadly snakes? Still, they have invited me here, knowing what they know. I wonder where her dad keeps the box of copperheads. He rises from the porch and drags his bad leg with his good leg, then hugs me with one arm and says, "Welcome to Tennessee, darlin'. You're always family he-ar." I almost cry to hear him say this, since I've felt so shunned. Before I can offer to help set up, he seizes my duffel bag and sticks a limp pillowcase in my hand. "What's this for?" I ask.

"We're going hunting," announces Kay. "Before sundown." She grabs a long stick with a metal hook on the end. "Catch a lively one," says her dad.

Kay is quiet as she steers me through the woods. We don't talk about my coming out process, her escapades in the barracks, the rickety railroad bridge between our lives. I wonder if she judges me, or if she still dates men. Over time, our letters grew polite and petered out. Her solemn brow twists like a point of wind turmoil on a grassy field, and I remember my first orgasm like it was yesterday. It makes my cunt throb to have our bodies so close. She rattles along with the snake stick, and I watch the rhythm of her shoulder blades. Kay might have had a hard time as a black kid in a white family, but people always kowtowed to her. Like those sturdy farm structures that just won't fall, Kay has an effortless way of making the wind bend around her skin. My pussy still remembers how she slid it open. At twenty-five, she looks like something decadent and tasty only adults get to eat.

Kay plods down the overgrown trail, pointing out poison oak. "Shhh. Be still," she orders, holding out her arm. Before

I can ask what's she's doing, Kay slides quietly to the left and scoops the snake stick down into a leaf-dappled area beside the trail. She lifts the thick, twisting body of a timber rattlesnake with the metal end. I hadn't even noticed its cryptic yellow and brown colors hiding there. She grabs the viper by the head while I jerk back. My heart rifles with adrenaline. "So you like to fuck girls?" she asks dispassionately, pointing the rattler's fangs at me.

"Hold on, I—" I protest. Then Kay bursts out laughing. "I need the pillowcase, fool," she says. "I'm not going to kill you for being a dyke." She rope-ties the end of the bag and the viper thrashes then goes still. "They call me 'charmer' now," she says. "I flush the serpents out." I nod and say, "I can see how you'd be good at that." Her eyes run over my own serpentine curves. "We've got time to kill now," she adds, nonchalantly. "Why don't I show you my favorite spot?" Then she takes me to a tiny shack in the woods, pulls open the vine-covered door and leads me in. She plops the snake bag on the plank floor. "It's an old hunting camp," she says. "Don't you love it?" The timber rattlesnake squirms and I try to move away, but Kay herds me near it, pressing me against the dirty wall with her whole body, keeping me scared. She is thrillingly present, her arms holding me there. "One thing I've learned about the power of venom," she says. "Is that you should keep it in the family." Then she grins. She puts her fingers through my hair and breathes heavy on my neck, flushing me out. What is she doing to me? I moan a little. Kay is so powerful up close.

We both look at the serpent when it rustles. "I bet it's the pillowcase I used to hump when I thought of you," I confess, reaching out to stroke her corn-silk-soft cheeks, to let her know I want her. She leans forward: she has a hot rock to warm my cold blood. She thrusts her hips a little bit, so I feel the lump in them against my body. "You feel what I've got?" she asks.

"Is that—?" I ask.

"It's a viper," she cuts in. "It'll kill you quick." She grabs my hand and rubs it over the lumpy curves in her jeans, then blocks me from touching it again. I can't believe Kay is packing a dick. "Oh god, Kay," I marvel. "I want to feel it."

"You just wait," she orders. "Wait for it." Then she shakes her hips until I hear a rattling sound. I don't know if it's a rattlesnake or gourd or can of dimes. I scrunch my brow. "Is that a real snake in your pants?" I ask, perplexed, and Kay pins me tighter. "Yeah, it's a serpent I caught for you," Kay says calmly, and puts my hand back on the lumpy mound that really does seem to wriggle. "Don't make me pin you face-first and give it to you *Deliverance* style." I hear the rattle growing louder, faster, as she grinds her hips against my pubic bone. I try to back away, to ascertain what's slithering in her pants, but she squeezes me against its cotton case. I get irrationally scared but Kay calmly holds my wrists in one hand. She unzips and pushes down my pants. "Can you handle the serpent?" she asks fiercely. "Are you a child of God? Are you holy and willing to prove it?"

She shoves me hard against the wall.

Then I feel the venom, the quietude, Kay's sweet cock sinking in.

The rattle comes from so far down, I cannot tell its origin. It rises up inside the room. It seizes me. It clutches Kay. My muscles knead themselves into a wild delirium. "Oh yeah," I groan, and try to pull her further in. But Kay slides out her cock and makes me look. I want to call it back. "Most people think the rattle is good luck," she says. Her dick is jutting out, and where the balls should be, there are the curving lumps of keratin: she's fixed a rattlesnake rattle there. "Some fiddlers put these rattles in their violins because they think it makes the instrument more masculine," she says. "Or that it sings along. I harvested this rattle from a tire track rattlesnake. No one can shred the rhythm in a body. That's why the serpent handlers rise up off their seats to praise." She starts to move her hips, and eases into me. I grab at her. Kay pierces me and I succumb. "I'm going to make you come so hard," she says. "For all the years I've held it in." And then my hot, adopted cousin fucks me good. I'm baptized in her sinuous religion.

ABOUT THE AUTHORS

D. Alexandria: dalexandria.com
Anna Bishop: bishop.anna36@gmail.com
Chuck Fellows: qchase.com
Violynt Femme: violyntfemme@gmail.com
Thea Hutcheson: theahutcheson.com
Debra Hyde: twitter.com/debrahyde
Lynne Jamneck: lynnejamneckdiaries.blogspot.com
Catherine Lundoff: catherinelundoff.com
Eric Maroney: ewmaroney@gmail.com
Peggy Munson: peggymunson.com
Radclyffe: radfic.com
Jean Roberta: jeanroberta.com
Sinclair Sexsmith: mrsexsmith.com
Kathleen Warnock: kathleenwarnock.com
Rose William: RoseWilliamErotica@gmail.com
Kristina Wright: kristinawright.com

ABOUT THE EDITORS

Eileen Myles (www.eileenmyles.com) has written thousands of poems since she gave her first reading at CBGB's in 1974. She is the author of many books of poetry including the Lambda Award–winner *Skies*, *on my way*, *School of Fish*, *Maxfield Parrish*, and *Not Me*, and the novels *Chelsea Girls* and *Cool for You*. She coedited *The New Fuck You: Adventures in Lesbian Reading*. She's a frequent contributor to *Book Forum*, *Art in America*, the *Village Voice*, *The Nation*, *The Stranger*, *Index*, and *Nest*. She is also an accomplished theater and performance writer, actor, and director, having contributed to many productions at St. Mark's Poetry Project and P.S. 122. She has read to audiences at colleges, performance spaces, and bookstores across America as well as in Europe, Iceland, and Russia; in 1997, she toured with Sister Spit's Ramblin' Road Show. Eileen is currently finishing up a novel about the hell of being a female poet. *And Hell*, an opera composed by Michael Webster, written and directed by Eileen, premiered at P.S. 122. For the past three years, she has been dividing her time between New York and San Diego, where she teaches writing at the University of California at San Diego.

Tristan Taormino (tristantaormino.com and puckerup.com) is an award-winning author, columnist, editor, sex educator, and feminist pornographer. She is the author of seven books: *Secrets of Great G-Spot Orgasms and Female Ejaculation, The Big Book of Sex Toys, The Anal Sex Position Guide, Opening Up: A Guide to Creating and Sustaining Open Relationships, The Ultimate Guide to Anal Sex for Women, True Lust: Adventures in Sex, Porn and Perversion*, and *Down and Dirty Sex Secrets*. She has edited 24 anthologies, including *Take Me There: Trans and Genderqueer Erotica* and *The Ultimate Guide to Kink*. She was the founding series editor of sixteen volumes of the Lambda Literary Award–winning anthology *Best Lesbian Erotica*. She runs Smart Ass Productions, and has directed and produced more than twenty adult films, from sex education to reality porn. She's written for a multitude of publications, from *Yale Journal of Law and Feminism* to *Penthouse*, is a former editor of *On Our Backs* and a former syndicated columnist for *The Village Voice*. She has appeared in hundreds of publications and on radio and television. She lectures at top colleges and universities and teaches sex and relationship workshops around the world. She lives with her partner and their dogs in upstate New York.